Also by Michael Ondaatje

DIVISADERO

DIVISADERO

Michael Ondaatje

McCLELLAND & STEWART

Library and Archives Canada Cataloguing in Publication
Ondaatje, Michael, 1943–
Divisadero / Michael Ondaatje. – Canadian ed.
ISBN 978-0-7710-6872-0
I. Title.
PS8529.N283D58 2007   C813'.54   C2007-900763-5

We acknowledge the financial support of the Government of Canada through
the Book Publishing Industry Development Program and that of the
Government of Ontario through the Ontario Media Development
Corporation's Ontario Book Initiative. We further acknowledge the
support of the Canada Council for the Arts and the Ontario Arts
Council for our publishing program.

Published in the United States by Alfred A. Knopf, a division of Random
House, Inc., and in the United Kingdom by Bloomsbury Publishing Plc.

This is a work of fiction. Names, characters, places, and incidents
either are the product of the author's imagination or are used fictitiously.
Any resemblance to actual persons, living or dead, events, or locales is
entirely coincidental. Some locations have been altered or renamed
and a few liberties taken with geography.

Printed and bound in Canada

McClelland & Stewart Ltd.
75 Sherbourne Street
Toronto, Ontario
M5A 2P9
www.mcclelland.com

1 2 3 4 5   11 10 09 08 07

For John and Beverly

and in loving memory of Creon Corea

—remembered by us as 'Egilly'

When I come to lie in your arms, you sometimes ask me in which historical moment do I wish to exist. And I will say Paris, the week Colette died. . . . Paris, August 3rd, 1954. In a few days, at her state funeral, a thousand lilies will be placed by her grave, and I want to be there, walking that avenue of wet lime trees until I stand beneath the second-floor apartment that belonged to her in the Palais-Royal. The history of people like her fills my heart. She was a writer who remarked that her only virtue was self-doubt. (A day or two before she died, they say Colette was visited by Jean Genet, who stole nothing. Ah, the grace of the great thief . . .)

'We have art,' Nietzsche said, 'so that we shall not be destroyed by the truth.' The raw truth of an incident never ends, and the story of Coop and the terrain of my sister's life are endless to me. They are the sudden possibility every time I pick up the telephone when it rings some late hour after midnight, and I wait for his voice, or the deep breath before Claire will announce herself.

For I have taken myself away from who I was with them, and what I used to be. When my name was Anna.

ONE

Anna, Claire, and Coop

The Orphan

By our grandfather's cabin, on the high ridge, opposite a slope of buckeye trees, Claire sits on her horse, wrapped in a thick blanket. She has camped all night and lit a fire in the hearth of that small structure our ancestor built more than a generation ago, and which he lived in like a hermit or some creature, when he first came to this country. He was a self-sufficient bachelor who eventually owned all the land he looked down onto. He married lackadaisically when he was forty, had one son, and left him this farm along the Petaluma road.

Claire moves slowly on the ridge above the two valleys full of morning mist. The coast is to her left. On her right is the journey to Sacramento and the delta towns such as Rio Vista with its populations left over from the Gold Rush.

She persuades the horse down through the whiteness alongside crowded trees. She has been smelling smoke for the last twenty minutes, and, on the outskirts of Glen Ellen, she sees the town bar on fire—the local arsonist has struck early, when certain it would be empty. She watches from a distance without dismounting. The horse, Territorial, seldom allows a remount; in this he can be fooled only once a day. The two of them, rider and animal, don't fully trust each other, although the horse is my sister Claire's closest ally. She will use every trick not in the book to stop his rearing and bucking. She carries plastic bags of water with her and leans forward and smashes them onto his neck so the animal believes it is his own blood and will calm for a minute. When Claire is on a horse she loses her limp and is in charge of the universe, a centaur. Someday she will meet and marry a centaur.

The fire takes an hour to burn down. The Glen Ellen Bar has always been the location of fights, and even now she can see scuffles starting up on the streets, perhaps to honour the landmark. She sidles the animal against the slippery red wood of a madrone bush and eats its berries, then rides down into the town, past the fire. Close by, as she passes, she can hear the last beams collapsing like a roll of thunder, and she steers the horse away from the sound.

On the way home she passes vineyards with their prehistoric-looking heat blowers that keep air moving so the vines don't freeze. Ten years earlier, in her youth, smudge pots burned all night to keep the air warm.

Most mornings we used to come into the dark kitchen and silently cut thick slices of cheese for ourselves. My father drinks a cup of red wine. Then we walk to the barn. Coop is already there, raking the soiled straw, and soon we are milking the cows, our heads resting against their flanks. A father, his two eleven-year-old daughters, and Coop the hired hand, a few years older than us. No one has talked yet, there's just been the noise of pails or gates swinging open.

Coop in those days spoke sparingly, in a low-pitched monologue to himself, as if language was uncertain. Essentially he was clarifying what he saw—the light in the barn, where to climb the approaching fence, which chicken to cordon off, capture, and tuck under his arm. Claire and I listened whenever we could. Coop was an open soul in those days. We realized his taciturn manner was not a wish for separateness but a tentativeness about words. He was adept in the physical world where he protected us. But in the world of language he was our student.

At that time, as sisters, we were mostly on our own. Our father had brought us up single-handed and was too busy to be conscious of intricacies. He was satisfied when we worked at our chores and easily belligerent when it became difficult to find us. Since the death of our mother it was Coop who listened to us complain and worry, and he allowed us the stage when he thought we wished for it. Our father gazed right through Coop. He was training him as a farmer and nothing else. What Coop read, however, were books about gold camps and gold mines in the California northeast, about those who had risked everything at a river bend on a left turn and so discovered a fortune. By the second half of the twentieth century he was, of course, a hundred years too late, but he knew there were still outcrops of gold, in rivers, under the bunch grass, or in the pine sierras.

There was a book, not much more than a pamphlet with a white spine, I found high on a shelf in the mudroom of the farm. *Interviews with Californios: Women from Early Times to the Present.* As most of those women did not write, archivists from Berkeley had travelled with tape recorders to capture these lives and the ambience of the past. The monograph included accounts dating from the early 1800s to the present, from 'The Dictation of Doña Eulalia' to 'The Dictation of Lydia Mendez.' Lydia Mendez was our mother. It was here in this book that we discovered the woman who had died the week Claire and I were born. Only Coop, among the three of us, who'd worked on the farm since he was a boy, had known her as someone alive. For Claire and me she was a rumour, a ghost rarely mentioned by our father, someone interviewed for a few paragraphs in this book, and shown in a washed-out black-and-white photograph.

All the people in the book had a humility, a sense that history was around them, not within them. 'We grew up in the Central Plain, north-east of Los Angeles, where my father worked the asphaltum pits. I married when I was eighteen, and that night we danced so many times to "La Voquilla," and "El Grullo"—the violin players and guitarists, my husband said, were the best in the region. The trestle table with food was set up by the great rock in the pasture. My husband's father landed thirty years earlier in San Francisco, and the same day, I am told, he caught the steamer to Petaluma, and built this house. By the time I arrived here there were a thousand laying hens. But my husband did not want others working on the farm so we kept only dairy cattle and grew corn—foxes were killing the hens and it took too much trouble to protect them. There were other animals in the hills—bobcats and coyotes, rattlesnakes in the redwoods, I saw a mountain lion once. But the devil's curse was thistles. We fought to cut them back. The neighbours never did it right, and their thistle seeds flew onto our property.

'There was a man further down the Petaluma Road who had a hundred goats, a gentle man. Sometimes he came and camped with his goats in our fields—a special small goat that ate thistles, and its digestion killed the seed, somehow it chewed the seed up properly. A cow doesn't do that. A cow eats thistles and the seed goes right through. If you hate thistles, you could have loved this man. . . . There was a terrible violence on the farm next to ours. The Cooper family was killed by a hired hand who beat them to death with a wooden board. At first no one knew who had committed such an act, but their son had hidden in the crawl space under the floorboards of the house for several days. He was four years old and he came out eventually and told who had done it. We took the boy in, to stay and work on the farm.'

This is all of the portrait we own of our mother. Whatever else she might have considered and thought remains in an unquestioned distance. She had spoken mostly of events that stumbled against her, so we had only her affection for the goat man, her brief joy in dancing, the details of the murder on the neighbouring farm that brought Coop into our household. There is nothing revealed here about her pleasures or her intelligence or her compassion. Things that must have been a guiding star for our father. Just two pages about this 'Californio' who would die in childbirth when she was twenty-three.

What is not in the small white book, therefore, is the strange act of our father during the chaos surrounding her death, when he took on informally the adoption of a child from the same hospital where his wife was giving birth—the daughter of another mother, who had also died—bringing both children home and raising the other child, who had been named Claire, as his own. So there would be two girls, Anna and Claire, born the same week. People assumed that both were his daughters. This was our father's gesture that grew from Lydia Mendez' passing. The dead mother of the other child had no relatives, or was a solitary; perhaps that was how he was able to do this. It was a field hospital on the outskirts of Santa Rosa, and to put it brutally, they owed him a wife, they owed him something.

Now and then our father embraced us as any father would. This happened only if you were able to catch him in that no-man's-land between tiredness and sleep, when he seemed wayward to himself. I joined him on the old covered sofa, and I would lie like a slim dog in his arms, imitating his state of weariness—too much sun perhaps, or too hard a day's work.

Claire would also be there sometimes, if she did not want to be left out, or if there was a storm. But I simply wished to have my face against his checkered shirt and pretend to be asleep. As if inhaling the flesh of an adult was a sin and also a glory, a right in any case. To do such a thing during daylight would have been unthinkable, he'd have pushed us aside. He was not a modern parent, he had been raised with a few male rules, and he no longer had a wife to qualify or compromise his beliefs. So you had to catch him in that twilight state, when he had ceded control on the tartan sofa, his girls enclosed, one in each of his arms. I would watch the flicker under his eyelid, the tremble within that covering skin that signalled his tiredness, as if he were being tugged in mid-river by a rope to some other place. And then I too would sleep, descending into the layer that was closest to him. A father who allows you that should protect you all of your days, I think.

More than a century before us, in August 1849, a group of men set up camp in a valley more than a hundred miles north of Petaluma. They built cabins at a place they called Badger Hill and began to search for gold. There were twenty of them panning the streams, standing knee-deep in the icy rivers, and they almost surrendered to the winter storms that overtook them. But within six months gold-laced quartz was unearthed in the place that would eventually be called Grass Valley. A hundred ramshackle hotels went up, and bizarre names for mines began to speckle the constantly reprinted maps—*Slumgullion, Delirium Tremens, Bogus Thunder, Hell's Delight, Graveyard, Lone Jack, Rich Hell, Ne Plus Ultra, Silver Fork, Rocking Horse, Sultana.* Men would be stranded in the mountains with no supplies and become hunters out of necessity, killing grouse, cattle, bears, with shotguns and pistols. Butcher shops sprang up. Steamboats travelled inland to the furthest point of navigation—as far as the Feather River. And a many-headed civilization arrived.

Gamblers, water entrepreneurs, professional shootists, prostitutes, diarists, coffee drinkers, whisky merchants, poets, heroic dogs, mail-order brides, women falling in love with boys who walked within the realm of luck, old men swallowing gold to conceal it on their return journeys to the coast, balloonists, mystics, Lola Montez, opera singers—good ones, bad ones, those who fornicated their way across the territory. Dynamiters blasted steep grades and the land under your feet. There were seventeen miles of tunnels beneath the town of Iowa Hill. Sonora burned. Weaverville burned. Shasta and Columbia burned. Were rebuilt and burned again and rebuilt again. Sacramento flooded.

A hundred years later, at the time of Coop's obsession, there would still be five thousand full-time gold miners along the banks of the Yuba and Russian rivers. They scouted out the old towns in the Sierras named after lovers and dogs and characters in novels—names that were a time capsule of hunger and desire for a new life. *Ne Plus Ultra!* At each filament-like dot on the county maps, something had happened. On this riverbank two brothers killed each other arguing about which direction to travel. At this clearing a woman was traded for a site. It was as if there were a novella by Balzac round every bend.

Prospectors now drove up in Airstreams, pulling gas-fuelled dredges to suck up whatever remained on the river bottoms. A century of flooding and storms had knocked loose the gold from the prehistoric beds, sluicing it down into the rivers. Miners in wetsuits were 'sniping' the streams, and swam in the underwater darkness holding giant cauldrons of light.

Everything about gold was in opposition to Coop's life on our farm. It must still have felt to him that he came from nowhere, the horror of his parents' murder never spoken of by us. He had been handed the habits and duties that came with farm life, so by now he could ride up to our grandfather's cabin on the ridge with his eyes closed, knowing by the sound of the breeze in a tree exactly where he was and what direction he faced, as if he was within safe architecture. Our land had been cleared of stones and boulders, the wood planks on our kitchen table were wiped clean as a page, the fence gates chained and unchained, chained and unchained. But gold was euphoria and chance to Coop, an illogical discipline, a tall story that included a murder or mistaken identity or a love affair. He hitchhiked two hours northwest onto the Colfax–Iowa Hill road and watched the men with crevassing tools working in the north fork of the Russian River. He was seventeen years old when he impetuously hired himself out for a pittance and the chance of a bonus to man the Anaconda suction hoses. He came home at the end of the week with a twisted back. He remained wordless in front of us, these two girls, his curious listeners, as to where he had been. Wherever he had gone, we could see, he had been somehow altered, been part of a dangerous thing.

He had jumped from the floating platform, the Anaconda hose in his arms, and sunk to the bottom of the river. A second later the generator broke awake and his body was flung from side to side as he tried to aim the live hose under boulders for the possibility of trapped gold. Sometimes, when it got loose from the suck of gravel, the jet hose leapt free of the water, into the air, Coop still riding it until he fell back onto the river's hard surface, submerging once more with the glass and leather and iron of the diver's helmet lolling rough at his neck while within it the thin line of air led amateurish and tentative and, he knew, unsafe into his mouth.

Coop sat in the small, dark farmhouse kitchen with us and attempted to talk of this, but he could barely take even one step into telling us of the absurdity and danger of what he had allowed himself to do. So we did not know what had occurred. I remember we sat there and chanted, 'Coop's lost week, Coop's lost week. Where did he go? Who was he with? Who was the woman who must have so exhausted him?'

The smooth rolling hills of our farm were green in the constant rains of winter and parched brown during summer and fall. Driving home, north out of Nicasio, we climbed to the peak of the hills, then abruptly swerved right onto the farm's narrow dirt road, which went downhill a quarter-mile before it reached the barns, the car clobbering over speed bumps made from the rubber of tractor tires that had been hammered into the earth with spikes. When Claire and I were older, returning from parties in Glen Ellen, half asleep and with full bladders, we cursed the existence of the bumps. In the darkness, at the foot of the hill, we had to halt the car. *My turn,* I said, getting out in my new cotton dress and tight shoes to push the too-friendly and wide-awake mules off the path at the foot of the hill, so we could drive on.

As sisters we reflected each other, competed with each other, and our shared idol was Coop. By the time he was in his late teens we discovered he had other lives, disappearing into the city, haunting pool halls, dances, returning just in time to drive Claire into Nicasio for her piano lessons. She'd watch his lean brown hands, how he handled the clutch, how he took corners as if guiding them through water, swerving back to the straight road in a single gesture. She loved Coop's easy, minimal effort towards whatever was around him. A year later, picking her up in Nicasio, he shifted over to the passenger seat and threw her the keys, pulled a paperback out of the glove compartment and began reading while she, frantic and uncertain about everything, steered the suddenly massive car—she felt she was screaming—

up the winding road to its crest and then slid down the hill to the farm. He never once looked up, never once said a word, maybe glanced at the face of an almost sideswiped mule as it caught his eye in the side mirror. From then on, Claire drove to and from piano lessons alone, missing Coop. Coop, who with his confidence would sweep a hay bale over his shoulder and walk to the barn lighting a cigarette with his free hand.

Sometimes Claire and I would come down the hill with the car lights turned off in complete blackness. Or we would climb from our bedroom window onto the skirt of the roof and lie flat on our backs on the large table-rock, still warm from the day, and talk and sing into the night. We counted out the seconds between meteor showers slipping horizontal across the heavens. When thunder shook the house and horse stalls, I'd see Claire in her bed, during the brief moments of lightning, sitting upright like a nervous hound, hardly breathing, crossing herself. There were days when she disappeared on her horse and I disappeared into a book. But we were still sharing everything then. The Nicasio bar, the Druid Hall, the Sebastiani movie theatre in Sonoma, whose screen was like the surface of the Petaluma reservoir, altering with every shift of light, the hundred or more redwings that always sat on the telephone wires and chirruped out loud before a storm. There was a purple flower in February called shooting star. There were the sticks of willow that Coop cut down and strapped onto my broken wrist before he drove me to the hospital. I was fourteen then. He was eighteen. *Everything is biographical,* Lucian Freud says. What we make, why it is made, how we draw a dog, who it is we are drawn to, why we cannot forget. Everything is collage, even genetics. There is the hidden presence of others in us, even those we have known briefly. We contain them for the rest of our lives, at every border that we cross.

Who was Coop, really? We never knew what his parents were

like. We were never sure what he felt about our family, which had harboured him and handed him another life. He was the endangered heir of a murder. As a teenager he was hesitant, taking no more than he was given. At dawn he'd come out from one of the sheds like a barn cat, stretching as if he'd been sleeping for days, when in fact he had returned from a pool hall in San Francisco three or four hours earlier, hitchhiking the forty miles back in the darkness. I wondered even then how he would survive or live in a future world. We watched as he muttered, thinking things out, while he stripped down a tractor or welded a radiator from an abandoned car onto a '58 Buick. Everything was collage.

Somewhere there is an album made up of photographs our father took of Claire and me that provides a time-lapse progression of our growing up, from our first, unconcerned poses to feral or vain glances, as the truer landscape of our faces began to be seen. Between Christmas and New Year's—the picture was always taken at that time—we'd be herded into the pasture beside the outcrop of rock (where our mother was buried) and captured in a black-and-white photograph on a late December afternoon. He insisted on modest clothing, although as we grew older Claire would arrive in chapped jeans or I would reveal a bare shoulder, causing a twenty-minute argument. He found little humour in this. The yearly episode was something he needed, like a carefully laid table that would clarify the past.

We would study ourselves in this evolving portrait. It made us secretly competitive. One became more beautiful, or reclusive, one became more self-conscious, or anarchic. We were revealed and betrayed by our poses. There was the year, for instance, that Claire lowered her face to hide a scar. In spite of having been almost inseparable, we were diverging, pacing ourselves privately into our own version of ourselves. And then there was the last photograph, when we were both sixteen, where our faces gazed out nakedly. A picture that I would rip out of the album a short while later.

Claire recalls whistling as she entered the horse barn, and reaching for a bridle when she heard a bucket kicked over somewhere in the darkness. A bucket would not be left loose in a stall, so it meant someone was there, or it meant a horse was loose. She stepped forward with her uneven walk, the bridle still in one hand. She didn't call out. She reached the corner of the passageway, peered around it, and saw my body lying inert on the ground in the dark silence of the barn. Then, as she approached me, the horse came loud out of the blackness and smashed against her, throwing her down.

There is a broken path in both our memories towards this incident, even now. We are aware only that something significant happened. Claire recalls herself whistling as she entered the barn, but in what follows, in what we have tried to piece together, she is still too close to the remembered evidence, as if she can see only grains of colour. For a moment Claire had been staring at me, who had already been knocked down by the attacking horse, and then the same horse had swerved out of the darkness and turned on her, and her senses closed down. Or maybe she remained like me, half awake on the concrete floor, unable to move, while everything around us was vivid and nightmarish, hooves smashing against the floor—I felt I could see sparks and flame to represent the loudness. The animal must have been crazed, claustrophobic, for it raced up and down the passageway, slipping on straw and concrete, banging into wood walls, charging the length of the barn, turning once more at the blocked exit, its eyes and heart frantic. Was she, was I, conscious during this, or unconscious? Or in a world of spirits, uncertain if we were dead or alive.

When Claire opened her eyes, I was apparently sitting up six feet away and not moving, just looking at her lazily. I didn't have the strength to rise, uncertain as to what exactly had happened. There were planks knocked loose all around us. No one had come for us. It was suppertime, I could tell by the light against the dusty windows.

Territorial was Claire's lovely name for that horse. I kept watching her. Later I told her it was because of all the blood on her cheek, though she said it was just her hands that hurt. We were both fifteen years old then, when Coop finally entered the barn and crouched down by me and called me 'Claire.' So that Claire herself became confused, uncertain for a moment as to who she was. But she was Claire, with what would become a thin scar like the path of an almost dried tear under her left eye, where all that blood had escaped.

Something happened in the horse barn, that early evening, between the two of us, in the confusion. We had stepped suddenly into the large uncertain world of adults, and we would now need to be distinctly Anna and distinctly Claire. It became important not to be known as the sister of—or worse, mistaken for—the other. From then on we would try to bring Coop into our fold. In the next few months we often slipped back into this 'incident,' to talk about it. There was a border now between us, something we had never achieved in the series of photographs that kept the two of us arm in arm. The album, I suspect, is still with Claire, on one of her bookshelves. If she studies it, she could parse more clearly how the two of us evolved away from each other. The year Claire cut most of her hair and grew more distant, the year I stared out, wild-eyed, everything in me a secret.

Why was Coop never in our father's photographs? There were a few pictures taken of him, but these seemed preoccupied with texture and light. And there were some abstract reflections of him in a window, or of his shadow on the grass or on the flank of an animal. How many things could you throw your image against?

In any case, it was Coop who had found us that evening in the barn and had mistaken our identities, who had eventually come over to me and lifted me into his embrace and said, 'Claire, my god, Claire,' and I had thought, Then I am not Anna, then that must be Anna over there.

Coop began living in the grandfather's cabin. From there, on the high ridge, he could look out onto black oaks and buckeye trees, where a glacier of mist appeared caught for an hour or so each morning in the roughness of the branches. He was nineteen now, in a desired solitude. He was rebuilding the cabin, working alone. He bathed in the cold water of a hill pond. In the evenings he slipped past the farmhouse and ended up in Nicasio or Glen Ellen, listening to music. Occasionally he ate with the others, abruptly rising from the table, bread still in his hands, and was gone—the exit and destination unannounced. The sisters knew that their days with Coop were finite. He was courteous and unruled, away most evenings. Returning, he'd cut the motor at the top of the hill and coast down so no one would hear him, then walk the half-mile to his cabin along with a shadow.

He accompanied the girls into town only if they insisted on hearing music. At the Nicasio dances, Claire and Anna wore their San Rafael dresses and graded the men in the bar, as if Coop, sitting beside them, were another species. He kept his distance, laughing silently to himself, barely speaking. Who is Coop, really? they asked themselves. Once, having decided to go to Rancho Nicasio an hour after he'd left, they saw him on that small dance floor, caught in its mayhem. Women were being swirled and then caught in his brown arms. He was not a good dancer, quite bad in fact, but girls buried their faces into his neck, their pretty heels next to his cow-shit boots. 'Well, he's a cowboy,' Anna claimed. They didn't want the spell broken, and melted away before he could catch sight of them in the crowd.

Still, being older, he remained the emotional negotiator and translator between them and their father, handed the moderating role a mother would have had. It did not fit his temperament, and perhaps it was the desire to escape all this that made him move into the grandfather's cabin. To rebuild it he needed money, and he earned it with extra work. His first job on the farm when he was a boy had been to help the father build the water tower that now was poised like a lookout over the fields. The grey structure had slowly risen on its skeletal struts, and even before it was completed, Coop would lounge on its sloped roof and gaze at the adjacent hills as though they were a road out. Now, a decade later, there was a leak somewhere within the tower's dark interior.

The minute Coop opened the trapdoor and looked down, panic hit him. There was in his mind the possibility of a snake or even a corpse in that unseen water. He stood for a last moment in the sunlight, pulled up the ladder he'd used to climb onto the apron roof, and dropped it down through the water. Then he removed his clothes, attached a slim hammer to the belt around his waist, and descended into the tank.

Around his wrist were tight rubber bands, and tucked into them pencil-shaped pieces of redwood. He'd been sent to Abdon Lumber in Petaluma. The old men there with furls of wood shavings attached to their arms had politely told him, after he asked to speak with Mr. Abdon, that Abdon was the patron saint of barrel makers. Coop assumed that once he found the leak he could pound in dry shims from outside the water tower, but these men who built and mended wine barrels proposed sharpened sticks of redwood or cedar, and recommended he drive them into the holes from the inside so that dampened they would eventually swell up. Redwood, they told him, lasted over a hundred years, even if it had lain sunk at the bottom of a river.

He let go of the ladder and swam into darkness until he reached a wall. The leak would not be under the water or above it, where the wood was dry, but somewhere around the surface line where the two met. Wood deteriorated at a boundary, it was where the weakness would occur. He was treading water, his fingers on the slippery edges. He had to feel for the leak, would not be able to identify it by sight. This could take hours, or days, in the numbing cold and in the windlessness of the tank. Even when his fingers discovered the initials he had cut into the wood years before, he was not appeased. It suggested a fate. How many times in his life would he or this family need to fix the tank? They had built a prison for themselves.

He climbed out shivering, put on his pants and shirt, and stood in the bliss of the sun. He saw Anna and Claire waving from the second-storey window of the farmhouse. When he got warm he went down again.

How we are almost nothing. We think, in our youth, we are the centre of the universe, but we simply respond, go this way or that by accident, survive or improve by the luck of the draw, with little choice or determination on our part. Years later, if he had been able to look back, Coop might have attempted to discern or reconsider aspects of his or Claire's or Anna's character, but when he had waved back to them, standing in the afternoon sunlight, Anna and Claire were interchangeable, one yellow shirt, one green, and he would not have been able to tell who wore this or that colour. And when he was back in the darkness of the water tank, there was just a retrospective image of the two girls, a tree branch partially concealing their identities and their waving arms.

Once more, as he swam in the water, his fingers touched the

wood for any clue of disintegration, some small tear. Coop preferred metal, the smell of it, oil in a crankcase, rust on a chain, all those varieties and moods of metal life. Reviving a car brought with it the possibility of another life, whereas this family rarely left the farm. The father had once ventured across the border into Nevada and spoke of it still as something foolish and unnecessary, perhaps dangerous. But Coop loved risk and could be passive around danger. He'd been gathered into this fold by a neighbour whose wife died a few months later in childbirth. He knew all things were held in the palm of chance.

He had covered most of the circumference of the tank before he found the leak. He gave a false, theatrical laugh and luxuriated inside the echo, then hung in the water the way he'd seen frogs loll near the riverbank. He inserted the bullet of redwood and hammered it in through water. He found a second hole near the first and filled that too, then swam over to the ladder. Up there, on the roof of the tank, even the sun couldn't warm him. He went into the farmhouse, undressed and wrapped himself in a blanket, then went back outside.

Coop finished the cabin and inserted a large window that allowed him to look out on the trees. Then he began work on the deck. By seven each morning the others could hear the echo of his hammer ricochet down into the valley. He had insisted on working alone, and the only living thing to keep him company during those months of building was Alturas the cat, who roamed everywhere and never settled within anyone's sight. Now and then the cat took a formal walk along the narrow man-made path that crested the hill but those were his only steps into their world. Though whenever Coop looked up from his carpentry, he'd see Alturas watching him, half hidden by the

crest of the hill, and the cat would then lower his head and disappear from view. No one had ever seen the cat sleep, no one
knew what the cat lived on. Yet when the great storm overtook
the region the following winter, none of them assumed Alturas
had perished.

Coop used rippled sheets of corrugated iron for the exterior
walls, saving wood for the eventual deck. He had poured concrete pilings, which allowed the deck to end in mid-air, ten feet
above the slope of the earth. He took his time, hammering down
the planks, letting himself be diverted easily by a hawk or its
shadow, or by mist moving like that glacier through the slope of
trees. He felt himself gregarious in this solitude, though what
happened a short while later may have been the result of his seeing no one for weeks. There was a hunger in him for something
as simple as the sharing of a laugh or a touch.

Was what happened a sin or a natural act? You live within the
crucible of a family long enough and you attach yourself to what
you gaze on as a boy or a girl, some logic might say to explain
what took place on that deck, in the silence where there was no
hammering, a silence as if no other life was being lived.

Neither one of them had made a move before the other. It felt
as if one heartbeat was at work. Anna—who used to leap
around like a boy or a dog; the one who'd broken her wrist,
which Coop had splinted up with willow before he drove her to
a sawbones in Petaluma, and who dared her sister to walk across
the highway by the reservoir blindfolded ('*I'll pay you, Claire*')
and, when Claire didn't, did so herself; the one who read so constantly and carefully she always had a frown, as if gazing at a fly
on the end of her nose—one day began walking up the east ridge
to his cabin in sunlight, along the curving path the cows, and
sometimes Alturas, took. She passed the tree with the pesticide
bag hanging from its low branches, under which cattle gathered

to escape the swarms of flies and mosquitoes, then walked through the circular corral. Coop, she thought, must have finished lunch by now. It was almost two. She closed the second gate to the corral, and as she drew the chain around the post and snapped it, a sudden and heavy rain began, so whatever she wore was transformed. Everything felt heavy, was darker. And then, after a few minutes, the rain ceased.

Coop was sitting, unaware of the brief shower, on the edge of the deck looking towards the thousand or so trees on the facing hill. There wasn't a creak as she moved across the new wood. Wind swept across the deck. He turned and she stepped into his gaze. The rain light made his face a shadow.

You're wet, she began.

Is that true . . .

His casual voice saying nothing more, abandoning her.

It would take a bird five minutes to swim through the air all the way back to the farmhouse, she thought. It would not, of course, move so formally, it would use sweeps and curves, preferring diversions, and be influenced by the surface of the earth. It had taken her twenty-five minutes to walk up here. A car could make it in four. An unhurried horse in ten. But now the farmhouse below seemed like a city one would spend days travelling towards. When she looked back into that distance, she felt there were a hundred valleys of mist and night travel that sheltered the two of them from the others.

Build a fire, will you, Coop!

It's a warm rain, he said quietly to himself, and then louder, It's a warm rain.

But build a fire for me. My clothes. They're wet.

Here. I'll do this.

The cotton shirt like seaweed as he peeled it off, and he startled to see it come away in one piece. She looked down, her face burning, at her whiteness, in the grey light. The freckles of rain on her small frame. *My turn*, she said.

There was silence, only water climbing down a chain from the spout. Everything else was still. Clouds, unseen tentative hills. She saw herself and Coop in this pause of weather, the sun coming out. A fox's wedding, her father called it.

In her memory later, in her unforgetfulness of that day, she sensed she had been present everywhere. With Claire by the stove in the farmhouse, saying, 'Oh, I got caught in the rain.' And Claire coming forward to help her, to (again!) undress. 'No, it's all right, I'll do it myself.' Or she was sheltered under the green curling trees across the gully, watching their two fragile, unprotected bodies on the deck. Anna and Coop, with the sun coming out from under the brief rainstorm so that there were actual shadows on her when his fingers moved back and forth on her stomach as if he were thoughtlessly or thoughtfully trailing them in a river. She watched his dark arm, his wild hair in this light, turned her head away and saw the damp hand-rolled cigarette he had placed on the lip of the deck, still burning.

He was, it felt to her, no longer Coop beside her, on top of her, his hands pinning her shoulders too hard into the wood so she was trying to shrug him off. Anna, he said, finally, as if that word was naked in his throat, so much an admission. Then his palms releasing the grip that held her against the deck, so that his chest now was on her and she could no longer see him, only his hair against her eyes and face, in this changing light.

They were on their sides facing each other. 'A fox's wedding,' he said, sharing the familiar phrase he had heard in their household; but it embarrassed her now, she wanted no evidence of a familial link, wanted wordlessness. As if . . . as if . . . if they did not say anything, all this physicality wouldn't exist, could not be tangible evidence anywhere.

~

Some days she would come up to the cabin and just watch him work. She would offer to hammer planks alongside him, but he did not want that. Sometimes she brought a library book and sat reading in the shadow of the corrugated roof's overhang until the sound of his sawing and hammering disappeared and she was in another country, in Italy with *The Leopard,* or in France with a musketeer. There were days they barely touched, when they would try to talk themselves out of this desire, and there were days when she would bring her book and there was no reading, no talking, in this sparse cabin that was colourless. One afternoon she brought an old gramophone that she had found in the farmhouse, along with some 78s. They wound it up like a Model T and danced to 'Begin the Beguine,' wound it up and danced to it again. The music made them belong to another time, no longer a part of this family or place.

Anna was sitting on the deck, hugging his black t-shirt to her stomach, watching him. She leaned over and opened her little satchel and unstrung the set of Buddhist flags she had bought through a mail-order catalogue. She put on his t-shirt and looked at the struts that bolstered the overhang by the door. 'Can you help me, Coop? I need to get up there. We can tack this to the rain lip over the door.' She already had his hammer in her hand, and a nail. He crouched so she could sit on his shoulders. 'Time for the heart and the mind,' she sang. 'You need to be wind-blessed!' He could feel her wetness at the back of his neck, as she reached up and attached one end of the strip of flags so the snake of it fluttered loose, free of the earth.

There are five flags, she explained. The yellow one is earth, the green is water, the red is fire—the one we must escape—and white is cloud, and blue is sky, limitless space or mind. Coop, I don't know what to do. She was on his shoulders, in mid-air, looking into space.

Do you think Claire knows?

Claire talks to me every night, and I don't say a word about you, and she must wonder why I don't say a word about you.

Then Claire knows.

Some afternoons she spoke to him in an earnest schoolgirl French—as though she were not someone who had grown up alongside him, almost a sibling. Or she'd move away from his desire and read him a description of a city. Sometimes she snuggled against his brown shoulders and after making love burst into tears. There were times she needed this boy or man, whatever he was, to cry as well, to show he understood the extremity of what was happening between them. When he was in her, about to come, looking down on her, his passive face looked torn open, but still he was wordless. It was easier for him. He did not accompany her down to the farmhouse each evening and eat a meal with her father and sister, and play a game of whist during which she'd look up suddenly to see Claire staring at her, attempting to break into her privacy. They were long, maddening, sterile games of chance and counting and collecting pairs or runs, with her father keeping score obsessively. (Besides, Coop was the only one among them good at cards. There were games in the past, Anna remembered, when he would sit laughing at their incompetence.) Worst of all, she had to sleep in the bed next to Claire in mutual silence.

Then Claire knows.

Had Coop loved anyone else? Did you love anyone else? she asked. He was shy at first. Then he said, 'A woman in Tulare.'

Tell me about her. 'No.' Tell—. 'No.' What am I like compared to her? 'It was just one night I slept with her.' Ah good, you *slept*. She kissed him on his doubtful face, then dressed and walked down the hill alone. Halfway home she approached tears, but refused them. She tried to imagine sleeping with anybody else. No one could ever know her as well as Coop did. No one knew Coop as well as she did. She felt this gave her some power, in her walk down to her other life. She was sixteen years old. Almost nothing.

Anna went into Rex's Hardware in Petaluma and bought a can of blue paint, a specific blue to match the blue on one of the flags, and lugged it uphill to the cabin. Coop brought his table out onto the deck. She eased the top off the can and stirred the paint. The weather was strange that day, the heat interrupted by gusts of wind, and they watched the flags bucking, almost breaking loose. Anna remembers every detail. She wound up the gramophone for music. They waited to make love. She sanded down the wood while conjugating French verbs out loud and then began painting the table. All that colourless wood in the cabin had driven her mad, and this blue was a gift for Coop. The wind died suddenly into silence and she looked up. The sky was a dark green, the clouds turbulent like oil.

Thunder exploded over the deck while they were lying there, holding on to each other, as if it had come down a funnel onto their nakedness. They didn't dare let go. It felt to Anna that whatever was in each of them had leapt out into the body of the other. That she'd replaced her heart with Coop's. She could hear nothing, the thunder crash still in her ears. She was trembling in his arms. Then she saw a hand come forward out of nowhere and grip the hair on Coop's head and pull it back, pull him off her, so that she saw sky for a moment and then her father's head looking down at her.

He had ridden up to the cabin to warn the boy of a storm, a possible tornado, had slipped off his quarter horse that was shying under the claps of thunder, and walked round the cabin onto the deck. It was not embarrassment that overcame him at that moment, but a fear. He picked up his daughter, naked as an infant, by her shoulders and flung her off the deck onto the slope of wet earth. Coop stood there not moving. Her father walked towards him, with a three-legged stool, and swung it into his face. The boy fell back through the collapsing wall of glass into the cabin. Then he stood up slowly and turned to look at the man who had raised him, who was now coming towards him again. He didn't move. Another blow on his chest knocked him onto his back. Anna began screaming. She saw Coop's strange submissiveness, saw her father attack Coop's beautiful strong face as if that were the cause, as if in this way he could remove what had happened. Then her father was kneeling above Coop, reaching for the stool again and smashing it down, until the body was completely still.

Coming out of shock, realizing that her father was not going to stop, that he was going to kill him, Anna ran onto the deck and tried to pull her father away. But she could not separate them. Coop looked unconscious, wasn't moving. The stool came down hard on his chest once more, and blood came out of his mouth. Again she tried to embrace her father and pull him away from the body, but she was nothing against his strength. She turned away from him, lifted a large shard of glass and pierced it into his shoulder, pushing it deeper and deeper into his flesh through the checkered shirt. There was a sound like that from a bull, and he turned and struck her with an arm that now held only half its power. He looked backwards and saw the triangle of glass still in him. Anna evaded him until her nakedness was between him and Coop. Her lover. Again her father swept her away. Again she put herself between her father and Coop's body. His strong left arm came up slowly and clutched her neck and began to crush her windpipe. Then everything began darkening and she dropped to her knees and went limp. She was near to Coop, she brought her face beside him and listened for the sound of his breath beneath that of her own frantic breathing, and finally heard a whisper of it. But he was so still. She nudged him and there was nothing. One eye badly closed, covered in blood. She stayed beside him, her arms around her chest, as if protecting Coop's heart safe within her.

Her father stared down at them. Then he walked slowly over to the bed, picked up a sheepskin, and came back and covered her with it. He ignored Coop's body. He carried his daughter over the broken glass until they were away from the cabin and he could put her down, back on the earth. Then he took her by the hand, and never let go of her on the twenty-minute walk down the hill to the farmhouse, the quarter horse nodding beside them, and Anna screaming his name.

He could see nothing, he sat up and could see no frontier between land and sky. Storms had filled the valley. Rain and then sleet. Hail clattering on the corrugated roof. He found himself in the very centre of the room, as far as he could get from the smashed window that sucked in the gale. Outside, the five bannered flags that Anna had strung up a few weeks earlier flew parallel to the ground. Blue, red, green, the hint of yellow, and the now unseen white.

Only the cuts on his face felt sharp and alive. The rest of his body was numb and cold. He was going to die here. He would die here, or walking down the hill. Who was at the farmhouse now? He stood up slowly. The noise around him was so loud he could not hear his own footsteps when he walked across the room, as if he did not exist. He sat at the half-painted table and picked up a book of Anna's. It felt cold.

When he woke he realized he had been asleep at the table. There seemed to be a momentary clearing, but the wind swivelled back and the cabin was again cut off by the storm. Just the flags snapping. He put his hand through the broken window, to test the weather. Was Anna at the farmhouse? All those times she had risen from the deck, laughing nervously, so that at first he believed she was laughing against him, or worse, at both of them. But she was frailer than he knew. She had pointed twenty yards away and said, 'That's what I want. A bathtub out there someday.' As if denying all that was happening between them.

An hour later he was on his knees, on the bare hill, scared he might veer from the path and be fully lost in the unseen landscape. He was keeping to the narrow path by holding on to its texture, brushing away snow to find gravel or mud rather than grass. After leaving the cabin, he had walked into a clutch of barbed wire, cutting open his cheek and tearing his thin coat. He had turned back. When he reached the cabin, banging his arm against its corrugated walls and moving alongside it to find the steps, his face brushed the flags, and he grasped them, wound them around his wrist, and pulled them loose. Come with me, Anna. And turned back down the hill.

The sky was darkening with sleet and he could sense leaves circling in the wind all around him. But nearly everything was invisible. The dead eye just ached. *If you were a Buddhist, you would rise above this. It would be a good thing, no?* He kept moving forward. A heavy push of water flung him sideways. He must have got onto the footbridge and the sluice water had risen over it, and he was tumbling within it down the hill, his clothes suddenly full of water and stones. His back slammed across a tree, and that held him. He had a fury in his head, and he didn't allow himself to lose it. Not letting go of the tree trunk, he stood up until he was touching the lowest horizontal branch, and moved along under it. His face was unprotected from the sleet, but he kept holding the branch, moving further; then his fingers touched the pesticide bag hanging from the tree. So he knew where he was. He knew that if he walked forward, in the direction the branch pointed, he would hit the fence just above the gate. As he began climbing the angle of the hill, he hung on to that small line of a direction. His body stepped into the fence, and he promised himself when he was on the other side he would sit for a while, rest forever. But when he was over it he kept walking, one hand holding the fence wire, in the direction of their farmhouse. It would be only a hundred yards more. He had no idea who would be there. The wire burned his hand and he didn't let go, but then he had to leave it, to cross the thirty yards of open space to the house.

Ten minutes later he was lost, wandering about in darkness. He brushed against a barrel and thumped it to make noise. He took another step forward and a vehicle blocked his way. At first he was angry. He discovered the door of the car and pulled at it. Nothing moved, but then it gave a little, so it wasn't locked, just a coat of ice. He pushed all his weight against it and then pulled the handle again. This time the door came free. He eased himself in stiffly and closed the door. It was quiet. He could hear his breath. He turned on the interior light. With a numb hand he brushed the felt on the ceiling and saw black blood on his fingers. If there was a key he could turn on heat, but there was no key. He pressed the horn for a long time and would not stop. Otherwise he might die here. He was listening to her, Yellow is earth and green is water and red is fire and white is cloud and blue is sky, limitless space, mind. Then he passed out.

Unlike her, you did not want to die. You got down here.

Did she want to die?

She did. Oh yes, I think she did.

Who was talking? Someone pressing down on his stiff bent knees. He was on the floor in front of the stove, stretched out and wrapped in blankets. A spark flipped over to him. Soon he was smelling burning wool. A good smell. Like food. He liked it.

Don't throw away my clothes.

Why?

I want the . . . things.

What?

The . . . the . . .

Flags, she said. Did Anna give you the flags?

Yes. They're not supposed to touch ground.

Well, unlike her you didn't wish to die, somehow you got yourself down here.

It was Claire talking.

Where is she?

They were here. He took her. She wouldn't say a word, even to me. She was screaming when they both came into the farmhouse. She wanted to die. He put Anna in the truck and drove off with her. There was blood on him. They were here just ten minutes.

He said nothing. He didn't know what Claire knew.

There was blood all over him, Coop. All over his clothes. I thought he was the injured one.

She'd had no idea that Coop had remained in the cabin during the storm; her father had said he was somewhere else, before he drove off with Anna. Then Claire had heard what she thought was a car horn, and she opened the door to a thick curtain of sleet. But there was nothing out there. A short while later she heard it again, and went onto the porch once more and looked out. The storm had lessened and she saw a faint orange light, and as she peered into the blackness, it faded. A minute later she would have missed it altogether. An interior car light. Thunder broke loose above the house. She stood very still for a while, then unravelled a circle of rope, tied one end to the porch railing, the other around her waist, and went into the storm in the direction of the light she had seen.

When she saw him through the windshield, she thought he was dead. Then his hands twitched in the ochre of her flashlight. The thunder began again while she was under it. Claire could hardly lift him, but she managed to pull him down out of the car and then to drag him across the hard stubble of the yard to the house and then up the steps. She untied the lifeline of the rope and wrapped him in a blanket and stretched him out before the fire in the empty, dark house.

The next morning there was a faint sunlight. She woke and remembered everything, what had happened to them all. In the barn Claire held the bridle up, and the horse dipped his head and brought his ears through the upper straps. She placed the blanket and saddle high on the animal's back and cinched the girth, keeping it loose for now. She leaned forward to smell his neck, there was always something about that smell.

The cypress trees along the driveway were still and she felt her senses fully alive riding out after the storm. The horse climbed the hill slowly while Claire's eyes skimmed every ridge for any small bump of life that might look like burlap or rock that could be a calf or some other creature. Going after lost things was as uncertain as prayer. Branches and fence posts were scattered across the slopes. An oil drum had rolled in from another farm during the night. The landscape off-kilter. She rode past their river, black with a mud that had probably never surfaced before. From the first hilltop she looked back and saw that the water tower had buckled under its weak legs.

Coop had left. Already. And where Anna was, where her father was, she didn't know. She was alone, sixteen years old, on a horse that bristled with nervousness and temper after his night in a barn full of crashing thunder. She talked quietly, constantly to him, the creature yearning to gallop, wanting to use the energy that Claire was containing.

A swath of buckeye trees had come down across from Coop's cabin. She dismounted and walked onto the deck. It was littered with glass. Through the broken window she saw the cat, Alturas, stretched out on the bed. Claire had never witnessed the cat indoors before. Its head was actually on a pillow, not expecting a soul. Even this one had been changed by the chaos of the weather. She gathered the dozing creature into a pillowcase, before it was fully awake, leaving his head free, and stood in the coldness of Coop's cabin. Years before, she loved camping here alone, when there had been just a pallet and a fireplace. It had been an eagle's nest for her in those days. Before it had become Coop and Anna's. Now, with the storm's destruction, it looked humble again. She was imagining what she could do to it. She imagined herself riding back and turning to see the building on fire, the black plume of smoke in the air. But this cabin was all there was left of the past, their youth.

Coop would never come back. Claire knew that. She knew about the two of them. She had lived in mid-air all those weeks. She'd witnessed Anna returning, sometimes as late as dusk, to the farmhouse, wild-eyed, her face holding nothing back, full of new certainties and knowledge, scared of everything. Anna hadn't stopped moving. She did not have to confess a thing as she circled and circled their small, dark kitchen.

Claire should have burned the cabin down then.

She walked out into the sunlight. She untied the reins and rose onto the horse with the cat in her arms, talking to both of them.

The Red and the Black

The Deadhead, or hippie, would be the one true ally Cooper found when he arrived at Tahoe. And the thing about 'the hippie' was that he seemed the healthiest person in the casino. He was a salt-of-the-earth hippie, cow-shit-on-his-Tevas hippie. From the first time Cooper heard rumours of him to the last night he saw him sitting at that card table with The Brethren, there was never a change in his outfit. There were his unironed Hawaiian shirts, there was the long hair, the loose beads that jangled whenever he moved, and the uncomfortable-looking necklace at his throat made from seashells. Cooper had been sitting on a banquette when he first overheard talk about him.

That friend of yours, that hippie . . .

Dorn's not a hippie. You can't gamble and be hippie.

Man's a hippie. He goes way back. Lives with that speech therapist he met at a Grateful Dead concert. That's hippie.

Dorn, slouching and robust, was the most collected card player to come down from the Sierras. He had a theory that two hours of handball a day justified and cancelled the drinking and cocaine and sitting in the presence of smokers during the long evenings.

Are you the hippie? Cooper asked. They were both watching a game.

Could be.

There's that line—'Hippies are living proof that cowboys still fuck the buffalo.'

I wonder how many times I heard that one.

Cooper had spoken to almost no one since he'd arrived. Now, in thirty seconds, he realized he had managed to insult one of the smartest and most anarchic players in Tahoe, who, the rumour went, had twice skunked David Mamet in a game. His new acquaintance put his hand on his shoulder.

Excuse me. Have to meet someone. My name is Edward Dorn. Like the poet.

The hippie left, and Cooper followed him outside and watched him get on a bicycle, and drift down the street.

Cooper was twenty-three years old when he first arrived in Tahoe and fell into the company of Dorn and his compatriots. He had begun his gambling career watching and playing pool in bars and halls along the coastal towns. He'd studied how the quickly aging players slunk around the pool tables, how they forgave themselves too easily with a grimace, how some were falling in love with the stroke. And he recognized those who were too bitter or ambitious, as well as those who could conceal the larger range of their talent. Cooper had known little about people before this. But pool was by necessity a game of disguises by which you coaxed your mark to the table. And then, when he started playing cards, discovering a technical skill in himself, he saw that in poker you did not need to hide your talent. No one refused a game because you might be a better player than you seemed. This was furious mathematics, a stone in your heart, luck, and the chance of an eventual card—the River—that would glance you towards your fate. He found himself at ease within all this chaos and risk. When he saw drunks steer themselves uncertainly between the card tables in Tahoe, as if avoiding whirlpools, he recognized the same look that had been on him and the other fooled youths coaxed back towards the great Anaconda hoses on the floating platforms of the Russian River.

The group around Dorn took Coop under their wing. There was Dorn, Mancini, and 'The Dauphin,' so named because he had been seen reading a European novel. They would enter gambling halls like royalty from Wyoming—save for Dorn, in sandals and beads, flash-frozen in the sixties. Gamblers scarcely remembered the name of the president of the United States, but Dorn followed politics with an obsessive aversion. He hated Born-Agains like Pounce Autry, whose group, nicknamed 'The Brethren,' formed a prayer circle on the mezzanine before coming down to the card tables. Dorn gave Autry a wide berth. Autry bounced between Tahoe and Vegas, but Dorn and his cohorts saw Vegas as the end of the world. They preferred to be based in Tahoe. Now and then they drove to Reno for a weekend on journeys that were non-stop arguments as to what was the best drug, worst drug, best breed of dog, who was the best cardsharp they had met, the best masseuse, the best or worst actor. Without a doubt, for all of them, De Palma's *The Fury* was the very worst movie ever made, that was a given. And at some point Mancini would insist that Karl Malden was the greatest actor.

Almost every movie—*On the Waterfront, Streetcar, I Confess.* There's *One-Eyed Jacks* . . .

You took those three fucking words right out of my mouth. Him and Katy Jurado—that's the whole movie.

He's in *Cincinnati Kid,* isn't he? Isn't he the mechanic in that?

Mancini, who'd been warming up, hesitated. You know, Karl has been in great fucking pictures, but *Cincinnati Kid* has problems. Remember they're having this game of no-limit five-card stud. And Steve McQueen has, I recall, aces and tens. And Edward G. Robinson—another grand master of the art, if he'd been a chess player, they'd have a statue of him—has three cards, no pairs. Now, you never ever give them a chance to draw, when that happens. You just don't give them a chance to draw again. Period. But Fancy-Pants McQueen puts in a piss amount and allows Edward G. to stay in and draw a card—he should *never* be allowed to get to that card. You'd put in everything, your wife, your *parrot,* to prevent him from drawing, you make it too expensive. . . . You know you have the best hand as things stand. You bet all your money.

So what happens? I forget what happens.

Edward G. lays down a straight flush he's just made, and busts him.

Cooper didn't know the movies they were talking about. The others were in their thirties and forties, he was the youth among them. They watched over him, knowing him as a compulsive risk-taker, dangerous even to himself. But what he could do, which surprised them, was imitate the way each of them played, as if he were speaking in tongues. Though in the mania of a game, when you had to be calm, Cooper could be either startling or foolish. Someday he might be their skilled heir, but it felt to them that for now he was still in hand-to-hand combat, mostly with himself.

Whereas Dorn's friends were in it for the way of life. They played twelve-hour marathons, crossed over from scotch to cocaine, read Erdnase and Philip K. Dick by the pool or in the back of an air-conditioned car, fucked glowing women with the Discovery Channel loud in the background, and shot up in the elevator going down. Cooper didn't participate, was an untouchable. He was sane everywhere but within a game. There was Peruvian flake to keep the others from getting tired. Asleep they could not win. That was the only logic. Several years later in Santa Maria, when a woman named Bridget attempted to give Cooper some, he held her face between his hands and said, 'I know you won't believe me, but one day you're going to write four hundred words down on the back of a matchbook and think you've written a masterpiece, you're going to believe you're invincible.' She smiled back at him: 'You're invincible, Cooper.'

In a deli one evening their group spoke of unusual winnings. Dorn mentioned a player called The Gentile who had won his future wife in a card game, with a pair of nines.

There were setups, larceny, and drugs everywhere. Two men asked Dorn to suggest a reliable card mechanic, and he mentioned Fidelio. 'Pretty name,' they said. 'What nationality is he?' 'Filipino,' Dorn said. 'No, thank you,' the gamblers said, 'we need an Aryan.' Cooper was appalled, but Dorn said, 'Fair enough, they want a dealer who's invisible.' It was a world where you needed to quickly forgive. You found yourself drinking with hit men or smack dealers who might have killed someone with an eight ball the previous week. Fast lives were ending all around them. The concern among their own group was which one of them would be the first to crash. The Dauphin or Mancini. They saw less evidence of disaster with The Dauphin. Though he took Quaaludes regularly, the odds were with him. And he seemed preoccupied with teaching his friends about the recordings and skills of the great concert pianists, as well as how to dress, railing against slip-on loafers, tattoos, men's cologne, the Windsor knot. He talked for hours on the proper length of the sleeve and the correct height of a collar. The greatest work of literature for The Dauphin, as far as clothes were concerned, was *The Tale of Genji,* and on those long drives he read the other passengers to sleep with paragraphs from Lady Murasaki. He had already lectured them on Japanese noir and the early femmes fatales. 'You've not met them yet,' he told Cooper, 'but you will. They'll come at you with a weakness. There is nothing more seductive to a man than a woman in distress. They're like priests, you never give them a handicap.

Cocaine fooled The Dauphin, however, and under its influence two Baptists lured him into a game of Deuce to Seven and he lost everything. A few days later a heart attack felled him. He placed his last bet on a football game that was showing in preop, and was dead a week later. When Dorn went to identify him, the orderly pulled back the sheet and they saw the Jack of Hearts tattooed on his calf, a mistake of taste from his youth.

That left Mancini the winner. (He continued his cicada-length relationships with women and surprised everyone by eventually becoming a drug counselor in Iowa.) They gathered in his apartment at eleven the morning after The Dauphin's death. The colour TV was on mute. There was some coverage about the buildup of the war in the Gulf, and Mancini switched channels and stopped when he found a programme with a female snake-handler wearing shorts. They watched her in silence, remembered anecdotes about The Dauphin, then got in the car and took a drive around the lake. They were more than six thousand feet above sea level and it was easy to get drunk.

They played shorthanded poker among themselves and learned new games and broke down percentages. Dorn's first principle had always been (as in the song) that you go with 'the one with hair down to here and plenty of money.' In the lull after The Dauphin's death, Cooper decided to show them how good a card mechanic he could be. He tore open a new pack, discarded the guarantee cards and jokers, cut at twenty-six and gave a series of faro shuffles, eight times in under a minute, so the deck ended in exactly the same order he started with. He confessed all this to them, even if it was something he would never use in a game, so they would trust him. 'Watch carefully,' he said at the start. 'You have the fingers of a good Catholic with his rosary,' Mancini noted. 'Why do you do this?'

There is a great history of people being given the wrong book, at some key moment in their lives. When Coop had been scammed a few years earlier in three-card monte on the pier in San Francisco, he went to a game shop to discover how he had been cheated, and instead found a reprint of *The Expert at the Card Table*, published as far back as 1902. Apart from explaining the three-card-monte hustle, the book became a Pandora's box for him. He found a subterranean world.

I thought I should discover everything that might come against me, Coop said. I found a treatise on the 'Science and Art of Manipulating Cards.'

Well, someday you must meet The Gentile, Dorn said, and learn a few more things from him. He's an old-time faro player. Maybe I will write you a brief letter of introduction.

A few days after The Dauphin's funeral, they scattered. Dorn returned home to Nevada City, where Ruth, his perennial girlfriend, worked as a speech therapist. He invited Coop to join him, and they drove a winding road bordered by pines and were caught in a swirling snow until they left the mountains. Dorn changed the radio dial to KVMR as they entered its frequency. In Nevada City, he turned out to be a pillar of the community, active with the local public radio station, and with helping transform an old forge into a community centre. At the same time, he remained obsessed with conspiracy theories that, like poker, had a disguised structure, revealed only by footnotes and glances. Dorn could always sense the contours of a setup or read a deceit. What frustrated him in his dealings with the Vegas Brethren, the born-agains, was that he hadn't broken their code, couldn't figure them out; he felt finessed by them. He was unsure whether Pounce Autry was a great poker player who hated to lose or whether he was always assisted by a mechanic or cardsharp who stacked or beagled every deck. Recently, during the buildup to the war, he kept seeing their lapel flags. Coop, disgusted by their adamant political self-righteousness, wanted to take them on.

Can't be done.

I think I could.

Well, visit The Gentile first, if you want to go up against Autry's crowd. The Gentile will teach you. He's become a civilian, but he hates everything about Vegas. Also, he ran off with someone's girl.

The one he won in the card game?

Yes.

So how do I get there?

First of all, you don't ever call him The Gentile. His name is Axel. Get a bus to Bakersfield, then you can hire someone to drive you the seventy miles into the desert.

❧

The no longer functional Jericho Army Base is where Axel and the woman have ended up, living in the 1980 Airstream they've hot-wired up to a transformer pole. They suggest that Cooper sleep in an old surveyor's tent not too far from their silver dwelling. Lina shows him the well where they bathe. There are still traces of gold in the water, she says. They cook all meals outside, and a propane tank hisses away during breakfast and dinner. At night Cooper can see other lights in the far reaches of the abandoned base. Two horses that belong to Lina drift near the camp.

Mentioning Dorn to The Gentile breaks the ice.

God, I knew his mother so well, I could almost have fathered him.

He's the smart one among us, Cooper says graciously.

The Gentile thinks, then mutters, And now they say he's a hippie.

It looks that way.

Coop watches Lina walk over and mount her horse, supple as a scarf, and suddenly he thinks of Claire. The way she was always serene on an animal. Lina has, according to The Gentile, a price on her head, her first husband still unforgiving about her escape from his bullying. *A woman in distress . . .* Cooper remembers. There are mesas and horse trails and old gold mines to explore during the day. The fact that Cooper knows horses surprises Lina. 'Hey, a gambler who rides!' So the two of them trek into the desert. Cooper has to wait for night, in any case—Axel refuses to bring out cards until it is dark, and then he takes Cooper into the Airstream's den and closes the door. They will emerge after three or four hours, at which point Cooper walks to his tent and crashes into sleep.

Some afternoons he wanders alone through the deserted cafeterias and abandoned barracks of the military base, which feels like a suburb of the moon. He meets no one, though at night he will sometimes hear a generator or see a fire. There are only Lina and Axel to talk to. It feels like a parody of guru–disciple teaching, except that The Gentile has a vociferous sexual life—he has even apologized for the noise, and his yells often sound like screams for help. Their sex takes place in the late afternoons, and shortly afterwards they emerge from the Airstream like humbled dormice. Cooper, in his tent forty yards away, has tied a thin cotton cloth over his eyes so he can nap in the three p.m. glare, but it's tough to ignore the shouts of surrender or epiphany coming from the trailer.

After a week, The Gentile doubles the hours of card-playing. The games now last at least six hours. At midnight they pause, Axel goes into the kitchen, and returns with scotch and two glasses, and they begin again. 'Beware the false ending,' he says, as if the previous hours had been only a rehearsal.

The Gentile records their theoretical credits and debits on a chart. By now Cooper already seems to owe him $30,000. 'Whoever loses rides into Miniver for groceries,' The Gentile announces, 'and I don't mount horses or mules.' Another night he raises the stakes. 'If you win, you may sleep with Lina. Try dealing from the middle of the deck. Anything goes tonight. If I catch you at it, the bet is cancelled. If you win, you can show that affection I know you have for her.' Cooper is deeply embarrassed. 'Some say I won Lina in a card game,' The Gentile continues, 'though in fact she won *me* in that card game. But of course I was the dealer. The CIA believes you can break anyone, turn anyone, if you know their weakness. It's usually sex, always number one, then money, or power. Now and then pride and vanity. What about you?'

They play with their scotch glasses balanced on the windowsill. 'It's easy being a mechanic playing a large table, so let's limit ourselves to a small one. Also, Vegas has distractions. We don't. So you can watch me carefully.'

Thus begins the second week of a more illicit education. How to be an undiscovered cardsharp. 'It's something we are not naturally inclined to do,' Axel murmurs, 'to handle things with skill and grace and make it appear that nothing is happening. You need to give the illusion of the unexceptional. Slow down your deal, in fact deal like a sucker. Then you can vanquish them. Now, show me your crimp work.' It is clear to Cooper that, as far as Axel is concerned, Vegas needs to be buried under the sands. 'I look at this military base and have high hopes that Vegas will end up the same, with entombed singers and comedians. A thousand years from now we will dig up the tomb of the great Wayne Newton, and he will be a god again.' Axel never stops talking. Cooper is reminded of hitchhikers who enter a car and rattle off biblical quotations with chapter and verse to prove that the end of the world will arrive before the weekend. The Gentile lectures about manner and style and focus. 'I am told that Tolstoy,' he says, 'was able to walk into a room that held a small group of people and understand everything about them in fifteen minutes. The only person in the room he could *not* understand was himself. That's what a good professional is like.'

The Gentile shuffles and deals quickly and angrily, listing what he loves in the world he has left—espresso, plots in Donald Westlake novels, the flavour of chipotle chilies—and Cooper keeps watching the deal. If he accuses The Gentile and he is wrong, he forfeits a thousand. 'Just a thousand,' Axel says. 'Normally if we are falsely accused, we pick up a handgun and blast your shoulder off. And don't forget—*if* you win this evening, Lina is beyond the door. I'll sleep in the tent. Probably howl like a wolf in jealousy. But a deal is a deal. I told her, and she approves of the stakes, by the way. I read of a similar bet in a Faulkner story.' 'Don't distract me,' Cooper says. 'I am distracting you. You missed two corrupt shuffles, during the story about Tolstoy. You were *listening,* there was content there, there was a maze-like thought there. You have to forget the content, think about the wheel. . . .'

Two in the morning. Cooper rises and marks his losses on the chart that's tacked to the varnished door. There is utter frustration in him. He thought he was skilled. 'Do you know what the best line in a movie is?' The Gentile asks, still in his seat.

'You can tell me that tomorrow,' Coop says. 'Good night.' In the other room Lina says, 'You lost, right?' He doesn't know whether she really is aware of the absurd stakes proposed by

Axel. She takes his hand. 'Great hands. So Axel tells me. Good night.' Cooper treads through the darkness, enters the tent, and is asleep instantly. A few minutes later he wakes to their loud laughter.

The two of them break from cards one night and walk with Lina for hours along a dry riverbed. They clamber to higher ground, where it is even darker, there's hardly a moon, and Coop feels barely attached to the earth. Lina comes alongside him, and her hand takes his so their fingers intertwine. For Coop, who has been solitary so long, it is full of intimacy, a secret gesture. She turns in the darkness, looks at his profile, and says, 'Oh, it's you,' and moves out of reach. 'I'm sorry, it was a mistake,' he hears her say, as she goes farther away from him.

She keeps reminding him of Claire. This woman who has been saved from a mistakenly chosen life by Axel. She has an abundance that emerges from her farm-girl's face. When Cooper leaves a few days later to catch the bus to Bakersfield, she offers a shy farewell. He kisses the plaid shirt by her neck. Then her temple. And Axel, who has rarely touched him in all his time there, gives him a bear hug.

He has, in any case, learned everything he came for. He has won only a few games against The Gentile, but Cooper knows—although his teacher doesn't say it—that he can now deal a pack of cards to the Supreme Court and get away with it.

In the half-light of the night bus he studies his hands, turns them over. The Gentile's hands looked like a girl's, like those of a princess. Coop, travelling to meet Dorn and the others in Vegas, suddenly feels unready. He realizes he has been living within intricate and private conversations with a possible madman, around one small light, at one small card table in an Airstream. He is a risk to himself as well as to the others. He looks up when the bus approaches Vegas, where the sky above the desert city seems to be on fire.

～

The Gulf War begins at 2:35 a.m. during the early hours of January 17, 1991. But it is just another late afternoon in the casinos of Nevada. The television sets hanging in mid-air that normally replay horse races or football games are running animated illustrations of the American attack. For the three thousand gamblers inhaling piped-in oxygen at the Horseshoe, the war is already a video game, taking place on a fictional planet. The TV screens are locked on mute. There are floor shows, cell-phone hookers, masseurs at work, the click-clacking of chips, and nothing interrupts the reality of the casino where the 'eye in the sky' looks down on every hand played on the surfaces of green baize. Simultaneously, in the other desert's night, orange-white explosions and fireballs light up the horizon. By 2:38 U.S. helicopters and stealth bombers are firing missiles and dropping penetration bombs into the city. During the next four days, one of the great high-tech massacres of the modern era takes place. The Cobra helicopter, the Warthog, the Spectre, and its twin, the Spooky, loiter over the desert highway and the retreating Iraqi troops, pouring down thermobaric fuel, volatile gasses, and finely powdered explosives, to consume all oxygen so that the bodies below them implode, crushing into themselves.

Dorn, his girlfriend Ruth, Mancini, Cooper. The four of them talk in the River Café. It's one in the morning. Mancini wants to be in on the actual game against The Brethren. 'I can't trust you,' Dorn says. 'You're a good actor, and then sometimes you're translucent. We need The Dauphin to be the innocent, and he's gone. So it will have to be me.' Dorn has taken charge.

Do I drive, then? says Mancini.

No. Ruth drives. It's best if you sit down with Coop for a few days and work on the hands, timing, the moves. All that.

So, The Speech Therapist drives. And I'm *translucent*. Thus, I am not on the floor at all. . . .

You can't be, they'll smell a crew. In fact, be somewhere else that night, another casino. How much have you discovered about Autry? Does he have a mechanic?

Sidekicks always play with him, so it's difficult to identify who is responsible. The cardsharp drifts from person to person, I think, every few hands.

Cooper interrupts. Then I suggest we just blow them all out of the water.

Then you'll never have an afterlife in this town. If they are corrupt, they will recognize corruption. The reason you went to The Gentile was to make what you are doing invisible.

I don't care.

I care, Ruth says. This is our world. We work here.

Dorn and Cooper step from the elevator onto the mezzanine level and walk down the flight of stairs into the swamp of card tables. The section of the casino where The Brethren always sit is a small room off the main poker floor where, beyond a blue rope, there is a single table. While strictly overseen by the eye in the sky, the hand-dealt games here have the dangerous air of an old faro game. No one is fully safe with the human element, but they have all been warned. Dorn, in a canary-yellow Hawaiian shirt, sips a glass of scotch and watches The Brethren hunting down a civilian. Autry gestures a welcome into their game. Dorn and Cooper hesitate. This is expected of them; normally they are gun-shy with the Born-Agains. They mime having another drink and signal a possible return, then continue their walk around the casino. An hour later, when they do eventually step over the blue rope and sit down with Autry and the two thieves, one on either side of him, it's quickly established that this will be a private game, there will be no house dealer. And it's Texas Hold 'Em. This is how The Brethren play.

In the first hand Dorn wins a thousand. It's the expected hook from The Brethren, and Dorn shows modesty. He leans forward with his long unwashed hair and his big smile. Autry begins a monologue about the state of the world, this desert, that troublesome desert. The hands go back and forth for more than an hour, the good hands essentially cancelling each other out, a familiar rise and fall. Whenever it is Coop's turn, he cuts the deck faithfully. The players are all watching the movement of hands, the buried habits. Coop notices where the player on his right habitually cuts the cards, roughly the same spot every time. The talk around the table is constant, interesting anecdote and data, but Cooper thinks of the wheel. He knows someone will make a move soon. 'Don't riffle-stack for just a minor haul,' Mancini has told him. 'Save the work for when everything has escalated.' So Cooper waits.

The plan is for him at some point to double-duke, creating two great hands during the course of the shuffles—one for Autry and a better one for himself. He will place this riffle-stacked slug of cards beneath a crimp, about where the player on his right usually cuts the cards. If the man cuts at the crimp, there will be no need for Coop to hop or shift the deck secretly; they will be able to bet everything on the known fall of the cards. Whenever he is ready to do this he will signal Dorn to provide shade so there will be some distraction.

The game began in mid-afternoon, and it is now seven. Autry's right-hand thief continues dealing Texas Hold 'Em. Shortly after this, Dorn suggests raising the blinds to make the game twice as big. There will be two hands before Cooper gets to deal again. He and Dorn have won and lost hands but have scraped through. A real assault against them has not yet taken place.

Dorn now describes some news footage he has watched of the massacre in the 'troublesome desert'—with American planes pouring down ten thousand rounds a minute onto a crowded highway of escaping soldiers. 'That's the news, as of yesterday,' he mutters. 'We're dropping five-hundred-pound antitank cluster bombs that spew out razor shards into the air at four thousand feet per second. We're burning up those bodies from a biblical height. The highway, they say, is like Daytona Beach during spring break.' 'Stop it!' Autry explodes, but Dorn doesn't. 'It's Resurrection Day. . . . Everything there, they say, is more or less charcoal.' Cooper completes his shuffle sequence and slips in the slug, low in the deck. A silence round the table. Dorn gives more details of the attack on the Republican Guard, until Autry puts his hand up and requests silence. Cooper takes back the deck, showing rapt attention as Autry remembers a conversion he witnessed in which a girl of six began speaking whole pages out of the Old Testament.

Cooper deals out the first round of cards—two face-down to each player. This goes on the table:

DORN	X	AUTRY	Y	COOPER
K♠	6♢	A♣	5♣	7♢
10♠	2♣	A♠	Q♠	7♣

Cooper asks Autry to continue his anecdote, diverting him from the surprisingly good hand he has been dealt. Dorn bets and Autry raises him. Cooper stays in and the two thieves drop out. Coop sits back now and relaxes. The fate of the entire dealing sequence has been set up during the shuffles. All he has to do is play out the hands. He burns the next card, discarding it as he has to, before dealing the next three communal cards, the flop, face-up.

DORN	AUTRY	COOP
K♠	A♣	7♢
10♠	A♠	7♣

The flop

A♡ 7♠ 4♣

Dorn has little of value but bets, and Autry, who now has three aces, raises. Cooper begins to sing quietly, *'You're gonna run to the rock for rescue, there will be no rock . . .'* and calls Autry's bet. Dorn folds. The game has been slowed to a crawl.

Cooper burns the next card before dealing the fourth street. It's an inconsequential card—an eight of diamonds—which doesn't alter the strength of the hands; it will simply create another round of betting.

Got any family? Autry asks Cooper. He has been X-raying the young man's nature.

No family, Cooper says quietly.

Got a girl?

Haven't got a girl. No, sir. Cooper clicks his tongue. You a married man?

Yes, I am.

Autry makes another large bet. Coop contemplates, shuffles his chips. Contemplates some more, and calls. It is about nine-thirty, and there is almost $100,000 in the pot, with nearly that amount again sitting in front of the two remaining players. Now even Autry is silent, and Coop deals out the last card—the River—his mind whispering it as he begins to turn it over. He will burn down Autry, humiliate him, with this humble seven of hearts.

AUTRY	COOPER
A♣	7♢
A♠	7♣

The board

A♡ 7♠ 4♣ 8♢ 7♡

Along with the communal cards, face-up on the board, Autry now has a full house, three aces and two sevens. He goes to town and moves all his remaining chips into the pot. Coop calls him. They put down their hands, Coop revealing his sevens. Voilà, he says.

Autry recognizes the dragon full of mockery. Coop pulls in the roughly $300,000, then stands up slowly.

Sit down, son, Autry whispers, a deeper voice.

Sit down, Dorn echoes.

Cooper stays standing, gathering the chips. He looks up at the eye in the sky that he knows is watching them, that he knows never captured what he has already done, and waves to it.

'You fucking idiot, you're a child,' Dorn says. Cooper, catching his real anger, looks at him. Then he walks to the cage and cashes out, watched by them all. Mancini is at the mezzanine railing, looking down.

Cooper bangs the button for the elevator and travels to the eleventh floor, gets out, and takes the stairs down to the parking garage, and searches for Dorn's car. Headlights blink silently and he walks towards the vehicle. Ruth is sliding over onto the passenger seat. 'It went okay?' 'Yes.' They drive out of the darkness of the garage into a world of swerving desert electricity. In twenty minutes they are out of the city.

There is war news on the radio all night. Ruth leans against the passenger door, watching him. Cooper, usually a person of humble acts, already feels foolish about his excess. She taps him on the shoulder with her finger, and he wakes from his focus on the road.

You know *Sophie's Choice?* Ruth says. The book? I heard the guy who wrote it, on the radio, once. They were asking him what he was working on, but he wouldn't say. Then, at some point during his excuse for not saying what he was doing, he said, 'You know, I think I have already written the most intimate and profound book I will ever be able to write. I don't think I can go as far as that again. From now on I should try comedy. Comedy is not easy, I know. But at least it is not the same road.' I loved that about him, what that writer said. And I read everything of his after that, but of course there was never to be a comedy. And of course you can't go back again.

I know that, Coop says quietly, so that she hardly hears it.

Then Ruth sleeps, knowing she has to drive back to Vegas by early morning. Cooper turns the radio knob, looking for further details of the war, but they are paltry. He is aware he has ended his career in Vegas and even Tahoe by winning so blatantly, with so much bravura. The Gentile, in his first lesson, warned him against flamboyance and unevenness. As a mechanic, Axel was of the Naturalist School, with the desire to always give the illusion that nothing was happening. And what occurred with The Brethren was not luck. Dorn will probably have to fan out the flames for himself, staying in the casino tonight, behaving in a manner that suggests anger towards Cooper. And Ruth, he knows, will slide the car back into the parking garage before dawn and be free of The Brethren's suspicion.

They stop for a drink in a roadside bar. Once back in the car, Cooper separates the money equally into four piles, and puts his in an old Northwest Airlines bag. Then they drive again, the last leg, with the windows down, the highway breeze sideswiping him. At one point he slows the car to a halt and she says, 'What is it?' There is an owl on the road, apparently unwilling to leave the heat of the highway, and Coop drives around it and continues. When they reach the bus depot at Tonapah, he sits a moment longer, his hands on the wheel, as if there were still miles to go. They get out and Ruth comes around to the driver's door and they embrace. Coop is going to disappear. He will never see these friends again. He pulls out the Northwest Airlines bag and walks away from the car. Ruth starts it and a moment later drives past him—a tap on the horn, her hand out the window—but he doesn't acknowledge the second farewell. He has already become a stranger.

At seven-thirty the next morning, when Dorn and Mancini arrive for breakfast at the River Café, Ruth is sitting alone in the slightly chaotic restaurant. Four waitresses in rubber boots are wading in the artificial river that has flooded, searching under large rocks in order to find the pump plug that malfunctioned during the night. 'River's in mourning,' Mancini says. They are aware that Cooper, their 'heir,' is the one blackballed for life, certainly from all the big casinos. They also know that the three of them are in some way permanently linked to him. But rather than talk about it, they watch the waitresses, who are now laughing and beginning to enjoy themselves, splashing in the water.

Le Manouche

She was following a path of gorse, her face and fair hair in the litter of light from the high branches of oak above her; she was moving at a fast pace ever since the incident a few days earlier when she had encountered the four men with their guns and dogs. They had been standing at a small crossroads in the woods, arguing, all barking at one another, and as she came near, the men threw out suggestive comments in French that she had understood but pretended not to. The atmosphere of threat had unnerved her. In spite of the episode, Anna had refused to give up her afternoon walks. She would take the forest path, come into the clearing, and then follow the river until she reached the paved road a half-mile from the village of Dému. It was a walk on the edge of a run. In Dému she bought groceries, put them in her backpack, and then turned home. At that speed she was there in an hour and a half. The house was a *manoir*, and she was a temporary tenant in the place. She had thought at first that it might be a château, but it wasn't quite that. She had never stayed in a French château, just as she had never seen a hunting dog until that afternoon with the belligerent men.

Most days Anna worked indoors at a kitchen table, reading the manuscripts and the handwritten journals of Lucien Segura. The *manoir* had once been the writer's home, and she found herself in some modest contrapuntal dance with him. So that when she looked up from her work, it took a moment to recognize the same doorways and the room around her—she had until that moment been immersed in unearthing and cross-referencing a detail from this French writer's life, delving below the surface of his work. A phrase among one of her colleagues described what she was doing as 'sweeping the translator's house.' And she knew if she ascended the flight of stone stairs and turned left she would be in his bedroom, could look down onto the branches of the large oak tree the way the Frenchman might have done as he dressed by the window generations before.

Once a week Madame Q arrived with her husband. She dusted the house silently, while Monsieur Q surveyed the garden and gathered branches and clarified the flower beds. He was also the postman for the village. They would stay the length of the morning and then leave. When no one inhabited the house, the couple came more often and behaved like full-time caretakers. As it was, they would step from the blue Renault 4L and bring news about the world, about local politicians, about various wars. Monsieur Q would look across a field and decide he could get away with leaving it for another week, while Madame Q attempted to teach Anna the basics of cooking a rabbit stew, assembling one large dish that would save her from making lunches for three days.

The husband, smoking his pipe, would walk the perimeter of the walled garden and consider how well the pollarding of the trees had succeeded. He would eventually circle the house to where the door leading to the back pasture would be open, and through the opening see Anna hunched over the table writing, or reading some large book, never looking up, never conscious of him a few yards from her open doorway, and he'd shake his head and drift away. The woman was from America, his wife had told him. When she stood up she was as tall as he was, light-coloured hair to the neck. She looked strong and healthy. She had asked him in her New World French where the good places to walk were, and he had drawn a map with the best paths, routes that weaved through other properties and crossed the river. He reminded her to close all the gates. When the owner of the *manoir* came there, he'd always be driving off immediately—to pick up *floc* from an Armagnac distillery or on some other errand. But this guest was different. She had no desire to spend time in town. She was content here. She might spend half an hour talking when they came their one day a week, but then she would be back at the table, with her books. He knew she walked into the village now and then. As a postman he travelled all the time, it was in his blood. Staying in a house the whole day seemed unnatural. So when she asked him into the back room, and escorted him through the lean corridor of the house to the kitchen, where he saw the open door leading to the pasture, which was where he had stood watching her work the previous week, and where now she offered him a sheet of paper, he drew the map for her clearly and to scale—his job had taught him exact kilometre distances and property boundaries and stream beds. He drew the rectangle of the house and a quick oval for the herb bed, then re-created the world outside, ending with distant copses and deer forests, dismissing places she should avoid, those that tourists inhabited. In Anna's terms the map was a 'keeper,' and she might one day frame it and hang it in her living room on Divisadero Street in San Francisco, a private core of a memory. In some part of her mind, she felt that if worse came to worst, she could always escape back here.

Anna carried the map with her as she walked. Since the day she had met the four hunters, she wore jeans instead of a skirt and shaved ten minutes off the ninety-minute walk. But where she was now, alongside the gorse hedges, the path was uneven, broken with stones, and she needed to slow down. Juniper grabbed her feet as she left the path, throwing up its smell. Sunlight fell through the trees and as she paused to look up at the splintered beauty, she heard music.

What she heard was a woman singing. If she had thought there were men there, she would not have walked towards the sound. But this was tempting. A woman's voice, a tune that seemed to have no scaffolding, almost too casual to be good, although the voice was clear, waterlike. Anna stood where she was a moment longer. She saw a sparrow leaping from branch to branch, clumsily, hardly adept. She strolled towards the clearing, stopping once or twice, trying to interpret the tune.

She came into the open field, where there was a woman, and also a man, sitting in a straight-backed chair, accompanying her on what looked to be a guitar. They didn't see her at first, but they must have sensed something—a sudden quietness in the trees above her, perhaps—for the woman turned and, when she saw Anna, stopped singing and strode away, leaving the man alone in the open field.

France had meant a quiet and anonymous time for Anna. Apart from the visits of Monsieur and Madame Q, she saw no one. And there was nothing in the house of the writer to remind her of North America. She was escaping the various aspects of her professional life—acquaintances, deadlines, requests for prefaces—all of which, if she were in her real world, would be essential duties. The only thing that had truly jostled her in the time she had spent so far in the Gers region of France was the group of men at the crossroads with their dogs, the men's tongues lolling in parody and their fists twisting in the air as she walked away. She felt at ease in the modest house, her curiosity almost aimless, as if she were beginning a new life. She was enjoying the process of filling a notebook with fragments and even drawings, something quite apart from her research. If there was the sound of a bird through the open door by her table she would try to articulate it phonetically on the page. She did this whenever she heard one clearly enough. And when she leafed through her obsessive notes, Anna would find a series of chords of birdsong, or her drawing of a thistle, or of the Qs' Renault.

The man with the guitar had turned his head to look at her. Feeling she needed to make a gesture to avoid being rude, Anna moved forward to say something, and he watched the uneven grass she crossed as she approached him.

Hello. I'm sorry.

As if she had come here and interrupted him to tell him she was sorry!

One thing, she felt completely safe. It was not the obvious fact that he was holding a guitar and not a weapon, it was his look, as though he had been just taken from refuge, and she was now insisting him back to earth. While she walked those last few yards towards him, she realized she must have also heard his playing when she entered the clearing, a subliminal hum and strum, a rhythm and a melody—which was why the woman had needed none in her song. The woman was accompanying *him*. So now it was as if everything she had heard was being replayed in her memory, recalled differently. He had been the one drawing her into the clearing.

It was a tattered guitar. When she got close she could see his hands had been bitten by insects, were scarred. His clothes, which had looked formal from a distance, were unironed, muddy at the cuffs; the waistcoat had lost buttons. But it was the hands that were too lived in, overused.

She looked in the direction the woman had gone, and saw a caravan in the shadows, within the trees.

This was the same clearing where Anna and her friend Branka had stood the second night after her arrival at Dému, more than a week before. The grass had felt like a flat receptacle then, a moon pasture. She was wearing a sleeveless dress, had just done a cartwheel and scooped up some golden broom, which had been colourless in that light. She'd had no awareness then that there was a caravan or *any* inhabitant in the vicinity, save for herself and Branka, who had driven her down from Paris. Branka, an architect, was staying for only a day. It was she who had helped Anna arrange the rental of the writer's house, through a contact in her firm. They had walked back to the *manoir,* clambering over the low brush, finding gaps in the hedges that were clear in the moonlight.

If Anna came any closer to the man with the guitar, she would be encroaching on his territory. If she remained more than four paces away, it would signal a fear, though there was none. He seemed a contained man, and he had one arm over his guitar as if it were a favourite hound.

I interrupted you, I'm sorry. But it was beautiful.

To be truthful, she hadn't really felt that. It had been just strange music coming through the trees to where she had been standing. It was something unexpected. So perhaps beautiful. She had not quite lied. The musical chords had calmed everything; even the insects had paused their noisy needle and thread. She looked towards the quiet trees.

I didn't know you lived here. I was here once before, one night.

The fingers of his right hand swept over the strings, six notes spreading towards her like a fan. He smiled briefly at her, then fell into a melody and seemed to be playing everything—bells, drums, a missing voice.

This was a field, he told her sometime later, that he had sat in as a boy, playing alongside his mother's singing. He would look not at the strings but at his mother's face in order to catch her rapid swerves of melody; there would be no clue about her voice's darting, except in her eyes—this starling, that wood thrush—and still he would be beside her, picking up notes as if counting kilometre stones as she flew down a road. As a boy he had always felt that his musical lessons were a net for holding everything around him—the insects in the field, the weather shifting in the trees—so that he could give it as a collected gift, like a hand cupped with cold water held up to a friend.

When he finished, he said, You did not sing. You did not join me.

No. I'd have been the extra wheel.

Music has many wheels, that's what makes it joyous.

The other singer . . .

Anna did not know what to say, whether she should inquire.

She comes from the village for lessons. Once a week I give lessons. You came from the house with the *pigeonnier*?

She nodded.

A bee landed on the neck of the man's guitar, and he pursed his lips and blew it off. When it returned after a quick circuit in the air, he flicked it away with his middle finger, and it spun wounded into the grass.

My name is Rafael, if you want to know.

Ah yes, ah yes, I was told about you, by the owner of the *manoir*. He said you might be here. She glanced behind. I should go, I suppose.

He said he would accompany her. But then he took no direct

path towards the house. He guided her, stepping over bushes. They had to bend almost double to walk under the low branches of the trees. He ignored a clear path a few yards to their right, as if he had the mind of a cow, or a crow in mid-air, perceiving a more natural route. If anything, going this way, they took longer to reach the house. The comfort she had felt in that field was replaced by scratches, and some annoyance towards him.

At the kitchen door she asked if he was thirsty and, under the gush of the tap, filled two cups and invited him to sit down at the table. It was covered with books and papers. His right arm pushed some of them aside to give himself more space, but he did not look at what they were. Instead his eyes searched around the room, the way a thief's might. You did not invite strangers in for a drink like this, but Anna hadn't spoken to anyone for days. He was looking at furniture and pictures, consuming them, the same way he had looked at her, with either curiosity or pleasure. That was how he now regarded the red enamel cup he was holding in his hands.

My father was known by some as a thief, he said, as though he had read her mind about how he was looking around the room. But he never stole from houses he was invited into.

That's civilized, she managed to retort soon enough to seem at ease with this information.

I think so too. Still, his craft taught him—and so he taught me—about the value of things I am unlikely to own. To me, for instance, what is most valuable in this room is this blue table. But I know it has no real value.

Does he live around here, your father?

He's not from France. But after the war he didn't go home, instead he met my mother. He was injured in the war. He later organized a small group who filched—is that the word?—from the houses they were not asked into. It had been difficult during the war, and I think he felt that everyone who had fought was owed more than they were given.

So he was a 'filcher.' A quaint term. And what did you say your name was?

Rafael.

And your father?

. . . never wished me to be a thief.

And your mother? Was she a thief too? He was grinning at her. Did they meet during a robbery?

Almost. It was in a jail. She had a part-time job at a police station. I believe he charmed her, even though he was older. May I have more water?

Yes, of course. She moved to the sink with the red cup. I met some strange hunters here, in the forest, the other day, she said.

There are terrible people, all over the place. Just like me.

She laughed then.

There's a big garden here, isn't there? I'd like to see it. I can cook you something.

It's out through that door. Pick anything . . .

Anna stood in front of the flecked mirror, washing her face and arms, then rubbed her legs with a cold, wet washcloth. Later, when she walked into the garden, she saw him smoking a cigarette, looking over the rows of vegetables.

Who were those hunters? Are they from the village?

I cannot help you there. We keep to ourselves.

I suppose, then, you wouldn't tell me even if you knew. . . . I was scared, to tell the truth.

As she spoke, he pulled a piece of green cloth from one of his inside jacket pockets. Tie this around your arm when you go walking, you'll be safe.

She took the cloth into her hands.

Your father, was he English? You speak very—

My father could speak it well.

Does he come here?

Not for some time.

Well, if he ever does, I'll be sure to invite him in.

Rafael crouched and began to snap off beans, passing them back to her, dropping them into the green cloth she held open.

Do you have a little beef?

I'll take these in, she said, and cut a few strips of meat for us.

He strolled into the house a few minutes later and unpacked rosemary and four figs from his pocket. He began working on a salad, slicing slivers of garlic into it.

So, how did you escape the life of crime—and your charming father?

Anna was talking with him as if he were an old friend from childhood who had changed shape into this thickset man. His musical fingers were now dicing tomatoes. The eyes that had darted around the room were now gazing easily at her. He seemed not at all awkward or tense about being in the house. His behaviour around her seemed effortless. So that when she went to bed with him for the first time, some days after this lunch, his hesitancy was a surprise. He did not pull away, but scarcely leaned forward. What had been familiar across the kitchen table was now shyness and perhaps incapacity, as though in the past he had been burned by something. They did nothing but hold each other. He would for now be content with her breath against his shoulder, the mole on her upper arm. He would fall asleep thinking of this small dark dot.

He was certainly not vain, freely admitting his thick girth, his imperfect health. After they had eventually made love satisfactorily (as far as she could assume for both of them), he stood and tested his calves in a naked leap, then strolled to the window, opened it and smoked a cigarette there, gazing out, not caring how he looked in that sunlit posture. He would mention later that he was unconcerned with his 'silhouette.' Anna had met no one like him. There appeared to be no darkness in him. Though he would tell her of an earlier relationship that had silenced him completely, and how he had almost not emerged from that. He was in fact coming out of that privacy for the first time with her. All over the world there must be people like us, Anna had said then, wounded in some way by falling in love—seemingly the most natural of acts.

He told her there was a song he no longer performed that had to do with all of that. It was about a woman who had risen from their bed in the middle of the night and left him. He would hear evidence of her in villages in the north, but she would be gone by the time the rumour of her presence reached him. A song of endless searching, sung by this man who until then had seldom revealed himself. His tough fingers would tug the heart out of his guitar. He'd sing this song to those who had grown up with his music over the years, who were familiar with his skill at avoiding the limelight. He knew his reputation for shyness and guile, but now he conceded his scarred self to his friends. '*If any of you on your journeys see her—shout to me, whistle . . .*' he sang, and it became a habit for audiences to shout and whistle in response to those lines. There was nowhere for him to hide in such a song that had all of its doors and windows open, so that he could walk out of it artlessly, the antiphonal responses blending with him as though he were no longer on the stage.

In the days before Anna slept with him, he had expected no gesture of interest from her. Their lunches had seemed innocent of courtship. And their first afternoon in the upstairs room of the house had been similarly genial, neither of them loved the other yet, so there was nothing fatal or fateful about it when they woke in each other's arms, facing each other, a breath away. In that small space between them was the smell of cilantro. He had a passion for it, and had crushed it into their salad a few hours earlier. His pockets always held a few herbs, basil or mint, so he could rip off a heel of bread and create a meal wherever he was.

When Anna had gone upstairs to wash that first day, he had stayed outside for a while, half dreaming among the green rows of the garden, then walked into a deep hollow in the earth, a *mare* that had a century earlier held water for cattle. He stood there blackened by the shadow of the great oak that rose above him, and soon he was stretched out on the grass, so that when Anna looked from the window he seemed to have disappeared.

Her early impression of Rafael was that he saw nothing around him as fully owned—his fingers removed leaves from a plant with the same ease as when, three days later, he wrapped his dark fingers around her wrist, barely grazing the skin so her pulse continued to pause and lift in his loose grip. She looked down at a scar across his knuckles, kept looking down, giving no gesture in response to this act of his, the captive pulse no doubt beating faster. She was thinking of the chords of music that had emerged from hands as scarred as these. She did not rest her face into his chest, into the cache of basil within the shirt pocket, until he let go of her. Come with me, she said then. Watch your step. They went up the stone stairs wide enough for three horses, along the corridor, into her small room, where she bent down to turn on the electric heater and waited for the appearance of its three red bars.

She laughed when he rather formally closed the door behind them. He shrugged.

Is that what you call a 'Gallic gesture'?

Garlic? He was perplexed.

Gallic! You know that turn of phrase?

'A turn of phrase'? Another shrug. We are in the smallest little room in a very big house, he said. Is there a reason?

You don't like it?

No, he said, we should take up the smallest possible space. But not *too* little space.

I'm embarrassed by the size of the other rooms.

Rafael sat on the bed, watching the strip of her energy, tall, erect. Dark jeans, blue shirt, a rolled-up sleeve on her brown arm. He noticed a mirror positioned low on the wall, a low sink.

This room belongs to a child.

∾

This 'smallest possible space' is where Anna wishes to be now. The truth of her life comes out only in places like this. There are times when she needs to hide in a stranger's landscape, so that she can look back at the tumult of her youth, to the still-undiminished violence of her bloodied naked self between her father and Coop, the moment of violence that deformed her, all of them. Anna, who keeps herself at a distance from those who show anger or violence, just as she is still fearful of true intimacy. Her past is hidden from everyone. She has never turned to a lover or friends when they speak about families (and she always inquires of their families) and spoken of her childhood. The terrible beating of Coop, the weapon of glass entering her father's shoulder as she tried to kill him. Even now she cannot enter that afternoon's episode with safety. A wall of black light holds her away from it. But she knows it damaged all of them, including Claire. She can imagine her sister riding her horse in the Sierras, wearing small bells on her wrists to warn wildlife of her approach, conscious of all the possibilities of danger. Just as she herself works in archives and discovers every past but her own, again and again, because it will always be there.

She and Rafael keep between them a formality that makes them careful with each other. They have stepped into this friendship the way solitaries in medieval times might have bundled together for the night before journeying on towards a destination of marriage or war. So that Anna is not aware that the casualness in Rafael she witnesses is inconsistent with his nature (save for the territorial precision with which he flicked that bee off his guitar in her presence a few days earlier), while he knows scarcely a thing about her. Who is she? This woman who has led him into this medicine cabinet of a room where most of her possessions exist—books, journals, passport, a carefully folded map, archival tapes, even the soap she has brought with her from her other world. As if this orderly collection of things is what she is. So we fall in love with ghosts.

Early in her stay at Dému, Anna watched three hawks flying low over the fields, half covered by mist, hunting for life. She noticed how the poplars held thrushes and blackbirds, how sumac built itself beside the wall of the house. One day while crossing a field, she trod her way beside a neighbour's linen drying on the grass and saw an empty wheelbarrow that must have carried the wet clothes there. Later a green lizard ran across the palm of her hand while she dozed in a kitchen chair. She has read in old manuscripts that troubadours in this region were famous for their ability to imitate birdcalls and, as a result, may have altered natural habits of migration. She has been told by Madame Q that at the first hint of winter her husband will wrap the water pump with straw and burlap, and likewise wrap the trunks and low branches of the almond trees on the terrace.

These are details that can construct a partial background of a writer's life. She knows that everything here in Europe has touched history or a literature. Besançon became prominent because Julien Sorel attended its seminary in *Le Rouge et le Noir*. The rough stone structure still exists, the dusk around it thick with the smell of limes from a nearby arbor. And there are all the other towns and villages etched by Balzac, page by page. Angoulême. Saint-Lange. Sceaux. 'I was born in Balzac—he was my cradle, my forest, my travels . . . he invented everything,' Colette wrote, glancing back to her youth. Just as she herself later created her landscape at Saint-Sauveur-en-Puisaye. And here in Gascony, where the fictional D'Artagnan was born, the writer Lucien Segura lived, composed his strange poems and novels, and disappeared.

Anna pulls her face back from an orange lily, aware of its pollen and of the hovering bee. Its ancestors must have done the same, shimmering down a stem of chicory some day in 1561, here or beside the church in the distance. She has noticed the *gardien* cycle past to unlock its doors. There must have always been a bee here to hear Catholic music and witness a verger's arrival. The past is always carried into the present by small things. So a lily is bent with the weight of its permanence. Richard the Lion-Heart may have stepped up to this same flower on his journey to a Crusade and inhaled the same presence Anna does before he rode south into the Luberon.

Within a few days of meeting him, she is conscious of Rafael's secular knowledge of every field. The row of linden trees that leads to the graveyard—he knows their height from when he was a child, for he walked between them then as though they were giants. Just as he has taken her back to the middle of that pasture where they first met, and said, 'This is where the old writer drowned. In the old days there was a small lake here.'

As a boy, Rafael crept from his parents' caravan before daybreak and stood on a wagon to watch the journeying light in the fields. The first evening he slept with Anna, he rose from her bed, left that smallest of rooms, and walked down the stairs in darkness, then made his way through the night fields. In the noisy pasture where everything was invisible he aligned himself with the rustle of a tree and moved in a straight line towards the trailer.

Where do you go? she asked later. Back to your home?

Yes.

I could come with you.

You wouldn't sleep well in that narrow bunk.

Outside, then.

We could, someday.

What night gave Rafael was a formlessness in which everything had a purpose. As if darkness had a hidden musical language. There were nights when he did not bother to even light the oil lamp that hung in the doorway of his trailer. He reached for the guitar and stepped down the three laddered steps into the field, carrying a chair in his other hand. '*I don't work, I appear*'—he remembered the line of Django Reinhardt's and imagined the great man slipping out from the shadows grandly and disappearing efficiently into his craft. The alternative was to arrive, as most musicians did, like an eighteenth-century king entering a city, preceded by great fires on the hills that signalled he had crossed the border, and then by the ringing of bells. But Rafael was not even appearing. Dissolving perhaps, aware of night bugs, the river on the edge of his hearing. His open palm brushed a chord that was response, just response. He had not yet stepped forward. This was the late summer of his life, the year he met Anna, and he had no idea whether he would ever be able to return to the corralling work that art was, to have whatever he needed to make even a simple song. Dissolving into darkness was enough, for now. Or playing from memory an old song by a master, something his mother had loved or his father had whistled, when he accompanied his father on a walk, for there was one specific song his father always muttered or whistled. In the past Rafael had travelled from village to village, argued a salary, invented melodies, stolen chords, slashed the legs off an old song to use just the torso—but he had come to love now most of all the playing of music with no one there. Could you waste your life on a gift? If you did not use your gift, was it a betrayal?

Earlier that day Anna had come behind him and slid the earphones of a CD player gently over his ears. He was, he remembers, skinning kidneys, and the music was almost skeletal, a bare list, a sketch. He knew who it was by, but not what the piece of music was. 'Bach,' she said, 'later Bach.' He listened, watching the blade slow its movement, now slicing the innards, then the mushrooms, a sleepwalking knife, his hand pouring a splash of brandy and dry mustard into a pan, while he was in this spare thicket of music. As if the half-uttered gestures and emotion of the musician were the desultory conversations of a wood pigeon.

Now he brushed the strings of his guitar into life with the calluses of his palm, and listened to what it was. What was adjacent to music was music. The night air held everything and pressed into his coat and his face.

Tell me about your father, Anna said.

Oh . . .

Is he a big shadow in your life? Did you tell me he met your mother while he was robbing a police station?

He wasn't quite robbing the police station, he was trying to take something off a man who was being held prisoner there. It was more difficult.

He wanted to rob a prisoner? So the prisoner was not a friend?

The prisoner had something that was important to a friend of my father's. I don't know why.

And where was this friend of his? Why couldn't he do it?

It was a woman. And she was another prisoner. In the same jail. It usually held men.

Naturally.

Sometimes there were more women than men. Not this time.

And your mother worked in the police station.

Yes, she came in for an hour or so while the jailer went on his lunch break. She was not supposed to go anywhere near the prisoners, but she had been given the keys, in case there was a fire. This was in a small town near the Belgian border. These were not major criminals in there. My father just needed to rob one of them. But it was going to be challenging.

Then?

He came into the police station, in a sort of outfit—an invented uniform, really—with a hose and a tank attached to his back, saying he was sorry he was late. 'I was supposed to be here earlier,' he said. 'I have to do this quickly, because I have three other jails today.' My mother, at the desk, had no idea what he was talking about. No one had said anything to her about his visit. He said, 'You will have to sign this when I finish.' He brought out some forms with carbon paper between them. This was shortly after the war, and you could hardly move with the red tape then. 'All men, are they?' he asked, and was told there was one woman, and he pretended to worry about that. 'Then you might have to help.'

What he needed to do, he told her, was DDT the cells, hose them down, and hose the prisoners too, which meant they had to push all their belongings and clothes out of the cells so they wouldn't get sodden. 'Sodden?' She asked him what that meant. 'Damp. Damp. Wet. Like flooded.' '*Ah. Je comprends.*'

Je comprends, Anna said, lying beside him in the bed.

So my father explained all this to the male prisoners while my future mother explained it to the woman. The men had to undress completely and push their clothes forward, through the bars. My father (not yet a father) took the clothes and carried them into the front office, then went and sprayed the DDT, essentially for lice and ticks—there had been a serious outbreak, he told them, that was tumbling through the region, two prisoners in another jail had even died. After spraying the cells, now devoid of sheets and books and papers, he sprayed the men's bodies, front and back. He then told them to stand still for ten minutes before they got dressed.

Meanwhile my mother had to get the woman prisoner to disrobe, and bring her clothes to the front office—as my father would have to check them for ticks and lice, and sprinkle DDT powder on them. The woman did not have to be hosed down, because, my father said, strangely the creatures never settled on women—a fact that my mother found peculiar, but if the man knew, the man knew. So my father sorted out the clothes, got the crucial piece of paper or whatever it was from the male prisoner's pocket and put it in the female prisoner's shoe, and everyone got settled back into their cells. He thanked the prisoners, he told the woman there had been three ticks in her clothes, he shook the hand of my mother and left.

He had made my mother sign the papers. She'd apparently needed to put down her age, other professions, and where she lived. She was a 'traveller,' she had told him then, what they used to call *gitans*, Gypsies. She was a *'manouche.'* Of course, the guards at the police station did not know this—she would hardly have been allowed to work there if they had known. She didn't really have an address, just a location she'd pointed towards, near the southwest edge of the town. Her family lived in a caravan. In this way my father met the enigma that was Aria.

No one was aware of what had taken place. The returning jailer held his nose at the smell of what seemed to be disinfectant. Maybe twenty-four hours later there was a cry of complaint from one of the prisoners. But by then my father had come courting, and had asked for 'Aria,' whose name he knew from the filled-out forms. He had been journeying up from Italy after the war ended, and had found himself in Belgium, where it was easier to obtain money the way he usually did. He'd been injured but now seemed to be back at his old criminal activities.

So he stayed with her and married her?

They never married, but she was his wife, yes. He stayed and lived in the caravan with her. My mother told me he had had another wife, before the war, but she referred to it only once. The war was a chasm for most. There was one life before and one life afterwards. Many decided not to go back to what they had been.

It's a good excuse. The war.

Yes. In this case it was because my father was besotted with my mother. She was quite a bit younger. He had never been a jealous person—after all, he was a thief who believed property was 'communal'—but he gave up everything he was and began living with her in the way she wanted to live. There was a strict moral code around her group.

So Aria . . .

Yes. Aria. And my father.

Turn around and face me. . . . Is that all true?

It's probably been aged a bit. But that was how my father, the DDT inspector, met her.

I suppose there are a lot more stories about him.

Oh, yes. For one whole month, when the police were suspicious of that community of caravans, he dressed as a woman. He was a woman for all that time, until the police gave up. He had been in jail during his youth, and he was never going back.

Then you can't blame him.

No. But the real reason he feared going to jail was that he became jealous of other men's interest in my mother. Though she was consistently faithful, as far as I know, but then, who knows . . .

Aria, she said again. As if it was some taste on her tongue.

After the disinfecting, his father noticed that there was still about fifteen minutes before the jailer was scheduled to return, so he sat down opposite the young woman and wondered aloud whether they would, and could, meet again. She was looking down at some cards. He watched her hands scoop them this way and that. Her dark hair was tied back with a few inches of green ribbon. Without a word she arced the Tarot pack across the table in front of him. He cut it, pulled a card out, and let it lie there. He knew nothing about what the cards meant, and he watched as she moved the other cards around it. She made him select another. He glanced at the clock above her beautiful head. 'I do not wish to be rude, but I must leave now.' She said nothing, continuing to move the cards from side to side, as if evidence, acknowledging him with a slight nod as he opened the door and slipped out.

She knew she'd see him again, and what she had on the table in front of her was considerably more significant than the need to look up and see his face or his strange dark hands again. When he passed the window, he glanced inside and saw her profile bent even closer to the table, studying the cards.

The next night he visited her caravan. She looked him up and down, making certain this was what she wanted. She'd seen a possible jealousy in his nature; perhaps the war had made him desire too much security.

So in the moment he was abandoning his wife and betraying her with Aria, he began insisting on no betrayal on Aria's part. As at the jailer's desk, she remained silent and uncommitted to this insistence. She refused to deny chance and fate with a permanent agreement, there was no such thing, and he himself was on no moral pinnacle to be able to negotiate. Through all their years together, she refused to give the needed comfort about her faithfulness to this man who was suddenly conscious of the sacredness of property.

Rafael did not recount their entire story to Anna. Even as a seven-year-old, lying beside his mother, he had been aware of Aria as the central being, his arms enclosing her, the way a boy embraced a dog with all the right in the world. When he was twenty he'd still undress and swim in rivers with her. So that nakedness was natural to him, as when Anna watched him standing by the north window, focused only on the smoking of his cigarette, listening to the sound of doves that had found harbour in the damaged wall of the house. If she had asked him, he might or might not have explained how his mother protected this mystery of her faithfulness, which was like a moat that no one could cross with certainty—there was always the mixture of carefulness and open desire in her. She would whisper something into his ear and then kiss it, to seal it there, so he could never give it away to another.

You're lucky you had a mother, such a mother.

I know.

It felt to Rafael that he had just turned from resting his face against Aria years earlier and placed it against the warmth of Anna.

~

Anna wakes early in the morning to begin translating the sparse texts by Lucien Segura that she has on her desk. For much of his life the man was unknown, save that he was a poet and later the author of a jeremiad about the Great War. And in the years since his death, knowledge of him has sunk into the fabric and soil of this region, so he is almost forgotten by his countrymen. Anna loves such strangers to history; for her they are essential as underground rivers. She wakes in this last house that Lucien Segura lived in, solitary in her bed, makes coffee, and is at work by eight. Rafael is absent from her thoughts until early afternoon, when he crosses the fields with a plan for lunch. He is her 'extravagant and wheeling stranger,' or perhaps she is his. In the afternoon, they nestle together in her small bedroom, and later, half dressed, still curious about the interior of the house, he will enter other rooms and glance at paintings, open what were once linen cupboards, and look down at the avenue of trees from an upstairs window.

During one of these reconnaissances he hears what sounds like a river's whispering in the corridor. He realizes the noise comes from above, from a closed-off section above the ceiling. He wanders off, returns with a ladder, and ascends through a trapdoor into a room where the air is thick with bird heat. As he rolls in shirtless, feathers paste themselves onto his back. When Rafael was a boy, he knew there was a *pigeonnier* attached to the house. But over the years the wall separating the dovecote from the attic must have partially collapsed, and now birds swoop in, assemble, pause in the portal for a moment, and fly out. It is a room busy with entrances and escapes. He has never desired to be a pigeon, but many times has wished to be a bird in flight over the landscape, moving in a long slide towards a copse, where its high secret entrance, invisible to humans, reveals at the last moment a path into the forest. What you experience in the high air is the petite life on earth, a drifting of voices, the creak of a wagon, the retort and smoke from a gun among the almond trees, somewhat like the music Anna has played for him in the kitchen, with only the essential notes of life reaching you through that distance of air.

Rafael stands quietly in the middle of the room. He knows what he will be able to see from the portal, from this bread-box-sized opening. He could look towards the wooded valley east of Dému, the Bois de Mazères, where the silent burial of his mother took place many years ago . . . he and his father digging and four others watching, and then, at the end of his mother's commitment to the earth, all of them stepped away from the grave and went their own ways like the spokes of a cart wheel, all of them carrying their own version of Aria, none of them wishing to share it, or dilute it within a group. No words were spoken. He was asked to play but did not; he would play later, when she inhabited him more, when she abided in him. Then he could represent her, just as he knew his father would take into himself the qualities of Aria he might unconsciously have fought against in the past. In this way she would remain with them. He can almost see the clearing in the forest where they took her that morning. They slipped her into the ground within three hours, so she lived the briefest death on the earth, as if earth were a boat that forced a quick embarkation. They had brought her back to the landscape she was most fond of. It was about five in the morning, and bird life was wild around them, as if it was his mother's leaving.

Rafael turns and walks along the struts of the loft. He thinks he has heard Anna calling. She has moved the ladder away and is standing there undressed, laughing at him when his head appears through the rectangle. He drops his legs through the hole and hangs on with his hands. When she sees he isn't going to ask her for the ladder, she scrambles to provide it, but he has already dropped the fifteen feet to the floor.

She stands there stranded, as if discovered naked on a stage with a ladder in her arms. He walks in slow circles around her, hemming her in. . . .

You've got feathers on you.

I've got feathers, at least I am partially dressed.

Let's have a bath. I will draw it.

No. The river. As you are. There will be nobody there. You need to just cross the meadow, then you will be in the trees.

His callused fingers hold her at the wrist again. So she goes with him down to the kitchen and out the back.

Next time don't move the ladder.

Oh, next time I will.

It isn't much more than a trout stream, so they lie on their backs against pebbles in order to be fully submerged. She sees a curl of water sculpt his hair and shoulders, as if he's being transformed. This is a first, she thinks. Then realizes so much is a first with him, her running up and down the corridor naked, the loose grip even now on her wrist, his almost sleepy sexuality where there seems no boundary between passion and curiosity and closeness, unlike one of her earlier lovers, who had been ardent but selfish.

And yet he keeps far away from her what else he is. As though he wishes in some way to remain a stranger. Why does that happen . . . with such an otherwise generous man? These men with art, like nineteenth-century botanists who, though wise and obsessive, claim only professional affection for the world around them.

But the next day, standing in the meadow, he invites Anna to visit the trailer, and she hesitates, thinking the offer is a commitment on his part, even a tentative one. It implies too much knowledge of the other—his home could be a capsule of the past or of a possible future. Her own hesitation at breaking their formality is interpreted by Rafael as shyness, or modesty, or a desire not to take the relationship further. And in some way this is not a misinterpretation of Anna. For she too has lived a stranger's life. There are layers of compulsive secrecy in her. She knows there is a 'flock' of Annas, and that the Anna beside this unnamed river of Rafael's is not the Anna giving a seminar at Berkeley on one of Alexandre Dumas' collaborators and plot researchers, is not the Anna in San Francisco walking into Tosca's or eating at the Tadich Grill on California Street.

She stands looking at Rafael in the middle of that meadow. Why doesn't she wish to visit her lover's home? She is curious, after all. But she knows this romance is a romance, in no way an agreement towards permanence, even though much of her wants to see his *silhouette* moving within that suitcase of a home that once belonged to the mysterious Aria. She wants to climb onto his narrow bed with him and brace her arms against the ledge of the window, look down on his weathered face and slowly bring her head to the patch of his body that smells of basil, next to his heart.

One of the dearest possessions that Anna has is an old map—*La Carte du Tendre Pays*—sweetly named, of emotions that fit into the shape of France. It was composed by women in an earlier century, during an era of male exploration and mapmaking. But this was a map of yearnings that courteously avoided sexual love, except for a darkly etched thicketed region in the north, listed as 'Terres Inconnues.' Well, times change. By the time she earned and saved enough money to pay for her university studies in French, she was told by a dean that the best way to learn French was to take a French lover.

In spite of everything that had existed between Coop and Anna for those two months on the Petaluma farm, they had remained mysterious to each other. They'd really been discovering themselves. In this way they could fit into the world. But years later, never having married, never having lived with anyone in a relationship that intended permanence, she still sidled beside her lovers as if she were on Coop's deck, glowing in secret with the discovery of herself. So there had always been and perhaps always would be a maze of unmarked roads between her and others. That emotional map of France was still true in the present, full of subtexts, social intricacies, unspoken balances of power. One still needed to move warily, with hesitance, within it.

She sits on his bunk, next to the sacred guitar.

So this is it.

Yes.

No books.

No.

No pictures.

He brings out a photograph of Aria. Anna looks for the person who has distilled in her mind as a result of his stories. There's a whimsy in his mother's face that Anna had not expected.

And your father? Do you have one of him?

He does not respond to this at first.

Somewhere I have a photograph that he is in, but you cannot see him clearly. He didn't like being photographed. You get in their books, he'd say, and you can never get out. If he ever needed a passport, he would use someone else's. Someone roughly the same age and hair colour. No one looks like their passport picture. Do you? Do you have a sister? You could probably use your sister's passport if you needed to.

I don't have a sister.

Don't you? I thought you did.

She shook her head.

She was lying again to a lover. Had a sister. Had a past. She would not tell him. Later, if she were brave enough. About their father turning like an axe on Coop, and her praying for his breath beside him, even for a small rise of his chest, the rest of her life splintered at that moment, with her becoming a creature of a hundred natures and voices, and with a new name. She envied this man beside her, as close as Coop had been to her on that cabin floor. This man's life seemed innocent. She envied the delightful adventures of his father and Aria. Perhaps she needed a man as content as this to tell her past to.

All your stories, Rafael—tell me, was there nothing terrible?

Oh, many things. Many things changed me. There was a love affair with a woman that silenced me, there was the writer who lived in the house you are staying in, there were the donkeys. . . .

See, that's what I mean!

Rafael's first encounter with a girl was when he was seventeen. On a Friday evening he was to walk the few miles into town, have a picnic with her beside the bridge, and then go to a cinema. He carefully picked some marigolds, and then, because he was late, decided to hitchhike. He felt the evening should go only one way, which was that he simply must not embarrass himself with a member of the opposite sex. If one minor thing went wrong, he was fated to die solitary. He could already list almost a hundred areas of danger, for at seventeen we are perfectionists.

He walked under the avenue of trees, his arm out every time he heard a motorcar, but no one stopped for him. Finally a Citroën 'Tube' stopped, with two men and a woman taking up the front. He walked to the back of the van, opened the rear door, and in his white shirt and ironed trousers, stepped into complete darkness. As the van took off, he began being nudged by three indistinct shapes that turned out to be donkeys. It was the longest ride of his life, and Anna insists that he relive every second of it for her, and the appointment that followed.

Le rendez-vous, he says, *n'a pas eu lieu.* The girl took one quick look at him when the van dropped him by the town fountain, staggering out with his shirt loose and his shoes wet and shat upon, and his hands holding—in an attempt at nobility— seven or so stumps of what had been flowers. His time in the Citroën had been spent mostly attempting to save the bouquet, holding it high, so that his frame was abandoned to the animals, which had been locked in the van since the start of their journey in Montricoux.

So what was the very worst thing about it? Anna asks.

The worst thing was that by the time I got home, after the girl left, saying, 'My father is ill, I must go,' after I had washed my arms and neck and cleaned the shit off my shoes at the fountain, after going to the cinema and seeing a Gabin all alone and then walking home along the dark road with the night sky so bright that I was beginning to feel good again—I'd bought some bread and herbs, as I was hungry, and I was walking with this food with a strange kind of joy, that was something to do with escape—the worst thing was that by the time I got home everyone in the village of Dému already knew about it. Even now, if you ask about the 'donkey boy' or the 'Citroën story,' they will know who you are talking about.

Rafael has added, in the many years since, a layer of casual irony to the trauma of the event. I try to imagine, he says, my donkey-odoured hand attempting to touch her naked waist or her sixteen-year-old shoulder during *La Bête Humaine*. I became used to the braying when I entered classrooms. And there was a sudden realistic neigh during the end-of-year exam a month later that made the students break into laughter, even cheering, and caused a knowing smile from the teacher.

I had no more 'appointments' with girls for the next four years—and then, knowing that the worst that could happen had already happened, I breezed into meetings with them unconcerned, the most relaxed suitor for my age. But during those four years I was in exile and I concentrated on the guitar. I owe my career to a bunch of marigolds and three donkeys.

So Rafael discovered the privacy of music, its hidden chords, all those disguised narratives. From then on, conflicts were to be within his art. And, being surrounded by the intimacy of his parents, he knew he had to somehow protect it. He was still the playful and loved son, but his mother noticed him removing himself easily from the conversations in their trailer. He had found his own enchantment, he had his own 'emergency.' He had an escape from the world. As if the chair he sat in was a horse to gallop into unknown distances.

Who taught him this secret? Once, as a young musician, he

witnessed a pair of dancers who began rehearsing on their own, before anyone had taken out an instrument, to a recording of piano music that they pulled across like a screen between themselves and the others who were there. They were alone already, in their intimate preparation. And he remembers something else—for Anna has asked him if he knew the writer—how, while he was a boy living near this writer's house, he spent long afternoons with him in the garden. The old man would sit at his table in the deep hollow that was once a *mare*, a notebook and a pen and ink in front of him, but would not write. So Rafael found another chair and walked down into the hollow and sat with him. He remembers how there was always birdsong falling out of the tree. The writer asked what was happening in the fields beyond, and Rafael said—a bonfire, a tilling, an execution of crows, and explained how his father had sculpted a large crow out of wood, placed it on a fence, and then with bloodcurdling screams attacked it violently with a knife. He claimed this kept crows away from their garden. I see, said the man at the table, looking beyond the lake towards that site of possible activity. Rafael visited him often at the blue table in the shade of the great oak.

When I wrote, the man said, that was the only time I would think. I would sit down with a notebook and a pen, and I would be lost in a story. The old writer, seemingly at peace, thus casually suggested to Rafael a path he might take during his own life, and taught him how he could be alone and content, guarded from all he knew, even those he loved, and in this strange way, be fully understanding of them. It was in a sense a terrible proposal of secrecy—what you might do with a life, with all those hours being separated from it—that could lead somehow to intimacy. The man had made himself an example of it. The solitary in his busy and crowded world of invention. It was one of the last things the writer talked to him about.

◌

It was three a.m. Rafael took the lamp off the hook and went outside. In the meadow there were two chairs, and he placed the lamp on one of them and lit the wick, then moved his own chair away so he would not be in the spill of light. He sat there, hands curled on his lap.

Before coming outside he had been listening to Anna's breathing in the dark trailer. She'd swept her arm back during the night and had relaxed into all of the bed. She was leaner than he was, but was used to American space. Asleep, Anna disappeared into her world, where even she was a stranger, and Rafael found himself alone once more. This was his night hour, when he was fully awake, conscious of the life of those trees that circled the field, the faint moon. Yet he was alone. The last time Rafael had laid eyes on his father was the morning he had seen him walk from Aria's grave. Rafael had needed him in the months that followed, to coax him back into the world. But there was no communication or evidence of his father's whereabouts. There was a maze of small towns, even cities, he could have been in. Rafael had become parentless. It was as if neither of his parents could exist without the presence of the other. Rafael had lost each wing of protection.

Anna came up behind him in silence and put her hands on his shoulders.

You went away again.

No, I am still here.

Good, I want to talk to you about something.

To do with us . . .

Not us, she said. Something about me.

Then suddenly Anna stopped thinking, her hesitation disappeared. Ahead of them a hare was peering from the border of darkness. She waited for it to take a leap into the light. Curiosity, courage, it was what they both wished for beneath their pounding hearts.

Out of the Past

For some years Claire had been living two distinct lives. During the week she had a job in San Francisco with a lawyer named Vea, a senior deputy in the Office of the Public Defender. The work was mostly arduous research, and Vea had walked Claire through the craft and process of it, noting there was something carefully obsessive in this woman who was able to recognize a mouse of information miles away. Then, on weekends, Claire disappeared. She would drive out of the city to the farm south of Petaluma and spend an hour or two of the Friday night with her father.

They sat and ate dinner across from each other. She noticed how much older he seemed. She was aware of how his clothes looked loose on him now, although he still appeared a severe man, precise as a utility in the way he moved and the way he talked at the kitchen table. He was the one who, in his twenties, had cleared most of the land, working long days, and fought back coyotes and badgers that were supposedly as ferocious as wolverines. She and Anna had heard that he'd once tracked a cougar for several days with a pair of bluetick hounds that eventually treed the two-hundred-pound animal, and that he had shot it out of the branches. The girls had yearned for him to dramatize such incidents, turn them into great adventures from his youth. But he had refused, always laconic and silent about the landscape of his past. Even now, he and Claire circled the episode that led to the absence of Anna in their lives, never speaking of it. It was as if the loss of Anna had consumed him and then exhausted him, until he had in some way concluded his emotion, the way he had probably done after the death of his wife, when his daughters were too young to know about it. And even if the pain and his fierce love of Anna were still somewhere, loose in his skin, he and this remaining daughter would now be silent about it. The last time Claire had spoken of Anna, her father had raised his palm into the air with an awful plea for her to stop. There was no longer a closeness between him and Claire; whatever intimacy had once existed had always been engineered by Anna.

During these visits Claire would see him again for a brief moment the next morning, before she rode into the hills with a rain slicker, water, and food for the next thirty-six hours in a pannier. She and the horse climbed into hills that some part of her had always believed were her true home. Here she was uninterpreted by family life, could be dangerous to herself, feeling the thrill at coming upon a campsite at night after being surrounded by a ground fog, that divine state of being half lost, half bewildered, and conscious of a wisp of smoke from some campfire.

She risked everything out there, taking narrow trails too fast in moonlight, swimming in turbulent river currents, cantering over No Hands Bridge with the reins loose and her arms outstretched. Her associates at work would barely have recognized her. Even her father might not have, though he had witnessed this love of escape from her youth. (She'd found him always to be a still man, rarely driving a car or riding a horse.) Claire assumed some ancestor in her changeling blood had been a horse person. She rose from her limp into the stirrup and was instantly free of it. It was in this way that she discovered the greater distances in herself.

The first time Claire had entered an endurance race, she'd

been thrown by her horse and went careening down a rock-strewn slope. The animal stood there patiently, in a cloud of red dust, as she managed to climb back on with a dislocated shoulder. She continued for two miles before giving up and turning with an un-bloodlike intelligence, something more to do with reason and survival, to follow the yellow markers back to the camp at Robinson Flat. The horse had balked as it descended a canyon and she had already forgiven it. Horses had their sudden demons too. Someone rolled her a joint, and she smoked that before she telephoned her father.

He got there an hour later with a horse truck. He came up to her and saw in her eyes the look of a dog who'd run too far and wild, injuring itself with a lack of knowing how much it could take on or achieve. She told him it was nothing, but at the farm, when she climbed out of the truck, she could hardly walk and he carried her into the house. It was the first time he had touched her in a year. He put her down on the long kitchen table and pressed a hot towel around her shoulder, put his knee onto her back, and torqued the shoulder up so that she burst into tears. When he did it again she passed out.

When Claire woke, she was where he had left her. There was a pillow under her head. She saw him sitting on the old tartan sofa, watching her, for safety. She tried rolling to the right and to the left. Then she got into her car and drove the forty minutes to San Francisco, where she was expected at work the next day.

The Public Defender's Office provided legal defence to those with no money, and Claire had worked there for five years. Aldo Vea, a state lawyer, had two assistants helping him with research; she was one of them. Vea met Claire and Shaun every morning at a café on Geary Street, and they ate while Vea discussed pending cases. He was brilliant at freewheeling the possibilities, conceiving and laying out angles for defence. By nine-thirty they'd go off to their phones, talking to anyone in the defendant's past—school friends, lovers, employers. Then they'd investigate the victim. There might be a hint of violence in the victim's past that could turn the case. They carried an obvious notebook and a hidden microphone. They were better than cops, Vea said. And they were a family. Claire knew everything about Shaun, and about Vea and his family. When Vea's wife was ill, Claire picked the kids up after school and brought them along on stakeouts. When Shaun broke her silence about her growing attraction to women, Claire and Vea had dinner with her and gave her a game plan.

Claire would always turn up on Monday mornings wearing a pastel-coloured dress. The homespun image and the sense of defencelessness was important, Vea said, but she suspected that he also liked it. She wore a ring she could move from finger to finger, depending on whom she was interviewing. To men her dresses suggested gentleness and courtesy; she did not appear to be in charge. If someone hit on her, the ring on her finger came into the foreground and she'd softly announce that she was pregnant. (When one dangerous-looking sort quizzically responded, 'With child?' she lowered her head to hide her smile. Now she was going to be treated like a Madonna.) She was supposed to be a creature of empathy, revealing no moral stance, just easiness and compassion. She knew the best times to get people to talk. Women were better on the phone, because they could do something else at the same time. During stakeouts, if curious neighbours knocked on her car window and asked what she was doing, she'd point vaguely towards a house. 'My boyfriend's in there, drunk,' she'd say. 'I had to get out. I'm waiting.' 'Can I get you something, dear?' they would ask. 'No, thanks.' She was dying for coffee, but then she would have to pee. In stakeouts you lived in a state of high awareness, and by the end of the day you were exhausted.

Most days Claire was investigating the provenance of an insurance scam or a molestation case. What the Public Defender's Office did in their work was essentially defend any indigent brought up on a criminal charge. Until the landmark case of *Gideon v. Wainright,* only the rich would get a lawyer. The Public Defender's Office had to respond to the police and the 'evidence orgy' that took place after a crime was committed. The police believed that if they didn't solve the crime in three days, they were never going to. They rarely gave a case more time than that, so they didn't want complications or subtleties. Public defenders were allowed to see the evidence only after the third day and had to quickly find witnesses and flaws, to prove either that the client didn't do it or didn't deserve to die. The latter applied to the penalty phase, and it was the only time the defence was permitted to try to influence the outcome. Claire had once researched the history of a man who was up for the death penalty, and discovered an earlier violent assault he had committed in the past, when he was twenty. She found that he had attacked a man who had been viciously beating his dog. Bingo. That turned out to be the detail that got him a life sentence, and saved him from lethal injection. As Vea had said at the time, if it had been discovered that he'd read all of Herman Melville, it would have had no effect, but the mutt had returned to save him.

After work, Claire would sometimes meet up with Vea for a drink at Fog City, watching that little oil slick on his vodka martini curling dangerously. Aldo Vea was the most principled man Claire knew, and he had taught her how to survive in this profession of crime and retribution, how to accept the flawed barrier between cause and effect, how to see that the present continually altered the past, just as the past was a strange inheritance that fell upside down into one's life like an image through a camera obscura. All that was consistent was a principle. 'You believe in the principle,' Vea would say, 'if you cannot believe in the man. You meet monsters and you help defend them. You believe in the principle of full justice. When a murderer fights the death penalty, *he* is not the one asking to be pardoned, he doesn't deserve to ask, *we* are the ones asking.' Vea had been in Vietnam between the ages of seventeen and nineteen, and he had seen the monster. He knew how the monster could come upon you.

They would have that drink at Fog City at the end of the day, and she would stop him from having one more. If he drank more she would leave, and if he didn't, she would stay and listen to him. He always needed to wind down, always. He talked Vietnam. He talked out the cases he was struggling over, but he was really talking Vietnam. One day she began to tell him about what had happened all those years earlier between her father and Coop, and how her sister had disappeared at that time. 'Well, these are not monsters,' he said, waving his hand as if dismissing an eyelash. 'There's always damage collected in childhood.' Vea was the only person Claire talked to about where she came from. 'Has she ever made contact with you?' 'No.' 'Then there is still sadness in her life. Were you jealous of your sister?' 'No. Only once.' If anyone calmed Claire and defused her past, it was Vea. She wondered whether her father and Coop and Anna seemed quaint to someone like him.

If she arrived too late at Fog City and he was already drunk, she would not sit with him. Instead she would take the car keys out of his pocket and wait until he struggled out of the narrow booth and paid the bill. They would find his car and she would drive him home, calling his wife to let her know. In his driveway she would put the keys back into his pocket and walk to the waiting taxi that she had ordered. She would wave to Vea's wife standing at their door, who would yell, 'Love you, Claire,' as she got into her cab. Vietnam.

Claire felt that Vea had implanted a cause in her, a guiding principle for what she could do with her life, and so she would do anything for him. He never approached her except as a compatriot, alongside the honour of his work, although god knows what his darknesses and hidden emotions were. Vea's wife, she knew, could map him intricately. She took Claire to symphony concerts and the ballet, things that Vea could not sit still for. Ballet had not enough words to keep him awake. The closest he got to formal was Thelonious Monk, whose music, in the neglected recordings, were, he said, like imprisoned birdsongs. When Claire went to the Veas' for dinner, he would be once more rebuilding his homemade sound system, and this always led to a discussion of the most recent eavesdropping equipment on the market. 'There's a laser scope,' he would say, 'that can measure the vibrations in the glass of a window across the street, and then translate them into sounds. From there it's one step to hearing the conversation going on in that room. And we're the ones who lost the war. . . .'

∾

Claire woke abruptly. She was in a hotel room in Tahoe. She had driven from San Francisco that afternoon and had needed to sleep for a few hours. Days before, she had been discussing a school board case with Vea, and he told her she would have to go to Tahoe. When she got up and looked out the window onto the town by the lake, she saw the casinos all lit up, beckoning.

But when she came downstairs, the bellman suggested that a club called the Stendhal might be more interesting than any entertainment in a card lounge.

At some point during her evening at the Stendhal, someone offered Claire a tablet. 'What is it?' she asked the person beside her, and he mouthed something that she could not hear. She broke it in two, then swallowed one of the pieces quickly, deciding on the lesser dose.

The Stendhal was a small city of moods. There were rooms for silence and for loud music, rooms for fruit juice and fresh vegetables, for massage, for films that seemed plant-based or planet-based—like *Baraka* or *Koyaanisqatsi* or the one in which a small section of plot from a thriller was replayed in slow motion so that a woman's arm packing a suitcase became as illuminating as a chrysalis in time-lapse. Claire had fallen under the spell of a brief scene from *Psycho* that was played slowly, Anthony Perkins walking innocently towards Janet Leigh with a tray of milk and sandwiches. Claire watched it just after taking the tablet, and as a result she was never certain whether the extension of the forty-five-second scene, which played out as a ten-minute sequence, was the talent of the tablet or the artist. In any case, she was now able to read, with a knowledge of what would take place in the future, all those innocent looks that went back and forth. When she turned away from the film she saw strangers moving cautiously around her, and a man who walked painfully slowly towards her with a glass of milk on a tray, so white there must have been a lit bulb within it.

She found the dance hall and remained there for an hour or two. Sometimes she was alone, and sometimes she was jammed up against several bodies moving together like the particles of a wave. She was in Tahoe for something, but she could no longer remember what. There was something she had to do, she just could not distinguish where it was in her memory. She would go into the silent room, behind thick pneumatic doors, and work it out there. The reason for being in Tahoe would then roll in her direction like a marble.

Some hours later she woke, and walked back from the club to her hotel. It was a cloudy morning, and gusts of rain were coming off the lake. The narrow streets sloped down towards the centre of town. She looked back to determine what a certain noise was and saw it was someone on a skateboard about to pass her. His eyes caught her look, and he made a quick decision and reached out, lifting her onto the board in front of him. He barely held her and she was holding nothing, just standing encircled within his arms, with her eyes wide open. They raced over the clacks of the sidewalk against the rush of the rain, hardly seeing faces as they slid past, everything was colour and rain. She began to relax, and at that moment he lifted her and placed her on the pavement, then sped away ahead of her. Claire turned to see the distance they had come, and stood there instantly still, immovable in front of the clapboard houses. She needed to find her hotel and lie down.

Somewhere during this somnambulistic walk, she entered a diner and sat down in a booth. She asked for mineral water, three eggs, sausages, and mushrooms. Did they have green tomatoes? Yes. A double order, then. The waitress brought her the food and she started eating, picking at it, feeling clumsy, tired, not controlling her knife and fork. That was when she saw someone who looked like Coop come into the restaurant.

Coop?

She didn't say it out loud, not quite sure if she had summoned him from the darkness. She just stood up in her booth. He looked across the room for a seat, and he saw her. Then there was an amazed smile. She went up to him and embraced him. It was him. She wouldn't let go of him, because she was sobbing. It was her tiredness, or the vapour trails of that pill. She was not expecting this, and the emotion of seeing Coop invaded her.

He sat down across from her. Both were silent. He kept looking around. He turned to look behind him, then back to Claire.

So this is where you live?

No. In San Francisco. I don't live here.

Coop said nothing, just watched her.

I work for a defence lawyer. I do research, investigations. I work for Aldo Vea. Do you know him?

Does he investigate gambling?

That's prosecution. I'm defence.

All at once she became conscious of what she was wearing.

I've been at a club. Not typical for me. Her eyes flickered. The excitement and exhaustion were hitting her simultaneously.

Listen, I want to talk, Coop, hear everything, but I need to . . .

Let's go, he said. He knew where her hotel was, and suggested they walk, for the fresh air. Once outside he told her that he made his living by gambling, and asked her again about the kind of work she did. He kept walking sideways so he could look at her. Are you investigating something here?

Just briefly. I'm looking in on a case for my boss. . . . You move like a gangster, Coop.

I'm a card player.

I see.

I live a few hours north of L.A. A small town called Santa Maria. I've been there some years now. I'm in Tahoe looking for someone.

Do you have a house? In Santa Maria, I mean.

I live in a hotel.

Jesus.

He waved down a cab.

What are you doing?

You're tired. I don't think you will make it to the Fuller.

He stood in the doorway after she entered her hotel room and asked when she was leaving Tahoe.

Sit. Have a drink, Coop. I can stay long enough to see you again, if you have the time. She fell back onto the sofa and toed her shoes off, watching him.

Coop walked over to the window that showed the still-pulsing lights of Tahoe.

There's a big card game down there, in the next few days. Somehow I need to get out of it. I need to get some help, from an old friend. Coop turned and saw that Claire had slipped sideways on the sofa and was asleep. He went over and stood looking at her.

He pulled her up so that she was against him, her face at his neck. He could smell a remnant of perfume. He had never thought of Claire as someone with perfume. She was a girl he had taught to fish, ride a horse, drive a car. Up close he could see the same warmth in her face, and he found himself smiling at her. It was years since he had last seen her. 'C'mon, you need a bed.' She half woke and her hands pushed him away. 'It's okay, it's me, Coop. I'm just helping you.'

~

During the next two days, Claire worked on the school board case, and waited for Coop to call. She tried the number he had left for her, but there was never an answer. Perhaps he had left town, after all. She went into a few card lounges, but when she asked players about Coop, they turned away or ignored her.

Anonymity seemed a courtesy in this world. She might be the wife of an errant gambler. She had nothing, no address for him, only his scrawled phone number. After all these years she had managed to lose him again.

She called Vea and said she was staying on for a while, and asked if he would track an address from a phone number for her. Someone she knew well, a sort of relative. She'd begun to feel something was wrong. That is, if he had existed in the first place. Perhaps the half of the pill she had swallowed had invented him, a little gift to end the very long night.

In Santa Maria, in the hills a few hours northwest of Los Angeles, during the years he had been there, Cooper would gamble long into the night, returning to his room at the hotel at three or four in the morning. He lived alone, mostly anonymous within the community of the town. A generation back, Santa Barbara County was populated mostly by migrant labourers, Mexican, Colombian, Vietnamese, Italian-American, who worked on the ranches and vegetable farms that spread over the landscape beyond the highway. The rich lived in the hills, and it was there one found the errant sons who loved to gamble. This was how democracy got a toe-hold in the valleys. Sometimes Cooper drove south and risked playing in bigger amateur games along the coast, but mainly he was at ease in this small highway town. Since the episode in Vegas, where he had cheated The Brethren, he was better off hidden. He went to movies in the afternoon, read legal thrillers, bought hookers when he needed them, and sat down at card tables at night. He would wake late in the day, then go running to burn off the staleness of the previous night. There was a balance to this spare life, and that was the trick. He didn't go to Vegas or Tahoe anymore. He was unknown to the strangers he played cards with. There was no desire in him to step back into his past.

In the early evening Cooper would drive to a steak house on the Taft road and stand at the bar and drink a bad margarita, then sit down at a table by himself. He was usually out of

Jocko's before the main dinner crowd came. He preferred eating alone. Later, during the night, he would be surrounded by gregarious company at the card tables, but here he silently watched the few other diners and the tells between couples. He had become preoccupied with a woman who came in every Monday and Friday with a bearded man. Jocko's wasn't known for its fast service, and while Cooper waited he tried to imagine the man's profession. A surveyor? Or one of those men who drove insectlike trucks up to planes at airports? The woman, in her black-and-white-checked woollen skirt, and with legs that barely seemed to fit under the table, was almost six feet, tall as Cooper anyway, and she was a ripple of energy. She'd leap up and talk to the staff, or check a name or a date on one of the posters tacked to the wall and come back with information for her partner.

She often had books on the table beside her. *Chemistry,* he thought he saw in a title once. She was in her early or middle thirties. She always seemed to be there at the same hour with the man. Her professor, perhaps. Or brother. They never touched each other, although they talked constantly while they ate. Like Cooper, they always sat at the same table. Sometimes he got there first, sometimes they did. Occasionally the woman looked over at him and acknowledged his presence—once charmingly in the middle of her laughter about something, and he had smiled back. So there was this small moment between them that he folded carefully away. Then sometime in the middle of a meal she would stretch her legs out. She did not fit or belong inside this wooden-walled diner, where the lighting clarified mostly the wrinkled necks of old gamblers and their season-long partners. Whatever the lighting was at Jocko's, it should have been bottled, he thought, and gone on tour with her, its sole purpose to follow this woman for the rest of her life, parting from her only after the funeral rites.

What he wanted was to simply look at that face that he couldn't read at all. That face, the blond hair. It wasn't the beauty, it was the variousness. Maybe in Vienna the woman might go unnoticed, but in Santa Maria she was this panther who came in and fit herself somehow between that chair and table near him every Monday and Friday, opposite a man who perhaps was an amateur magician in this semi-suburban California town—who sawed her in half in some unhealthy bar down the road. She leaned forward to whisper to the friend, or whatever he was.

Cooper went back to his room at the Santa Maria Inn, curious about her interests. He had to admit to himself that he knew nothing about her. He had not even caught the timbre in her voice. He simply arrived for dinner faithfully at eight o'clock before driving to his card games. And he ate those Spenser steaks cooked on the swimming-pool-sized outdoor grill at the back of Jocko's—a medieval scene—the t-shirted staff guiding the meat with giant tongs. Then he played cards until three in the morning, as the twelve-ounce steak digested slowly within him.

One night he looked up and she was there, sitting alone. As his head rose, she turned towards him, and without thinking he gestured a greeting with his hand. She acknowledged it and he sat there not knowing what to do. Normally he would glance at the couple, who were so engrossed in conversation they were never aware of him. She moved her fork around, on and off the placemat, which gave diners a history of the restaurant. Cooper's eyes skimmed his own placemat. The saga had begun in 1886, when

Emery Knotts opened a saloon. One of his eight sons was 'Jocko' Knotts, whose wife was the region's first telephone operator. They had children called Pookie, Jissy, Noonie, and Beagle, they had white lightning during Prohibition, slot machines throughout the forties, and a card room for poker. 'It was not unheard of for people to travel hundreds of miles to get to Jocko's,' the placemat read. 'For years there was a monkey in the bar. . . .'

So—may I join you? She stood and brushed her skirt. He said nothing while she sat down opposite him.

Where's your friend? he asked.

Oh, who knows. He probably won't be here. She was still settling in. Her clear voice was inches away from him. There was an absence of perfume on her. A strange first reaction, but in most card lounges women were encased in it and men had their talcums and sprays.

She was mouthing something to herself, a little prayer or a chant perhaps. He would discover this was a habit. But now, this first time, he sat forward, quizzical, as if missing something she was trying to impart. *'As I was motivatin' over the hill . . . I saw Maybelline in a Coupe de Ville.'*

I'm sorry?

Chuck Berry . . .

I played cards with him once, Cooper told her, when she'd identified the source of her lyrics.

Did he beat you?

No. He paused, to break it gently. No, I skunked him. He was not too bright about the game.

Who else?

Who else famous?

She nodded.

Oh, I don't know. No one else. He had come across no one

else as important as the singer and writer of 'Maybelline' in the card halls. As far as he knew, he had not dealt a pair of aces to Alfred Brendel.

They spoke haltingly, unable to find a subject that allowed a wide field of conversation. She said nothing about the relationship with her usual dinner partner, though she mentioned that he owned a hardware store. She was reading books on science, but no longer had a university connection. She travelled a lot. Her dad had been in the army, but she didn't see him anymore. 'I'll have a Spenser,' she told the waitress. And a glass of wine? She shook her head, she didn't drink. Cooper had already noticed that. They threw little clues back and forth across the table until about nine-thirty, when he announced he had to go.

Oh.

Card game at the Guadalupe Dunes, west of here, with some archaeologists.

Oh.

He had been able to witness her more clearly when she sat at the other table, at an angle from him. This close he had to keep up his end of the talk and also think before offering his answers. This close too many other things existed between them.

Will I see you again?

Mondays and Fridays, he said. He got up to pay the bill, and she remained sitting.

Bridget, she slipped him her name as he left.

He nodded. Hello, Bridget.

If Bridget had not been an addict or a dealer, if she had not been one whose life seemed engaged with many others, if these qualities had been absent among the clues Cooper had intuited in their first meeting, he probably would have avoided her, would not have had another meal with her at Jocko's the following Friday, or taken that walk to her apartment. Just as, in an earlier century, he would not have picked up the carefully dropped glove and returned it to the strolling woman. The knowledge of all he assumed made him feel safe. If Bridget sucked a milky-white smoke up through a water pipe or put a needle into her veins, if she found more pleasure in that than in romance, it meant he would not be important to her. He would remain at most a fragment in her week. She might, he thought, not even recall him a few months from now. As a competent gambler, his instinct told him she would not be a danger to him.

They walked to her apartment. He followed her into the large kitchen—its dimensions surprised him—and watched her cook up heroin. Then she was sitting on the carpet, the checkered skirt had ridden up her thighs. And all he kept thinking was that she looked healthy. As if it was impossible for health to be a segment of this life. He shook his head when she offered him some, although it was only a quick courtesy on her part—you offered salt before you used it yourself; a girl brought up by army rules—she was already hungry, and he had in essence disappeared. And then she moved back, away from him, and her gaze froze, balanced on a far tree, no longer in this world. He thought this surfeit of pleasure in her was like some unreachable beauty he would never know, beyond any won purse he might scoop from a card table into his arms. Her shoulders and head were resting against the fireplace. And her look returned to the room. 'Come and hold my hand,' she said quietly. She didn't use his name.

She lay on her back, her knees up, and guided his head across her white shirt, down to her stomach, her skirt. Her arm started pushing him away and then pulling him towards her, as if he were a log, or something she was trying to get loose and then into her possession. He wasn't expecting such strength or energy. He had imagined a languid seduction. She climbed over him, saying, *Cooper,* as if she had finally found his name and were now holding it up like a sword pulled out of a lake, as if it were *he,* jaded, on his back, who had to be revived with her surrounding force, white-shirted and gold-legged above him.

She would let him fuck her only when she was stoned, after she peaked and came back from the twilight of it. Two or three afternoons of the week, it was almost always afternoons, within the sunlight and motes of her apartment. Sometimes she asked him to hold her—she was cold—while she vomited into a sink. Sometimes when he returned from work at three or four in the morning he'd find her in the lobby of the Santa Maria Inn, asleep in a leather armchair. She would have left a message for him at the desk, as it was a confusing, rambling lobby with several alcoves—one for games and crosswords, one with a piano, one with historical photographs—and it was easy to miss someone waiting for you. He'd pull her to her feet. He would be tired and she would offer him pills, but he never took any from her.

On those nights when Cooper still felt wide awake, they would get into his car, fill up at a Texaco, and drive almost into Nevada, the windows down and music by The Clash pouring like tacks onto the highway behind them. Bridget snapped on the interior light and they were a lit bubble gliding through scrubland. She unwrapped an oblong white package of cocaine, and shook up the cocaine with sodium hydroxide till it was milky white, then added the ether. She siphoned the ether into a dish, then turned off the car light and continued in darkness with just the knowledge of her hands. He could see her faintly within the light of the dash, picking the crystals off the plate and dropping them into the pipe, could hear the pipe hissing with the burning of the crystals, then her breathing in the smoke, until she sat with the sledgehammer of euphoria against the open window.

The darkness of the car held them together. He felt it was Bridget's body, with whatever drug sparkled and pumped away inside, that steered them easily through the towns of Duncan and Erica. She placed her bare feet against the dashboard and guided the car, her head against the frame of the open window, the thump of the bass coming off the door panel against her neck. They stopped, left the car door open so music filled yards of the desert night, and she bent over the hood of the Chrysler, the heat from its engine against her t-shirt. He could hardly grip her because of the sweat on her shoulders, and he knew even in careless moments like these never to touch the bruises on her arms.

She had been the woman who brought a chemistry book with her into a restaurant, whose seeming mystery and boundlessness he had been drawn to before this flashed-by month. '*Her hair was so yellow, the wine was so red . . .*' At first he believed he would remember her that way, as someone in a song. She slept against him with her young secrets and her senses doubled by substances that constantly waved their arms, so he could not look at what was behind them. Her world existed only here, only now. There wasn't a single tale he knew from the past or from another place that he could ask her to retell or enlarge on. When she mused—in those floods and rivers when she was high—it was about what drugs were capable of, what desire was capable of, so uncontrolled it was illegible. Sometimes he woke just before dawn and saw her hunched on the carpet over an inconstant blue flame. Once he opened his eyes to see her a few inches away, watching him, and he feared suddenly that she

looked like Anna. He did not know whether she was a lens to
focus the past or a fog to obliterate it.

'I love singing. My dad used to sing while he drove, when I was
a kid.' Bridget was looking over Cooper's shoulder. It seemed to
him as if a catch had been released on a small door. She was
handing him something. Even without her direct gaze it felt intimate. A father's tune that drifted into the backseat of a car
where she sat alone as a child. Cooper did not take his eyes off
her remembering face. The way her blond hair fell across her
cheek, the shadow of light under her shirt. He swallowed these
moments and textures, as if preparing for an eventual drought.
Her becalmed voice interpreted the traffic of small things around
her. Here was where importance existed, within this small firma-
ment she turned over and over in her hands, alongside the quick
code-talk of border drugs—'the parakeet,' 'the rooster,' 'the
goat'—in that sweet and, yes, becalmed voice.

Sometimes a car with musicians came by and picked Bridget
up. She would be away all evening, returning in the early morning, about the time Cooper got back from his card games.
'Why don't you come with me,' she asked him. 'Singing is my
pleasure.'

He was hesitant, accustomed to her only in close quarters. To
witness the way she behaved with others would release him from
what he knew and wanted. She was his willing and diligent lover,
even as she shot up and loosened the sallow tube from her arm.
She was already various to him, even in her habits. Some days
she would go running with him, equal in stamina, then come
home and unpack her paraphernalia of eyedroppers and sodium
hydroxide and contact-lens-shaped discs, waiting patiently for
the crystals to appear. Or she would read restlessly into the

night. So when Bridget asked him to accompany her, along with the musicians, he swivelled his hand, meaning 'Not a good idea,' assuming wordlessness was more polite. Her mouth made a not-quite grimace, more pensive than annoyed. The exchange was thus a gesture of his hand, a tightening of her expression. She left the room, and when he followed her into the bedroom later she was looking out of the window at the slow traffic along the collector lanes of Santa Maria Boulevard. Thirty minutes later her friends picked her up. She was always good-humoured on returning.

The next time they went, Cooper joined Bridget and her friends. He had called the day before to cancel his presence in a game, and when the musicians showed up, he simply accompanied her downstairs. She kept watching for him to turn back.

Are you coming with us?

I thought I would.

That's great, Cooper, but take off the tie. Here, give it to me.

The Dauphin had taught him to dress well, and he'd never been able to shake the habit. Something like a tie, or a shirt with French cuffs, gives you an edge, The Dauphin had told him, even on a losing streak.

Bridget sat up front with the driver, while Cooper sat next to a bass guitarist who explained during the drive that he was an editor of a California nature magazine that was owned by a couple of robber barons. 'Conservatives love California,' the guitarist said. 'They're dying to get their hands on the rest of it.' Bridget spent the time chatting, barely audible to Cooper. She had told him they all performed in a bar up the coast, and after an hour they arrived at a roadhouse on the edge of the two-lane highway. Bridget got out and brushed down her skirt. That was another thing, it was a skirt he'd never seen her in. The neon above them reddened her face. 'I'll leave you here,' she said. 'See you later, okay?' 'Okay.' 'Meet up with me after the show.' 'Okay.' The building looked anonymous, one of those basic rectangular shapes. It could just as easily have been a bordello with wheelchair access. But it was, apparently, a boxing gymnasium and bar. There were already about forty cars, several half-ton trucks, even a honey wagon, parked on the gravel around it.

It was a night when Cooper was in the slipstream of Bridget's agenda, and was at ease. He walked around the building to kill time. One side of the structure was unlit, and beyond were unseen fields, suggested only when a car turned around in the parking lot. He imagined Bridget in her dressing room, preparing herself, changing her shoes or painting her nails a burnt sienna. He felt avuncular towards her. He really knew nothing about women. A door opened out into the dark, and a slice of light landed on the ground about twenty feet from him. She came out with two men, and they peered into the blackness and then moved closer to one another. She had her hand on one of the men, and there was a tug and she fell against him. She stepped back, and Cooper saw her remove what looked like his blue tie from her bare arm. He'd seen a man collect poison in Taos, forcing the serpent's jaws open harshly against a beaker and squeezing the venom out of whatever gland held it so that it dripped against the hard plastic, a little click from the tooth of the creature almost inaudible, like a brief protest. Cooper watched Bridget and the two men, not moving from where he was. When they opened the door wider to return into the building, the path of light actually reached him, but they had their backs turned towards him then.

The bar ran down one side of the lounge, and Bridget was on the stage at the far end. She had changed into a cream-coloured dress with a low neck and was wearing his tie loosely around her throat. The Dauphin would not have approved. When she began to sing, what was surprising was not the power of her voice, or its range from rough to tender, but the confidence she had up there, as if a great actress were sculpting the air with her arms while drawling like Chrissie Hynde. It was a persona Cooper had not met in all the time he had spent with Bridget. Her subliminal dancing, her yelling back to the crowd, her translation of 'Season of the Witch' into a rough, dangerous blues, left him unmoored from everything he knew about her. He'd never met this woman before. All he recognized was his tie, loose around her neck. She was the only thing he watched. That evening, every approach to a song was a new side of her nature. Even when he saw that she was growing tired, she had a focus and a presence. She moved back and forth among the other band members, banging into the contained light, breaking across the structures of songs, her white arms catching the sparkle off a globe, her hip fucking the audience. There was nothing too prepared or controlled about the performance. She was enlarged.

When it was over, he watched as she came down from the stage with the band. She was handed, and swallowed it seemed in one slide, a tall glass of beer. The determination in the songs was now replaced by a childish happiness at the flattery and hugs from acquaintances. Now and then she looked out beyond them to see if he was there, but she could not see him. He remained further back, watching her out of the darkness. He was curious about every detail of this moment, when she was still partially caught up in what she had been onstage; he didn't want that person to dissolve into the air with his appearance.

Her eyes were darting over shoulders. She was sinking. Cooper came forward into the limelight (so this was limelight), and he saw her unsure smile, which seemed to shrug it all off for his sake. They embraced and he felt the sweat on her arms, her wet dress, her wet hair against his cheek.

The next night he went to a card game, and when he returned was unable to find her. She was not in his room at the Santa Maria Inn, or asleep in the lobby, or in her apartment. It had been cleaned out and paid for. He realized he had no contacts for her, no idea how to reach her. There was only the man from Jocko's, and he didn't know his name. In the morning he drove to every hardware store within twenty miles of Santa Maria. He was worried that Bridget was not safe, wherever she was. Even though her rooms had been efficiently emptied.

He started sitting in coffee shops and bars along the town's three-mile strip, and walking around Santa Maria, hoping this was a way to find her. He kept up his habit of running in the mornings, but now, more frantic, he flung himself beyond the outskirts. He was conscious, after all these years, of his wakened sexuality. He went into a gym and began sparring, using the regimen of rope and heavy bag. This was harsher, a better escape for his mind than running. He felt strong, but the strength grew, he knew, out of his own powerlessness. When he went back to his hotel one day, he looked at himself in the faint light of the lobby mirror for a clue of some sort. The realization hit him that he had been the one who was addicted.

The desk clerk said he had mail. It was a postcard from Tahoe with no message or signature, just his name and address in the handwriting he recognized. On the other side was a picture of Harrah's casino glistening in a dusk light. It was Bridget, telling him where she was.

Within an hour he was going east, away from the coast, along the same roads he had taken with her on those late nights when they would drive towards Nevada. At the Carrizo Plain Monument he curved north and then travelled up the San Joaquin Valley on Highway 99. Visalia, Fresno, Modesto, and then Sacramento. The sacrament. In Carmichael he ate a meal. By the time it was dark he was climbing into the Sierras. There was rain and a mist, so that towns like Silver Fork and Strawberry, settlements he'd driven through a hundred times in the past, slipped vaguely by. Shortly before Tahoe he checked into a motel, shaved and bathed, using up the thin wafer of soap he'd been given. He put on a clean shirt and a tie. It was about two a.m. when he drove away.

He descended into Tahoe, into its lights and its subdued universe around the glow of the lake. He got out of the Chrysler to look at the mountains he had come over. He could already sense the change in altitude. He was back in the past, it was a conscious risk, and everything could change. Then he drove the car into the garage at Caesars Palace and walked to Harrah's—he knew that you never parked where you worked.

As soon as he entered the Grand Hall, the pumped-in oxygen hit him. He'd driven all afternoon and much of the night, and now the buzz of tiredness in him dissolved. A pompous decor surrounded him. He sat on the twenty-foot-long leather sofa and stretched his legs. When a waiter offered him a drink, Cooper tipped him a ten-dollar bill and asked for a wet espresso. He carried the tall glass towards the tables. So far he'd seen no one he knew, but the Tahoe night was young. Fifteen hours ago he'd been boxing his heart out, sparring at a gym where there was Astroturf for carpeting.

Cooper knew that if he made himself visible, Bridget would find him, so he moved through the palatial rooms, the waterfall of noise, the haphazard slow motion. Eventually he sat down to play. He lost the first hand intentionally, as he always did. The game was faster than in the south, but these were amateurs around him. It was four a.m. He was still wide awake.

An hour later, looking up during a deal, he saw her. Something lurched in his body. How long had she been standing there like that, so still, watching him? She was taller than most of the onlookers. He finished the hand and swept up the chips. He'd made enough tonight in any case to rent something good on the south shore, if he or she needed it.

Cooper.

She gripped his arm at the cash grill. He put his face against her neck, white, almost gold, the muscle there taut, perhaps the centre of her confidence.

They walked up wide carpeted steps. As soon as they escaped the Grand Hall they were free of its noise and a memory came into his mind of himself as a boy canoeing round a bend of San Antonio Creek and losing instantly the roar of a nearby set of rapids. He followed a step or two behind Bridget. She spun around and said, 'I've just been for a swim.' She was drifting on a light foot. No one else in Harrah's appeared to have such casual strength. There was an efficiency in her he hadn't seen before. In the elevator she held off his embrace.

Wait.

As if that word explained it all.

Wait for what?

We have to talk. Are you checked in here?

No.

Because you can't stay here, in this hotel.

He said nothing to that, and they rode the rest of the way in silence. His car was at Caesars, he could have stayed here.

It was now about five-thirty, and the two of them sat down to breakfast. He looked out the windows from the eighteenth floor, and the sky was still a magenta dark above all the lights. Cooper didn't raise the issue of why he shouldn't stay here. It felt to him that Bridget was armed in some way, and he needed to circle her carefully. He needed to know what her intention was. Though if she was up to something, it would be wise to keep quiet about it in a building where the eye in the sky could be anywhere. He realized she'd coaxed him into a place where he couldn't argue and accuse. Instead he brought up her old dinner partner at Jocko's. 'That hardware store fellow . . .' he asked. She lolled her head side to side as an answer. 'What's his name? You never told me. Does he live in Tahoe? Is that why you are here?' She waved everything away except to admit that the man from Jocko's was here.

Underneath Caesars Palace he unlocked the Chrysler, and let her in the passenger side. There was that familiar sense that the air and the uncertain lighting in the underground garage were left over from an earlier decade. He walked slowly around the car and got in beside her.

I should go back to Santa Maria.

Huh? Her head jerked towards him.

Why did you leave? What are you getting me into, Bridget?

Let's just drive out of this place.

No.

Can we drive—

I'm not ready for that sun yet.

Okay. She ran her hand slowly down his arm. Well, you didn't go to seed.

Oh, I hit bottom, don't worry.

She kissed his right eye, then his forehead, then his mouth. He accepted everything. Her hands on him. They were not kissing now. It was more intimate, their faces staring at each other, almost touching. A breath, no words to accompany this, only watching each other's naked response. His tired eyes alive upon her.

On Nevada Inn Road, twenty minutes later. 'I'm taking you to meet my friend,' she said. 'There's something I want to ask you to do. . . .' She began telling him about the hardware store owner on the drive, and how he had recognized Coop that very first night at Jocko's. His name was Gil. She owed him money, and she worked for him. 'Is he your lover?' She'd known him for a long time, she said. He was a card player. There would be his two friends with him, they were all card players. They knew everything about Cooper. They had heard about him before he ever sat down for a meal at Jocko's. Cooper was silent, whispering to himself, wanting to slam the heel of his hand through the windshield, as if it were her foolishness. She was a part of a setup to bring him to Tahoe.

They parked, and he walked with her into a short-lease condo. Three men sat in the large, almost unfurnished apartment. She introduced Cooper, and right away the men began speaking of his episode with The Brethren, even about his infamous gesture to the eye in the sky that would find no documentary evidence of his cheating; they were impressed he had been that good. He looked over at Bridget, who was staring at her hands, as if she had nothing to do with any of this. Then Gil put forward the plan. It was clever, intricate, and Cooper refused right away. He stood up. There was an exhaustion overtaking him. The men kept giving him more details so that he felt surrounded by talkative demons. He moved away from the light coming through the big windows. Cooper kept replaying the moment in the car when Bridget had admitted her connection with these men so casually. He had no idea who these people were. They were newcomers. They were older than he was, but he had never heard of them. He waved them off when they wouldn't accept his refusal. He'd made that one mistake in his life; he wouldn't do it again. He started to walk out of the room. One of the men touched him on the arm, and Cooper wheeled around and almost hit him. They were aware of that. When Cooper got to the door, Bridget came beside him and put her hand on him, exactly where the man had touched him, as if he should understand the difference. He turned and saw the three men, over her shoulder at the far end of the enormous room, watching them.

Cooper, can you help me? This has to work. I need my life back.

This life?

I need money to pay him back. . . . It's a lot of money. It's just a card game.

He laughed at her.

Can you do this? She reached out and he stepped back, would not be touched. He remembered how comfortable she and her friend had been at Jocko's. Always talking, always interested in each other.

You can step away from here, he said.

You don't understand, Cooper. You have to help me through this.

Tell me.

There's this dream. I don't know. It's a long-standing dream. You walk into a room and the white lines are laid out, or the crystals are forming, and you think, Just walk out, don't take a hit, you're going to feel bad if you take a hit. But an addict never just walks out. You always take the hit. You get the high, even in your dream, and you know at the same time it's going to hurt. If only you had just walked out.

Why are you whispering?

Why do you *think*? It's the truth about me.

I see. He looked back towards the men.

I've known him so long. But I'm unsafe now. You have to help me. Do you need more time? He and his friends . . . they could give you another day to decide. I'm sure. Think about it. Don't decide against it now.

He drove along the south shore of the lake and found a chalet to rent. Neither anger nor exhaustion had kept him away from Bridget when he arrived in Tahoe. But even in his passion for her, Cooper had refused Gil's proposal. He could have done everything the three men wanted him to do, but then he would be imprisoned in their world forever. He knew when he'd stacked the deck against Autry and The Brethren that they were familiar with larceny. These men were about to hit an innocent. And they already had too much knowledge of him. They'd selected him before he knew of their existence—long before his first sighting of Bridget at Jocko's. He had *never* been invisible. And Bridget was there only to bring him to Tahoe, with the crook of her finger, with a swirl from her sea-green skirt. He saw another version of their romance, where the only thing being gratified and comforted was him, not her. He saw himself in the frame, surrounded by the con.

The telephone rang in the chalet, and it was Gil. All communications would come from him. Cooper had one day to decide. The phone went dead. So they knew where he was. They had followed him. Cooper sat down at the Formica table and pushed a kitchen knife back and forth to the edge, as if its weight and balance might contain a crucial clue about how he should respond to all this. Win the right games, lose the right games. People did this every day in their lives, in their careers and friendships and love affairs. It was the moderate virtue of compromise. He stood up, leaving the knife balanced where it was.

Bridget was within that array of lights across the lake. If she had appeared on his porch at that moment and allowed him into her jet-white arms, offering herself like a genuine truth, he knew he would, in spite of this new hate, move towards her, though the odds were blatant and foolish. He could not stand her absence. Her laugh was too far away from him, he was not in a steamed-up bathroom beside her, where she stood drying her hair, twisting the cone of the machine so it blew across her body. He needed the familiarity of her talking in that calm, low, grainy voice, detailing things; he needed the nine or ten glimpses of her in the bevelled mirror of an elevator, and her energy beside him as he drove the coast, her feet jacked up on the dashboard like a twelve-year-old girl's. He wanted all of that. He would have taken all of that, over the odds.

Then a strange thing happened. He drove into Tahoe the next day to eat a meal. He fantasized he might actually see Bridget somewhere, but instead there was Claire, in a diner. After all these years. Her lean brown shoulders, madrone-coloured, her dark beauty like a brown flower, her inquisitive face, as if she had all at once invented an adult look and manner. She had fallen into his arms, and in that second he recognized the original Claire, right through the years. She made a gesture that was familiar, and he looked around, as if Anna should also be there. But there was no one else. Claire appeared tired, and he accompanied her back to her hotel and said he would contact her later. He returned to the chalet and got into bed, but he couldn't sleep.

He recalled Claire mostly on horseback. He was used to seeing her in the context of currycombs, a bridle slung over her shoulder, or kneeling in the grass and peering at a ring-necked snake's thin red collar. She'd been the one to discover him half frozen in the car. He could still hear the voice yelling. But he had been too cold to move. His head had turned slightly and he had glanced at the girl, with one half-open eye, at that figure pulling on the door with all her strength. Then she had disappeared. She had given up. He had been too slow and had not helped in any way. He began falling back into unconsciousness, then woke abruptly as an axe splintered through the passenger-side window and glass leapt into the darkness and into his hair and there was suddenly the noise of wind around him in the car. A hand came in and tugged at the door frame, breaking it free of the casing of ice, and then Claire was in there trying to pull him out through the passenger door. He could not straighten his legs, so she got into the passenger seat, covered in glass, and put her legs over him and kicked the driver's door open. That was easier. Then she was carrying him out from the driver's seat and dragging him through the dark yard.

He was being pulled out of his bed, half asleep. The men hoisted him and took him into the living room of the chalet and made him sit in a cane chair, then duct-taped his hands to it loosely. For a while there was a silence as they stood around him. He felt he was still within his dream. Then Bridget came in. A skirt, her grey sweater, for the cold Tahoe evening. She came and sat on a low stool near him and leaned forward. Moved her face closer. He could feel the breath from her mouth. One of the men behind her said, 'The deal, Cooper, the choice—say you will work with us, or we'll beat the hell out of you.' 'I've been there,' Cooper said quietly.

Gil came forward and put his hand on Bridget's shoulder as if it were something he owned. 'It's just this—you can't fuck her for a couple of months and then not work for us, because you're "principled." You're a mechanic, Cooper. You need to pay your way. We're going to beat that principle out of you.' He gripped Bridget's yellow hair for a moment and then moved back, leaving the two of them alone.

'Look down,' she said. A whisper. 'I can give you this, so you will barely feel what they do to you.' A syringe lay in the palm of her hand. She tilted it and the fluid swayed back and forth; it was like a floater pen in which a woman's black dress would slip off, or a train would vanish into a tunnel. She was screwing the needle onto the syringe as she looked at him. 'It's a favour. . . . Or you can say you will work with them.' She hesitated, then the words stopped. He was conscious that everyone was watching him. He said, 'Do you only fuck him when you're stoned?' Someone struck him in the face so hard he fell backwards with the chair, his head hitting the floor.

They pulled the chair with him back onto its four legs. Gil was now sitting on the stool Bridget had used, as close to Cooper as she had been. He swung his elbow hard against Cooper's mouth. 'You can't walk away, not now. Let's admit we're all whores.' He took a deep breath—Cooper sensed a movement but dared not look away from the man's lips—and then Bridget crashed into Cooper, and under the shield of her body stabbed his neck with the syringe, compressing it fully, and dropped it. The three men were all struggling to pull her off him. Cooper lay on his side by the fireplace, his head capsized with the rush of the drug. She was in Santa Maria, saying, 'This is for you. There are five flags. The yellow one is earth, the green one is water, the red is fire—the one we must escape.'

He remembered nothing after that.

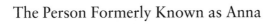

The Person Formerly Known as Anna

I came to France, in the thirty-fourth year of my life, to research the life and the work of Lucien Segura. I had flown into Orly, my friend Branka had met my plane, and we drove through the darkening outskirts, passing the smaller peripheral towns that were like blinks of light as we travelled south. We had not seen each other in over a year, and now we were catching up, talking all the way. Branka had packed a hamper of fruit, bread, and cheese, and we ate most of it, and drank from a constantly refilled glass of red wine that we shared.

We reached Toulouse around midnight. Nothing was open, and we still had another hour to go before we got to Dému. Branka proposed a diversion to the village of Barran, where her architectural firm was involved in the restoration of an old church belfry, and forty minutes later we navigated the car through the narrow streets of that town. We parked beside the graveyard.

Of course she had an arc light in the trunk of her car, and she lifted it out and beamed it towards the strange steeple that rose high into the darkness like a spear, or a giant beanstalk, though what it reminded me of mostly was the shambling water tower that we used to climb as children. But this was stranger. Built in the thirteenth century, the belfry had been constructed like a coil or a screw. It had one of those unexpected, helicoidal shapes—the surface like a helix—so that as it curved up it reflected every compass point of the landscape. We circled the church in the dark. Who had conceived and constructed this? Branka said that early historians claimed its builders were inspired by the form of a snail shell. Other explanations were that carpenters had used wood that was too fresh, so it ultimately warped, or that a very strong wind had created the torsion. My friend disregarded these theories of fresh wood or strong winds. The belfry was for her an example of visionary craftsmanship, its fifty-metre elevation 'like a fire in the sky.' She added there had been a fight during the recent restoration, in which a man had almost been killed.

We returned to the car and drove towards Dému.

All my life I have loved travelling at night, with a companion, each of us discussing and sharing the known and familiar behaviour of the other. It's like a villanelle, this inclination of going back to events in our past, the way the villanelle's form refuses to move forward in linear development, circling instead at those familiar moments of emotion. Only the rereading counts, Nabokov said. So the strange form of that belfry, turning onto itself again and again, felt familiar to me. For we live with those retrievals from childhood that coalesce and echo throughout our lives, the way shattered pieces of glass in a kaleidoscope reappear in new forms and are songlike in their refrains and rhymes, making up a single monologue. We live permanently in the recurrence of our own stories, whatever story we tell.

There was now not a single lit streetlamp in the villages we passed, just our headlights veering and sweeping along the two-lane roads. We were alone in the world, in nameless and unseen country. I love such journeying at night. You have most of your life strapped to your back. Music on the radio comes faint and intermittent. You are wordless at last. Your friend's hand on your knee to make sure you are not drifting away. The black hedges coax you on.

~

Whenever there is thunder I think of Claire. I imagine her, content by herself, though as far as I know she could be comfortably married. There is a poem of Henry Vaughan's that describes the way 'care moves in disguise.' I don't know if this is what I am doing, from this distance, imagining the life of my sister, and imagining the future of Coop. I am a person who discovers archival subtexts in history and art, where the spiralling among a handful of strangers tangles into a story. In my story the person I always begin with is Claire.

Claire's limp made her appear serious to those who did not know her well. It was the result of her having had polio as a child, and I remember our father during that period carrying her constantly from room to room. The limp always led to ardent gestures of courtesy towards her. Men on a trolley car or the Larkspur Ferry would rise and give her their seats. But Claire never felt this seriousness in herself. It is in fact I, Anna, who should be identified as the serious sister, who always insisted on some determined path to be taken. Claire was in many ways the adventurous one, with a wildness in her. Her journals about her travels—on horseback, of course—contained a range of friends unknown to the rest of us. . . .

January 7. We rode the cliffs looking for Keene's dog. He was always yelling at him, goddammit this, goddammit that, but we knew he loved it. We split up going along the creeks, looking for something that was either dead or alive, we didn't know. We all had done this before, looking for animals, then we would come across them dead, as if there had been a small massacre in the snow. In the late afternoon, we found the dog, shaking beside the creek at Richardson Bend. He had never been a friendly animal, except to his master, and now he had almost too much company. We crouched and 'paid court,' as Anna would say. Keene wrapped George in a blanket, and the rest of us led our horses into the water. I listened to the sound of their drinking, soosh soosh soosh, the sound a baby makes at a breast. A buck appeared, about twelve points—a deity. It came out of the trees and looked around. That must have been what it was like around George all that time when we thought he was alone. Keene so relieved, he held the dog in his arms and talked nonstop all the way home.

October 3. Old white trees. We take a brush light in one hand and ride into the aspens at night. There were horses in there, half asleep, walking like an ocean inland. I was there for two hours smelling their necks. I wanted to find one and sleep on her back.

December 5. Bobby has a girlfriend so thin she gets hammered on one beer. When Bobby's father died, she crawled into Bobby's bed and quietly embraced him. White-Jacket by Melville, that was Bobby's favorite book. Men like him, it's almost as if they are hiding behind depth.

In my work I sometimes borrow Claire's nature, as well as her careful focus on the world. Though no general reader will recognize my sister, not even she, I suspect, if she would happen to pick up a book of mine. For I have changed my name. Perhaps, if she were reading my work, she might be impressed by my details about halter buckles and cinches in some medieval episode, or by the realism of the swivel of a walk caused by childhood polio. It was a swivel, not really a limp, and I have parsed that walk of hers carefully—how it would be different on a hill, on grass as opposed to pavement, how she could disguise it in a room of strangers.

And like Claire, I have become cautious of what I take in and nurture—the carefully chosen portion of experience. I once read an essay by a writer who was asked to imagine an ideal career, and he replied that he would like to be responsible for just a brief stretch, perhaps two hundred yards or so, of a river. I think this would have charmed Claire utterly, she would have safely put her life in that author's hands. Perhaps it is because small things repeat their importance on a farm and make them indelible in our memory. She will remember Coop picking her up after a birthday party, and how they drove home along the coast road with the sky yellow and the hills purple-black. And the time he stood on the top of the water tower as the two of us watched him. And Alturas the cat. And probably the strange episode with the fox. I am sure Claire could draw a diagram of the cup of wine and the heel of bread and the deep gold of the cheese on the table at five a.m. in that dark kitchen of our childhood before milking began, and recall how even at that hour it felt raucous with the noise of the starting fire. But then, I remember that too.

I feel I can imagine most things about Claire accurately. I know her. But Coop I know only in one distinct way—as the twenty-year-old I fell in love with, who took one step beyond the intimacy that was handed to him. It is almost natural, is it not? He had grown up alongside these two sisters, an orphan, in our small desirous field. He had taught Claire and me how to build a rail fence, how to grind up a buckeye nut and sprinkle it on the surface of a river to tempt fish. All these rules and habits had created a bond between us. But when I reconstruct the arc of Coop's life I can take it only as far as the knot of the moment when he, that shy alien one, became my secret lover, ironically at the very moment when he was exposing himself by this act of sharing.

The discovery of us in each other's arms, under that green sky, a father attempting to murder a boy, a daughter trying to attack a father, is in retrospect something very small, something that might occur within just a square inch or two of a Brueghel. But it set fire to the rest of my life. I was witness to madness—fully mad myself—clawing his body and face with a piece of glass to be free of him, as he held my neck in that grasp. I have come to believe that no girl has had such an intimacy with a father, who was trying perhaps to strangle the devil out of her. Whatever anger existed, there must have been some grains of a fearful love for me. But I did not believe that then. All I thought was that I still had Coop's heart in me as my father lifted my body out of that cabin, gripped my hand and took me down the hill. I was screaming when we entered the farmhouse. He said nothing to Claire. Minutes later he forced me into the truck and drove me away, down the coast, as if distance would dilute whatever existed between Coop and me. I had only a moment to collect what I wanted. I ripped out from a photograph album a picture of myself and Claire, took one of her journals. I knew already I would not be back.

I would never see Coop again.

And then, somewhere south of San Jose, at a truck stop on I-5, I slipped away. I went in one door and immediately out another and caught a ride. I disappeared. I was probably ten minutes ahead of him by the time he realized what had happened. He must have careened down the interstate looking into the windows of every car he passed along the coastal route, alerting the police about his lost daughter, searching for me in towns like Gilroy and Santa Clara and San Juan Bautista. He would not have gone back to the farm for several days. And by then the abnormal ice storm and blizzard that hit the region had left the Petaluma hills. I was now a runaway. And Coop would no doubt be gone.

Who recovers from such events? You meet people even in middle age and discover that at some point, in the delicate path of life, they have been turned into the Jack of Hearts or the Five of Clubs. This is what has happened, I suspect, to Coop and to me. We have become unintelligible in our secrets, governed by our previous selves. Just as Claire, in some way, will always be adjacent to our romance, the one who lost her family because of it.

'One fetal twin may absorb the other without malice, and retain in its body a loose relic or two of one of the absorbed twin's femurs. (The living twin grows and becomes an adult; the femur stays fetal.)' That marvel, Annie Dillard, wrote that. And perhaps this is the story of twinship. I have smuggled myself away from who I was, and what I was. But am I the living twin in the story of our family? Or is it Claire?

Who is the stilled one?

∿

Those who have an orphan's sense of history love history. And my voice has become that of an orphan. Perhaps it was the unknown life of my mother, her barely drawn portrait, that made me an archivist, a historian. Because if you do not plunder the past, the absence feeds on you. My career exhumes mostly unknown corners of European culture. My best-known study is of Auguste Maquet, one of Alexandre Dumas' collaborators and plot researchers. Another is a portrait of Georges Wague, the professional mime who gave Colette lessons in 1906 to prepare her for music-hall melodramas. I work where art meets life in secret. An archive is Utopia to me, a poet said, and my acquaintances no doubt feel contemporary life must seem a thin and less interesting pasture for me. That may be true. When Rafael asks, for instance, in which historical moment I desire to live, I say, without pause, Paris, the week Colette died, when at her state funeral Georges Wague made certain a thousand lilies were sent by the Association of Music Halls and Circuses. . . . I want to be there, I tell him, in my 'Contre Sainte-Beuve' t-shirt, looking up at her apartment on the premier étage of the Palais-Royal, where 'no more amorously selected words would align themselves on the pale blue paper under the light of the blue lamp.'

Georges Wague, who taught Colette mime, taught her two important things. He had recognized a hidden art in her, that she could represent herself not just with words. This woman, he could see, contained other qualities. She could be as powerful when she was speechless. He took her hand and they walked away from others in Natalie Barney's garden, and as she began to speak he put a finger across her lips and her eyes caught fire, full of life. They watched his face for a signal. He let his hand fall back in a surrender so she knew he was not manipulative, and they walked on. He told her then that mimes live long lives. The second thing he told her she already knew. That there was nothing more assuring than a mask. Under the mask she could rewrite herself into any place, in any form.

This is where I learned that sometimes we enter art to hide within it. It is where we can go to save ourselves, where a third-person voice protects us. Just as there is, in the real landscape of Paris in *Les Misérables,* that small fictional street Victor Hugo provides for Jean Valjean to slip into, in which to hide from his pursuers. What was that fictional street's name? I no longer remember. I come from Divisadero Street. Divisadero, from the Spanish word for 'division,' the street that at one time was the dividing line between San Francisco and the fields of the Presidio. Or it might derive from the word *divisar,* meaning 'to gaze at something from a distance.' (There is a 'height' nearby called

El Divisadero.) Thus a point from which you can look far into the distance.

It is what I do with my work, I suppose. I look into the distance for those I have lost, so that I see them everywhere. Even here, in Dému, where Lucien Segura existed, where I 'transcribe a substitution / like the accidental folds of a scarf.'

I am uncertain, even now, what made me fall upon the life of Lucien Segura and wish to write about him. Or what made me explore in the Berkeley archives the almost worn-out paths of his life in the Gers. I had read the French writer while studying at Randolph-Macon Woman's College. But then, more important, in a carrel in the Bancroft Library at Berkeley, I heard for the first time his voice, reciting his poems into a lacquered tin funnel as if into the large ear of a stranger. This documentation by the Académie Française in an early-twentieth-century recording had positioned him too far in the background, so that close by was what sounded like a seacoast or a crackling fire. Nonetheless I felt there was something in the articulated voice that suggested a wound, the way one can sometimes recognize a concealed ailment in the slow movement of a king in newsreels. And I remember that, after his poems, Lucien Segura read something on that cylinder about his father—his stepfather, really—who had been a clockmaker, and I looked up from the notes I had been taking in Dr. Weber's semester on peasant life and began to listen more intently. There was a sweet shadow and hesitance in Segura. It was like a ruined love, and it was familiar to me. Till then all I knew of his life was his odd departure from his family; that late in life, comfortable, successful, he had climbed into a horse-drawn cart, and disappeared. His voice with the wound in it kept haunting me. I travelled to France, to the last house he had lived in, during the final stage of his life. I pieced together the landscapes he had written about. I took long walks. I swam in the nearby stream, I walked his avenue of trees. I met Rafael.

Seven minutes after I escaped from my father at the truck stop near San Jose, this person formerly known as Anna climbed into the passenger seat of a vehicle going south. We drove all night, a shy black man in his commercial refrigeration truck giving a lift to someone he thought was a French girl. (I did not wish to talk or explain anything.) We stopped now and then for food, though I barely ate, my stomach hurting from fear. We sat in roadside diners and I watched him eat guacamole and chiles rellenos, while the weather stations on every truck-stop television screen reported the freak ice storm invading northern California. It had been a sunny afternoon on Coop's deck, before the windlessness and those moments of thunder, and here I was, a day later, across the table from a polite and generous stranger. I did not speak. English never escaped my lips, and the only words that existed between us as we travelled into the Great Central Plain came from the truck's radio.

The Central Valley of California that we drove through had been, in an earlier time, a sea of flowers. John Muir describes how it used to be a 'continuous bed of honey-bloom, so marvelously rich . . . your foot would press about a hundred flowers at every step.' And at times the region had resembled a sea. 'The whole Valley was turned into an ocean. Most of its people were drowned. Some tried to swim away but frogs and salmon caught them and ate them. Only two people got away, swept into the Sierras,' says a Maidu myth on the birth of the Great Central Plain. Explorers came and gave the Sacramento and Merced rivers their names. Sacramento. Mercy. The trapper Kit Carson hunted along the 'shaggy river-beds.' It was raw, unstable country then, with gunfighters and thieves—Joaquín Murrieta (who claimed to have eaten ostrich), Johnny Sonntag, Tres Dedos (Three-Fingered Jack), the Daltons. They camped around Visalia, now a sleepy atonal town. Succinct histories tell us something—that anything peaceful has a troubled past.

Nowadays this flattened stark land is etched by railway crossings and a remarkable symmetry of river channels, as if God has impressed a circuitry down onto the earth and given it reason. So we have the low hill civilizations of Pixley and Porterville, the lights of Buttonwillow and Tulare. Coop once slept with a girl in Tulare, that tense, frantic night of his remembered with a coy term. He had 'slept' with the girl in Tulare as he had 'slept' with me. The damnation that came down on us is not quite extinct. Someone from the past might still say of me, 'There's a black flag in that woman's life.' But this is unlikely to happen. A family keeps its secrets. Just as all that remains from the Central Valley's past are muted rumours of anarchic outlaw girls and the furious Eugene Key, who took over as sheriff in Tulare and cut off the left hand of Three-Fingered Jack, and sent it to Visalia by Wells Fargo as evidence, to celebrate a victory of sorts.

Our truck that day crossed that antique seabed. We slipped past fruit farms, entered brief bouts of rain. I have read up ever since on the history of the Great Central Plain, about cattle in Fowler's Junction, and about the beautiful and haunting Allensworth. I've read *The Octopus,* in which Tulare is renamed Bonnerville, and read about the waves of immigrants who came here with their music of languages—Tagalog, Spanish, Italian, Chinese, and Japanese—to cut open the ditches for irrigation, to turn swamps into fruitland, or to mine asphalt in the intense heat, as my maternal grandfather did, working practically naked, coated in that oil they used for flux for what they were mining near the spur line of Asphalto. Just another place named after a mineral on the map of the world. How many are there? A greater number, I suspect, than named for royalty.

I was sixteen the year I took the roads travelling south, running away from my father, with Coop's heart in me. And I kept travelling it seemed for another ten years among strangers, alone, never intimate, slowly building a confidence in my solitude. But during that first journey, I sat in the spacious cab of that commercial refrigeration truck and stared and stared, swallowing everything I saw, so that whatever existed in me would be washed away. KUZZ-AM played Buck Owens singing 'Under Your Spell Again,' and I swallowed that as well. I had run out and jumped into the driver's cab at the truck stop on I-5, and he, luckily, was going inland first, to Merced, *Mercy,* and then south on 99. It was a route separate from my father's. We continued to Dinuba, where he ate Mexican food, then Cutler and Visalia. It began to darken and my mysterious new friend headed south and west to a place he said we could stay. We drove alongside orange groves and a state prison in the moonlight, and finally entered the deserted town of Allensworth. He said it had been abandoned for more than forty years. We would be the only ones there.

All I could see at that hour were the outlines of a score of houses. We drove beyond them till we were in a campground, and he climbed out and left me the cab to sleep in. I stretched out on the old leather seat. It would be the last night of my youth. And I kept my eyes open for as long as I could. I heard the night birds. Then the trains that shook the earth under me all night.

In the morning I walked among the beautiful pastel-painted

houses of Colonel Allensworth's abandoned town. The two of us climbed the steps up to each home, walked along their verandahs, reading the plaques that described the general store in 1912, the hotel, a school, a library. We peered in the windows and saw an old player piano, a picture of Lincoln. He said he always stayed in Allensworth on his journeys, a former depot town settled by blacks. We returned to the truck, which he had parked under the trees, and soon we were on the highway again. It was early and we were in one of those valley fogs called ground clouds. We could hear birds through the open windows, and we saw red-winged blackbirds dart out of the whiteness across the road.

He kept talking to me in English, but I still returned mostly silence. If I spoke, I spoke my mother's Spanish, or my tentative French. He knew I was raw with something, that I had some poison within me. He spoke to me anyway, telling me about Colonel Allensworth and the trains that since 1916 had refused to stop at the depot run by the black community. He must have known I could understand everything he said, for he spoke openly, and had stopped waiting for answers. At some point during that last morning with him, he went on about books and how they signalled the possibilities of our lives, and he recited to me what he said were the most beautiful lines. 'Whether I shall turn out to be the hero of my own life, or whether that station will be held by anybody else, these pages must show.' I know where those lines come from now, but I didn't then, and when I did eventually stumble on them I froze and burst into tears for the first time in my adult life.

At Bakersfield he dropped me off, and slipped some money into my pocket. I started to walk through the sparse town, my life ahead of me. He had never touched me that whole time. I gave him a kiss at the truck stop. My last good kiss. I kissed no one for a long time after that. I have come to believe he was Mister Allensworth guiding me south.

This is the story I wished I could have someday told Coop— perhaps in a letter, perhaps in a phone call. But he, my first darling, was lost to me, and I was too far away by then, in another life.

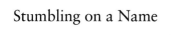

Stumbling on a Name

It took Aldo Vea two days to locate Coop from the phone number that Claire had read out to him. 'It's a chalet, along the south shore of Tahoe,' he said. 'He must be renting the place.'

Claire parked at the foot of the hill. 'Chalet' was perhaps too grand a word. Halfway up the steep walk she called his name. When she reached the deck she saw the front door wide open and the body, face-down, a cane chair taped to his hand. Coop had always been strong, but it looked as though someone had beaten half the blood out of his face. He was conscious and he glared up at her. Turning him she saw dark bruises on his neck. This hadn't just happened.

When the medics arrived, when they asked questions—Who had done it? Where did it hurt most? Was there still pain in his head?—he waved them away. She told the medics she would stay with him. Then he's lucky, they said, he's going to need help. They left and she remained beside him, waking him every few hours, as they'd told her to do, to check on him. Later he woke on his own and she fed him soft-boiled eggs. He could talk, but he was essentially reflecting the questions awkwardly. She remembered that embarrassed smile of his when she accused him of walking like a gangster. That had been only two days earlier.

What happened? Was this connected to your work?

Work, he said in a monotone. Then, What work?

The poker.

She watched him searching for an answer, as for a misplaced thing, a pencil, a lighter. He doesn't know what I'm talking about, she thought.

You play poker, Coop.

There was a grimace of a laugh then.

You are a gambler. That's what you do. Do you know my name?

He said nothing to her.

Do you remember me? Do you remember Anna?

'Anna,' drawn out as if it were a new word he must learn to pronounce.

Thank you, Anna, he said when she took away the tray and the bowl that had held his eggs.

Gotraskhalana is a term in Sanskrit poetics for calling a loved one by a wrong name, and means, literally, 'stumbling on the name.' It's a familiar occurrence in the Restoration-like fables of marital life and love affairs collected by the scholar Wendy Doniger. What these verbal accidents do is aim a flashlight into the brain, reveal its vast museum of facts and desires. So when Coop assumed quite logically that her name was 'Anna,' a bulb lit a surprising pathway Claire never would have believed could be travelled. Just for now, she thought to herself, just for a thrill.

Coop's memory, the Coop she knew, seemed to have sunk without trace. Only his motor skills remained adept. When she went for groceries, she bought a deck of cards and a Sharpie pen. Deal, she said when she returned to the chalet, and he immediately and efficiently slid fifty-two playing cards out of his fingers into four piles. But there was no knowledge of the game until she explained the basic rules. Then he knew where he was. Whatever Claire said to him he learned, though if she gave an alternative possibility he became confused. When she tried, on the second day, to correct Coop about her name, it proved too difficult. We remember the first things we learn.

With forgetfulness, what remains of the desire that consumed Coop? Where does it go? Obsession, so finely tuned, is misplaced with this dramatic loss of autobiography. So that someone watching him on his hands and knees on the thin chalet carpeting is perhaps witnessing a frantic search for that physical half that longed to lock itself like a claw in the body of another. A few hours later he is no longer aware of what has left him, the body's role muted, the brain refusing to give any clue as to what he once wanted so badly. He falls into a relieved sleep in the single bed, unaware of the panorama of his week, unaware of a motive for these wounds, unconcerned with the need to avenge himself. Desire and obsession so slight. One organ, the hippocampus, closes down, and we are redirected into an emptiness.

Faces become anonymous to him now, like shadows in the grass. Who is this woman who is here with him? Another woman rises from a bed. When does that happen? He sees himself pulling her into the spray of the shower, her yellow hair turning brown around her face, he cannot connect this person with anything—a house, a street. He likes being in the small bathroom with her, and her lazy strength. Flecked with water, she opens a drawer and pulls out a hair dryer, tests it on her arm, and lets it blow into her hair, lightening it, tossing it like wheat. Her face changes as she does this, her head surrounded now with a texture. She diverts the cone of hot air across her body and pulls the cord out of the wall, and he hears that subliminal sonar tumble in its dying sound.

∿

She would wake in the night and go to kneel beside his bed and listen for his breath, stare at him. She kept trying to recognize the young face she had known, beneath the bruises and the stubble. Coop. She had spent half of her life with Coop and Anna, and now there was only this unclear shadow of him in the moonlit room. As she watched him he opened his eyes, and she could tell he recognized nothing. It was as if she did not exist in the room. Do you want some water? Yes. Here. She held the glass to his dry mouth.

They took slow walks on the trails above the chalet. If Coop went alone, Claire would write her mobile number on his arm with the Sharpie. One night, when he had been gone for a while, she looked down from the deck and saw car lights at the foot of the hill and then three men struggling their way up the chalet stairs. They were surprised by her presence. When they asked for Coop, she pretended no knowledge of him. The previous tenant skipped town, she said, left a few things behind. She was leasing the place now. She gave them the owner's name, which Vea had mentioned. They took Coop's things and said they might return, in case he came back. She called Vea then and told him what had happened, what she had found when she got to the chalet, that she was sure the three were the men who'd almost killed Coop. 'Okay, Claire, the two of you leave now. Just drive. Wherever you feel like, don't make it logical.'

They left as soon as Coop returned, and drove deep into Nevada, into the desert. They stopped whenever they were hungry or tired, sometimes at night, sometimes during the blazing afternoons. She bought a Polaroid camera and took a picture wherever they stopped. She thought it would help him remember the present. She balanced the camera on the hood of her car, set the timer, then ran to where he was, and waited for the click to release them from their pose. The extra seconds felt long, falsely intimate, their eyes half closed because of the bright sunlight around them.

Do you remember how to drive?

It looks easy.

Yeah, sure. You can deal cards, you can drive.

They climbed out to switch seats. In the driver's seat he twisted the rearview mirror so he could see his bruised face, the marks of iodine, then repositioned it to look behind him, as if he could now clearly see where he had come from. She leaned against the passenger door and watched him handle the clutch and the gearshift with ease. She was fifteen years old again, and he was teaching her to drive.

She began to think where they should go. A danger had focussed itself on Coop, and she did not know whether it was only Tahoe that was unsafe for him. She had no knowledge of the extent of his world. She remembered Vea's remark about randomness and made Coop double back, and they entered California and went north through the old gold towns. She bought a local map and discovered a place called Hass, nestled in the hills. They arrived there in the afternoon and checked in to a two-storey brick hotel. There was one room available, so they shared it. When Coop removed his shirt, she saw that the bruises on his chest and arms were now an ugly yellow. He had not complained of pain since they'd left Tahoe. She recalled the Absorbine horse liniment that she and Anna used to rub on each other as kids, its smell—cowboy perfume, they called it. Claire gave Coop the bed and took the sofa. They were silent and separate in the attempted darkness of the hotel room, knowing that outside it was still bright daylight.

You okay?

Yeah.

The hum of the drive was still in her body.

So tell me about yourself, Anna. How do we know each other?

She was silent.

You knew I could drive.

What?

You said I knew how to drive.

Well, yes, most people do.

I was a gambler.

Yes, you said that, the day we met.

There was a pause, and Claire tried to slip him back, into the past. Do you remember the day with the fox?

The fox . . .

Then they were silent. He must have fallen asleep. Coop's 'How do we know each other?' burned in her. Anna and Coop and Claire. The three of them, she had always believed, made up a three-panelled Japanese screen, each one self-sufficient, but revealing different qualities or tones when placed beside the others. Those screens made more sense to her than single-framed paintings from the West that existed without context. Their lives, surely, remained linked, wherever they were. Coop had been adopted into the family in much the same way that she had been taken from the hospital in Santa Rosa and brought home beside Anna. An orphan and a changeling . . . they had evolved, intimate as siblings, from that moment. She'd lived one of her essential lives with Coop, and she could never dismantle herself from him.

She went over in the dark to his bed and saw his face; it was sallow in the shut-away afternoon light. Once more he opened his eyes and looked at her, looked, she thought, at nothing. His lips were dry. There was no water in the room. No tap. The shower was down the hall. She spat onto her fingers and rubbed them over his lips and saw him trying to swallow. He took her wrist before she could withdraw it, and held it for a moment. Anna, he said. No, she said. No, not Anna.

Claire went back to the sofa and sat across from him in the dark, trying to retrieve any other details he'd mentioned that day when they had met in the diner. He'd suggested there was a problem. 'Things are difficult for me right now,' he had thrown out, almost too casually.

Do you gamble always? she had asked him then.

One or two games a week now. I used to play endlessly.

I don't understand such a world . . . what its blessings are.

It's no different from any compulsive work. Some live a full life. I had one friend who was a Deadhead, but he was also involved with local politics. He'd play cards socially in a casino in Grass Valley.

Is he your friend still?

Unfortunately no.

Sounds like you should have stuck with him.

Then she had said, Do you ever think of our farm? And he had not said anything. And she had let his silence fall between them.

What is your mission, do you think? Vea had asked her once. And she didn't know. In spite of her desire for a contained universe, her life felt scattered, full of many small moments, without great purpose. That is what she thought, though what is most untrustworthy about our natures and self-worth is how we differ in our own realities from the way we are seen by others. What Claire later remembered, for instance, of her walk with Coop back to her hotel in Tahoe that day was her pleasure in his presence, and how invisible she believed herself to be in their brief hour or two together. She was simply happy to be walking beside him, nursing her tiredness, listening to him talk about the world he lived in. This extraordinary recurrence of him back into her life, the grandness of the names of the towns—Vegas, Grass Valley, Nevada City, Tahoe—seemed iconic, something discovered on an adult's map. If she had been told that Coop mused on her brown shoulders, that he had been remembering how she had saved his life in that ice storm, that somehow *she* was perhaps the heroine of their meeting, she would not have believed such a truth. We relive stories and see ourselves only as the watcher or listener, the drummer in the background keeping cadence.

There was sunlight in their room when Claire woke. Coop was waiting for her, already dressed. 'We need to visit Grass Valley, to find someone,' she said. 'We need to go back the way we came.' So they headed towards Nevada City and the neighbouring town of Grass Valley, where there might still be the casino in which Coop's friend, the Deadhead, used to play. She had no idea if the man still lived there or even what his name was.

They reached Nevada City and had a meal, and afterwards Coop sat in a chair in the foyer of the National Hotel, while Claire went out and bought some poster board. That evening she stood outside the Gold Rush Gaming Parlor in Grass Valley, with a sign in front of her that said ARE YOU COOPER'S FRIEND? At about ten o'clock a man with shells around his neck walked up to her and asked her who she was.

Dorn got into the car and looked at Coop. He put his palm up to the bruised face. A gesture, not a touch. He suggested they leave her car in Grass Valley. Dorn helped Coop into his station wagon. There was a hound, alert in the front passenger seat with no intention of moving into the back.

Dorn's home was a modest bungalow a mile or two from

town. He began cooking a meal he called 'broccoli surprise,' and a short while later Ruth arrived with their six-year-old daughter to find the house busy with strangers. Ruth walked over to Coop and embraced him. Dorn explained the situation to her, and they moved some of their daughter's things out of her bedroom so Coop and Claire could use it.

After the broccoli surprise, in which no broccoli could be found, Ruth began to examine Coop's wounds. She turned to Claire. It's been a long while since I've seen him, she said.

Did you know him well?

Yes, I was one of the boys, then. And Coop was 'The Untouchable.'

Claire was enjoying watching Coop, now in the context of his old friends, even if the affection and concern flowed only one way, towards Coop's unawareness. Dorn lit a joint, passed it over to Claire, and spoke of the incident with The Brethren, and then moved to various anecdotes in which the well-dressed Dauphin drifted in and out. Then Claire told Dorn and Ruth about their childhood in Petaluma. The three were slowly piecing together Coop's life as he sat there uninterested, studying the small movements in the room, the billow of a curtain, the leather sole of Claire's brown shoe, tapping whenever there was music. 'If we can stay with you a couple more nights, that would be good,' she said. 'Then we'll go.' 'Fine, stay longer if you wish,' Dorn replied. The dog was sitting on the sofa beside Dorn, listening to him with a concerned and dutiful look. His Master's Voice. Claire was finally beginning to feel safe, with Dorn, this family man. He must have at one time been a lean hippie, she thought, a lovely elder brother for Coop.

That night, lying flat on her back, Claire heard someone moving in the dark around her bed. She could hear breathing close by. She feared it might be the men who had beaten him, who had just come into the house. There was a leap, and Dorn's dog, who had been deciding from which side to enter the bed, burrowed next to her under the covers, its claws towards her. For a while it was still, and then, wanting more space, it pressed the claws gently, then more firmly, like tuning forks into her back.

By eight the next morning, Ruth had left for work. Dorn spread a large piece of velour over the sofa and with Claire's help began stitching costumes for the medieval feast that was an annual local event. It was to be held that night in the historic Miners Foundry, now a community centre, where everyone would be arriving in royal, peasant, or troubadour costumes. Dorn interrupted his brutal sewing by flinging a giant flank of meat, garlicked and herbed, on the barbecue. He insisted that Claire and Coop participate in the ceremonies. It was just a local crowd. He broke into his favourite songs all afternoon while they worked on capes and hoods. '*In Delaware when I was younger . . .*' He sang verse after verse of that song, and made up a few others. 'Now, that's a great song. Great song!' Ruth and their daughter returned home at five, and soon they were all transformed into fourteenth-century European villagers, Dorn's nonremovable beads and shells the only hints of the contemporary. Coop and Dorn carried the giant platter of meat, and Ruth brought a bowl of edamame beans. But the narrow streets of Nevada City were full of war protesters amid the music of mandolins and flutes. Twelve years after the American bombing of the Gulf in 1991, America was poised to attack Iraq again, and Pacifica and NPR stations had been updating information all day. So Claire found herself alongside medieval monks carrying antiwar placards to the event.

Dorn pulled his squirming daughter out for the first dance of the evening, and fifteen minutes later dragged Claire out too, crushing her to his doublet. She leaned against this Delaware-born (as in the song) anarchic hippie conspiracy-theorist, now a comfortably successful poker player living like a gentleman farmer in this town in the foothills.

The night ended with Dorn's breaking the time capsule of the Middle Ages by persuading the high school band to play 'Fire on the Mountain.' But much had happened before that. During the dinner, a five-year-old sat beside Coop at one of the decorated trestle tables. There was almost no conversation between them, because the boy was listening intently to a transistor radio. Finally he switched it off and turned to Coop and told him the Americans were bombing Baghdad. Coop was startled. The child was speaking about it casually, and insisted on giving him details, until Coop said, 'Tell that man over there,' pointing to Dorn, who was with a chiropractor, submitting himself to a complex arm hold. So the boy went over and waited until Dorn was released, then tugged at his arm. The two adults bent down, and the boy said something they could not catch because of the noise around them. Dorn lifted the boy into his arms. 'What's up, Finnegan?' Coop heard him say. And the boy told him.

Dorn put the boy down and stood there a moment. Then he walked over to his wife and slid his arm around her, listening while she continued talking to a friend. Ruth looked at Dorn, and he moved his hand down her arm, not letting the contact go even for a moment. He gave her a little tug, and she followed him to a side door. Coop watched the man they said was his friend profiled in the doorway, where coloured triangular flags of red and blue and yellow and white floated in a light breeze. Ruth kept staring at Dorn as he spoke, then turned away to look into the dark beyond the flags. She was hearing about America bombing a civilian city.

Coop began walking towards them, his brain struggling to hold on to something. He heard Ruth say, as he approached, 'Look at your friend, even he's not innocent. No one here is. Not me. Not you. Not even you. We're the barbarians too. We keep letting this happen.' Dorn was not responding, until her hand ripped at his neck and a hundred small shells paused on his chest for a second, then clattered to the floor. Children began scrambling for them. Coop in his silence had something by the tail, and he couldn't name it. He stood in front of them and didn't know what to say. He could see tears on Ruth's face. The music got louder, suddenly.

What had he been about to say to them? Something about her? Something he'd seen? She went up to him, weeping, and put her arms around him. 'Dance with me, Coop. Will you?' He put his arms up and she moved gently in against him, remembering the bruises. They aligned themselves to the dance. More and more children came onto the floor, then adults, as if coupled in another time, at an outbreak in the Hundred Years' War. Much later, Dorn, very drunk, grabbed the mandolin from a six-foot-tall teenager and joined the band, insisting on the endless version of 'Fire on the Mountain.'

The next morning nobody woke early, except for Coop, who sat alone at the kitchen table.

Was this his life before this life? What he was looking at felt familiar only because he had been here in this very same place the day before. There was nothing older than a few days in what he remembered. And what he held now, like a smooth doorless object in his mind, was his dance with the woman named Ruth. He had been able to tell right away that if he had danced in his earlier life he could not have been good. He had thought about this for a moment and then said it out loud to her. And she had said, 'That's right.' 'Begin the Beguine,' he said. And she had not responded.

He pondered now her manner, the way she had said, 'That's right.' As in, 'It was certainly a well-known fact among us.' What was she to him? A friend? Nothing? Was she speaking only of the present when she said, 'That's right'? But that was not the way the remark had been said to him. Who was Ruth? She had a name as small as a keyhole. She had danced with him. She'd wept in his arms.

Coop's mind held only a few distant things. A Polaroid of him by the highway, an owl on the road, a woman bent over a blue flame, a dance to the sound of flags. Otherwise his mind was this scrubbed table that could barely remember holding cups, or plates, or slices of bread, or a girl's tired head.

Driving to San Francisco, Claire reaches for Coop's hand.

I need you to meet my father.

Your father . . . Why?

He brought you up, Coop. And he's old now. So old. After you went away, and after my sister went away, he barely talked. Not even to me. He made himself alone. I want you to see him.

I don't know him.

He will want to meet you, Coop. And you need to say your good-byes. Perhaps this is important for you.

She did not want to explain any more to him, knowing this act could be terrible, even brutal. Or it would be generous. Or break her father's heart again. All of these things were possible. But so much had been wasted. She had only a distant father, and now Coop, like this, a boy remembering nothing. She wanted to fold the two halves of her life together like a map. She imagined her father, standing now on the edge of the cornfield, his white beard speckled by the shadows of the long green leaves, an awkward, solitary man, hungry for the family he had brought together and then lost—his wife in childbirth, this orphan son of a neighbour, and Anna, whom he had loved probably most of all, who was lost to them forever. There was just herself, Claire, not of his blood, the extra daughter he had brought home from the hospital in Santa Rosa.

From San Francisco they drove north over the Golden Gate Bridge, then left the highway and took a country road until they came into Nicasio. She said she was tired and asked Coop to drive. They went on, and saw the bent tree growing out of the great rock by the reservoir. The car wound along the Petaluma road into the hills, bordered on one side by giant poplars. She bit her tongue, looked out of her window seemingly unconcerned. As the car reached the peak he swerved the steering wheel with one hand casually to the right and they drove down the narrow farm road. He turned the key off, and they were gliding between fences towards the farmhouse. They went over the old speed bump of tires, and she saw her horse approaching the fence, and she saw Coop looking over the steering wheel into the old world.

*R*afael and I follow the river that disappears under a chaos of boulders and emerges once more a few hundred yards further in the forest. We walk in silence beside it. Eventually we come to a ford where our river meets a road and covers it, or from another perspective, where the road has come upon the river and sunk below its surface, as if from a life lived to a life imagined. We have been following the river, so that now we must look on the road as a stranger. The depth of water is about twelve inches, more when the spring storms come racing at low level over the fields and leap into the trees so nests capsize and there is the crack of old branches and then silence before each plummets in their fall. The forest, Rafael says, always so full of revival and farewell.

They merge, the river and the road, like two lives, a tale told backwards and a tale told first. We see a vista of fields and walk through the clear water that floods the gravel path, leaving the background of forest with each step.

TWO

The Family in the Cart

The House

The writer Lucien Segura moved through an overgrown meadow abundant with insects that sprang into the air as he approached. He had been following a path. The grass was chest-high, even higher, so he was using his arms in a swimming motion to move forward. How long was it since this grass was last cut down or burned? A generation, or more? About the time when he was a boy?

After ten minutes he stood motionless in the claustrophobia and heat. He had no idea how far and for how long he would have to keep moving to be free of it. There seemed to be a clearing about thirty metres away, for some charm trees stood there, barely moving. As he looked at them he saw, unbelievably, a peacock flying over the sealike surface of the rough pasture. The bird reached and settled within the darkness of one of the trees, its blue shape disguised now as a horizontal branch.

A poem from his youth about a strange bird from the foothills had been one of his most famous verses, memorized, explicated, exfoliated in schools until there was nothing left but a throat bone and a claw. The lines had become a mockery for him. There had been, in fact, no such rare bird in his youth. None had ever flown across his stepfather's fields. And now, suddenly, one existed as a reality.

He wished he had worn a hat. And the shirt he was wearing was wrong for this labour. He'd simply begun walking into the

field as part of a brief reconnaissance of a property he might purchase. The house had come with a formal driveway of plane
trees and several hectares of abandoned land. He began moving
forward again and, unable to see what was below him, stumbled
across a wooden object. A bench or a pump. He got to his knees,
cleared the grass away, and discovered it was a wooden boat.
The sound of insects thickened around him, and he felt even
more alone.

Three weeks earlier he had left his home near Marseillan,
which his stepfather had willed to his mother and which his
mother had willed to him, and he had left his wife and family.
Lucien Segura, in old age, was traversing the region of the Gers
in a horse-drawn cart, in search of a new home. Now and then
he gave travellers a ride in order to escape the strictness of this
new solitude. They were of varying ages, from all walks of life,
some alone, some who swung themselves onto the cart with one
or two children and a dog. He conversed with them openly, as he
always did with strangers, and heard the stories about forests
they had worked in, their settlements by rivers, the gardens they
manicured for a week's pay. As he listened, he entered their
worlds invisibly.

Until suddenly, one day, Lucien Segura had clambered off
the cart and asked the family that was travelling with him to
stay with his belongings. Then he had slowly walked like a
pawn along the formal pathway of trees and found a shut-
tered and closed-up house. He broke the lock off with a heavy
stone and entered a hallway full of dusty light. A door led into
a kitchen, another to a dining room. He walked along the
hollow-sounding corridor not even glancing at rooms, reached
the back door and pushed it free of an old clasp, then stepped
into the garden and beyond that into the depth of the long
grass.

Now on his knees, the old writer touched the porous planks of the abandoned boat. It was the size of a child's bed, half boat, half raft, with space between the planks. There was a manacle-like remnant of an oarlock on the side, and the tail of a rudder. It was a dried-up object, baked for years by the sun and tunnelled into for years by insects. But it meant there was possibly water nearby, and as soon as he assumed that, he began to smell it in the air and stood up, lifting his face to the sky. He bustled forward and within moments came upon the small lake. He stripped down and slipped into the water, all the scratches and bites on him covered now in its coldness.

For most of his life he had been regarded as a solitary. He was described once by an acquaintance as being 'difficult as a bear,' and this rough, impolite image projected onto the contained world around him was useful as well as false; it gave him space, and a border. But it was true that in spite of the gregarious situation of his family he lived mostly an imaginary life. When his marriage was dying, he found somewhere within himself the *grisette* Claudile and wrote three books about her divergent life. The fictional girl had kept him company. If this was sickness or a perversion of life, it was a sickness that had helped him overcome that difficult time, and he would never demean it, or her. He would remain faithful to this person in the town of Auch whose fate he'd invented and shared with readers. Some had come to love her, and wrote him letters as though he knew her in real life, not just in a fiction.

> *Cher Monsieur—*
> *I have recently reminded myself of a dinner in which Claudile Rothère and her sister spoke of fig jam, telling how they love it.*
> *So I have kept a pot for you, made by a friend*

*living in the countryside of Cahors. I hope, sir, you
enjoy it.*

> *With my deepest regards,*
> Sarah S

Lucien had received this package a few days before leaving
Marseillan, and now and then on his journey he carefully
reopened the envelope and reread the letter—the formality and
kindness of it—as if it were a billet-doux. He had brought the fig
jam with him, and during the afternoons he would, with a similar formality, open it and share it with whoever was in the cart
with him, most recently with three travellers—an 'old thief,' as
the man called himself, and his younger wife and their son. They
had been with him for several days, and by now Lucien was
accustomed to them. Like him they were looking for a new
home, so theirs was a journey similar to his. 'La confiture de
figue!' he announced. 'Faite par une dame à Cahors.' The eyes of
the young son at first pretended to gaze at nothing, like a falsely
polite dog. Then he watched the knife's spread of the jam, and
like that dog, he watched the adults eat first, swallowing when
they swallowed, so he could feel he had already eaten three por-
tions of it before he consumed his own.

The thief would disappear early in the mornings, before anyone was awake, returning at noon with berries, fresh herbs,
sometimes a hare, all rescued, as he called the act, from the surrounding fields. Coming over a rise, they would first smell the
smoke of a fire and then see him beside it, cooking by the edge of
the road. He had a rough grey stubble that made him appear
ponderous, as if used to lazy movement, but he could disappear
in an instant or arrive just as quickly, providing the alfresco
lunch. Lucien therefore felt he himself should be responsible for
other meals—first of all, beverage and fig jam at four in the after-

noon, and then dinner, to be purchased at an inn in one of the villages they passed through.

The cart would halt whenever Lucien smelled the possibility of an available house. He spoke with mailmen and carpenters as to where there might be an abandoned farmhouse for sale. Meanwhile the thief's young wife would go off on the spare horse, the boy riding behind her, to search along the side roads for a possible settlement for her family. The three of them were travellers, Gypsies, *gitans,* who had left their caravan in the south and were coming north to find a new home. They might, he knew, at any moment curl off and decide to remain in some anonymous field. Already Lucien felt he would miss them. He was enjoying the man's company, as well as the woman's singing in the mornings. Which had come first, he asked her, her name, which was Aria, or her pleasure in singing? 'Who knows,' the husband said, 'She's Romani, they have so many names. The secret name, which is never used but is her truest name, which only her mother knows, that's hidden to confuse supernatural spirits—it keeps the true identity of the child from them. And the second name, which is a Roma name, is usually used only by them. And that one is Aria.'

And *your* name, then? Lucien asked.

I am not Roma, the husband said. I have simply attached myself to her, I live in *her* world. I am not important.

The whole family felt half dreamt, especially in the way each of them wandered off whimsically, the man in the morning, the woman and the boy in the afternoon. Sometimes Lucien would be in front, guiding the horse, talking about something, and would realize all at once that there was no one else with him. They had slipped off, as if from a boat, and were swimming towards those poplars.

No, I don't have a name, a permanent name, the husband said, when asked again. I know the Roma language, enough to survive, but . . . His sentences were halfhearted, unpersuasive. He appeared uncertain of all things, and was content to reside in a state as humble as a sparrow. The boy, whose name was Rafael, longed for information and practical lessons and constantly asked the opinions of the old writer. Because of this, Lucien assumed there might be a jealousy from the father, but the man turned out to be happiest listening to their discussions, while pretending to take none of them in.

From the beginning each man regarded the other almost as a mirror. Two or three times a day one would catch the gaze of the other. Even Aria recognized the echo between them. They had a similar build, and the writer, in spite of his supposed fame, had a hesitancy that made him as guarded as this shyest of thieves. *If* the man was a thief. Lucien would never witness any illegal act by him. And while the writer was considerably older, it was Aria's husband who was not quite of this world, his remarks porous, his talents invisible, the paths he took almost erased. Once Lucien picked up a book that the thief had been reading, and saw a sprig of absinthe leaves used as a bookmark. That felt like the only certain thing about the man, and from then on, every few days, the writer carefully noted the progress of the absinthe, making its own journey through the plot.

'I went to the war and I never came back,' the thief said, crossing a field with the writer one day, and it was the most personal thing that would ever be revealed by this new friend. It had come in response to the writer's speaking of what he had witnessed in an earlier war.

What is his name? Lucien had asked the wife that first day as the family climbed into the cart.

You will need to ask him that, she said.

That had been the start of the evasiveness.

I cannot call you a thief all the time. I shall certainly acknowledge the title when it is apt, but I need a name.

Aùguste? Peloque? Liébard? Any of those . . .

All right, Liébard it is.

He kept the man's joke to himself, he was fond of *Un Coeur Simple*. So the name Liébard was used for a while, the first of many aliases, though Lucien eventually forgot most of them. What he did remember was that in all their time together he rarely saw Liébard eat, even if he had just cooked their meal. Aria would shrug if Lucien brought it up, as if that was an explanation, as if she was saying, *Men*.

Each evening during the journey, they arrived at an inn where the writer would buy them a meal; he himself would then sleep there while the family camped in the fields. The country air and the journeying brought an appetite for sleep. But one night, Lucien Segura woke, not knowing where he was. He was suffocating and threw off his blankets. Then he unbuttoned his nightshirt and went to the window. There in the darkness he saw Liébard walking along a narrow wall that ran along one side of the inn's garden. There was enough moonlight for Lucien to recognize his travelling companion and this strange act in the middle of the night. He clapped his hands, and Liébard paused and looked up and gave a slow wave. Lucien put a coat on and went outside. They began talking quietly. He told the thief he'd been unable to sleep. Then you should not sleep, he was told. Darkness has many potent hours. It is often a waste of time dreaming through it.

I need your help, my friend.

Liébard was instantly silent. Lucien paused also, waiting for a reply to his dramatic statement, but there was just the invitation of the man's silence. After a moment Lucien continued. I need you to kill someone for me. A further silence. I feel my wife has become a nightmare. She will damage our children. I feel that for the rest of my life she will haunt me.

I have a wife too, in another life. (Liébard was talking cautiously, as if aware this might be remembered against him.) There are other ways to stop a haunting. I agree that men and women haunt each other, but your children will take care of themselves. The problem, the difficulty, is not the killing. It is harder to steal a healthy chicken and cook a good meal. There's no skill in killing, it's not equal combat. And as well, it will destroy you. You have lost or misplaced your wits. Perhaps your breathing, your sense of suffocation, is related to this, may have brought this on. I can tell you of an herb—*la bourrache*—the flower is like a little blue star and is good for your heart. It will calm you. We can locate some. . . .

Lucien had not thought about his difficult, abandoned wife for weeks. So it was peculiar that she had all at once risen to the surface of his thoughts on this night as an enemy. Now he was embarrassed he had said such a thing to a stranger he had known for mere days. He thought perhaps he might still be in a dream or in half-sleep.

Forgive me, he muttered.

No, I am honoured that you trusted me with the possibility, said the calm voice back to him. Lucien did not quite laugh, but smiled in the darkness.

It was the morning after the last of the fig jam, that is how the boy Rafael would remember it, shortly after they had passed through the village of Dému, that they found the home for the writer. They were resting in the back of the cart—the writer, the boy, and his mother—when they felt it halt, breaking the sleepy rhythm, as if they had stopped casually at the edge of a precipice. The boy's father sat up front with the horse, looking silently to his left. What was tempting him was a lack of care along that pathway of trees. The grass had not been scythed for months, and the branches of the plane trees tangled into the opposing limbs. The writer sat up and followed the gaze. 'Yes, perhaps,' he said. 'Perhaps. Will you wait here?' All first investigations of possible houses were to be made alone. The family in the cart could not select a home for the man any more than he would know how to choose the correct field for the family—he would not know, for instance, that it should contain a number of exits for them to feel secure. Finding the final home for one's remaining days was like a decision to be made in a fairy tale, with the prince or princess needing to select a marriage partner before twilight. It had to be a wise but also private desire, knowing what was honestly needed, although at first it might seem appalling—a blind girl instead of a chatelaine, a hedgehog instead of a blue-blooded suitor. The outside world would not know best. And so the family remained in the cart and watched the writer kick his legs to remove the stiffness of sleep and begin his cautious and suddenly youthful walk towards the possible home.

Astolphe

Two days after the writer bought the house along with the nine hectares of land that surrounded it, the two men, Lucien and Liébard, entered the chest-high grass with scythes. Within minutes they had disappeared from each other. Only if one of them paused could he hear the other's movement, the ceaseless sweep of a blade or, during longer silences, the sharpening of its metal with a stone. They began before dawn, while it was still cool and half dark, and even then insects rose into the air and surrounded them. Their scythes swept above the ground to avoid stones and roots. It would truly have been easier to burn the grass. But Liébard, who was helping Lucien in his campaign to reclaim the overgrown field, had insisted that the meadow needed the ant and the cricket whose lives would be destroyed by such a fire. The unseen traffic was necessary. And the writer might long for that cricket in the grass, or a cicada within the trees in the future.

They pulled the tough blueberry roots out of the ground and burned vines along with the cut grass on the perimeters of the field. They raked open the soil and began crop-seeding it so that bacteria in the mustard and clover would eventually draw in nitrogen. At dusk they walked onto other properties, gathered seeds, and returned with *légumineuses,* scattering this family of beans and peas onto the writer's land. Why not? demanded Liébard, who was as much of a traveller in some ways as a blown seed or a bee.

Liébard knew what comforted winged creatures in terms of

domicile. He proposed not just birdhouses, but holes drilled into blocks of wood for flying insects. He collected sunflowers and split their stalks and tied them against branches to create a home for bugs. He crammed hay into jars for centipedes to use, for they would eventually eat the larvae of bugs that attacked fruit trees. He was aware of the awkward moral balance in nature. You gave and you took away. Wasps lay eggs that ate the larvae of butterflies, but then wasps were better for plant life than the beautiful flutterers, just as Liébard knew that it was lazy wealth in the fluttering class that made them mean-spirited. In his *mépris* he knew a thing or two about them—the result of sightings and witnessings over the years, first in towns and now in fields. Although Liébard would never claim to be a moral man. He himself could be diverted by a feather.

On the second day some distance from the writer's house, the boy discovered a field full of exits. Hearing of this, Lucien suggested the family camp there if they wished. Before actually making the offer, he told them he was giving them a field, not suggesting that he needed companionship. Perhaps they would not even talk much again, but he had a limit of hectares and it was unlikely he would ever journey beyond the small lake. And the field in question was a distance beyond that.

The proposal was this: If Liébard would help him clear the overgrown fields beside the house and clarify the lawns under the full-branched chestnut trees, then he and his family were welcome to stay on that land for as long as they desired. Lucien would sign any formal document if Liébard wished, but Liébard waived that possibility. He disapproved of putting pen to paper—that and excessive dialogue had always got him into trouble in the past. And while they were talking, in a footnote to the conversation, Liébard announced that he was relinquishing the name he'd been using, and was now taking the name Astolphe.

Within an hour the boy, who was used to these changes, began calling his father Astolphe. Lucien realized the man used names like passwords, all of them with a brief life span. But this time the thief wished that he had owned the name earlier in his life. He spent the first day imagining moments from his past when he could have been 'Astolphe,' when he might have behaved and participated with more ease and subtlety just for having the epaulette of such a name. It led to the kind of biographical reconsideration a man might make when looking at photographs of a wife or lover in an earlier time, in her teens or twenties, which always brought the wish to have known her *then*—even that dress from another decade, whose tender buttons he might carefully unfasten; even to taste the fruit in the flowering tree behind her. . . . The thief liked the sound of the name, its aftereffect, its airiness, with a hint of an echo. With such a name it would almost be possible for this thickset man to turn into a three-ounce bird or a subtle grammatical form.

The writer watched him with the absinthe-smelling book on his lap. The name Astolphe appeared in the sixteenth-century *Orlando Furioso*. How had this man come across it? Would he have stolen such a book in the past—did thieves even steal books? How did he gather such things into his pockets?

Journey

While the two men worked in the fields, Aria and the boy returned south, to where they had previously lived, to collect their caravan. Their journey on horseback took several days, and they crossed the fan of rivers—the Ardour, the Baïse, the Gimone. They went south and east, riding into the fertile lands. On the fourth evening they arrived in darkness at the outskirts of Saint-Martory, where they had left their horses and caravan. There was a bonfire and music, and they sat talking to others for a few hours and later slept in their narrow familiar beds. The next day they dug up herbs and plants from their small plot that would survive the journey back to Dému, and decided what goods and property to leave behind.

Soon they were heading north, returning by a different route because with the swaying caravan they needed wider roads. There could be no more shortcuts by simply opening gates and crossing fields, or even fording a stream where the water was deep; there was too much weight for the horses to pull from the sandy soil. They were going towards Plaisance, and from there they would leave the company of the Arros River and turn west.

They took their time and stopped wherever they wished. Rafael built a fire while Aria coursed over the fields, looking for things to eat. An onion or two, rosemary, leeks. Lunch was a collection of minor plants and shoots as if gathered by a pair of birds rushing and diving over the fields. It was barely there on their tongues. When the meal was over, if the stream or river was private enough, they would strip off their clothes and swim. Aria was determined that Rafael never have a fear of water like his father, so she would laugh as she ran down the bank and then grin at him when she surfaced out of the river. She did not want a fearful child. The boy swam into her arms and embraced her, kissed her shoulders. There was a sensuality between them, as there was between the boy and his father in their cuddling affection. Back on dry land she bowed her head and he dried her long, dark hair with his shirt.

Sometimes during their journey great storms came at night, out of the west, from the ocean, near Ségalas, at Buzon; and when they were west of Saint-Justin, lightning lit up the river like a path through history and she grabbed the boy to stop him from leaping into its brief beauty. It was a season of storms. She imagined the old writer up at Dému, trying unsuccessfully to persuade her husband to sleep in the mostly empty house.

She and Rafael kept the caravan in the middle of open fields and let the horses loose. Released, they hardly moved, as if pretending that there was nothing dangerous, that it was safer than galloping into darkness. There were evenings when Aria and Rafael stood on the dry night-grass with a hundred layers of stars above them. Uncountable. A million orchestras. The boy could scarcely store the delirious information. That journey south with his mother and the return north broke his heart again and again with happiness. It was when he felt most clearly that there was no distinction between himself and what was beyond him—a tree's sigh or his mother's song, could, it seemed, have been generated by his body. Just as whatever gesture he made was an act performed by the world around him.

They were a few miles north of Plaisance when the eclipse paused over the Gers. The darkness came fast into the afternoon. Rafael was lifting a pail for a nervous horse to drink from and became conscious of the darkness only because it was growing cold. He spun around and saw his mother looking at him with concern. Grey rain started falling in the half-light, though it was the wind that bewildered everything, arcing the trees down so they hovered almost parallel to the ground. He saw the horse's eye lolling, distracted, in front of him as if it too were part of this peculiar nature. He didn't know what an eclipse was. He thought it might be some vengeance that came with the end of the world. He was holding the horse's neck, looking for rope to secure the animal, but there was none, so he held on to the mane with his hands. If the horse got loose they would never find it. When the animal began to pivot, he swung himself onto its back, just as his mother yelled out *No!* and the horse burst through the trees into further darkness with the boy upon it.

Rafael put his head down against the horse's neck, and he became the animal's eyes, witnessing the quick choices of direction. He was saddle-less, clinging to the wet-coated creature in its stumbles and swerves until it emerged into a vast field where the sky was a shade lighter than under the trees. The horse now doubled its speed and flung itself into the open. The boy could hear his own breath alongside the breath of the horse, he could hear the hooves in the long grass, their sudden clatter over a wooden bridge after the muted sound of the earth. He was holding on to the warm blood of the animal. For perhaps a minute—time was measureless now—they had gone through a village where only the two of them moved in the blackness, the boy's leg brushing a cart, then a child, and then they had come through it, into fields again beside a river. Then there was a slow return of light, and there was heat once more around them and in the wet grass. Time was in a broken state. The sky appeared filled with a bright moonlight, though it was day. The horse calmed, aware now of the flylike rider whose knees clutched it, the boy's feet bare from another time, when they were serene under the trees, and he had approached this animal with a pail of water.

Rafael rode back slowly, field after field. They were all new to him. He looked for the village, but whatever community they'd rushed through he never encountered again. They crossed over the wooden bridge, then saw the black horizon of forest and soon he could make out his mother pacing on the edge of it. He never hurried the horse. He finally dismounted lying back and sliding off the slippery wall of the animal. He could hardly stand in front of Aria, though he did, shaken by her and then embraced.

Two Photographs

There are two photographs pinned up on the wall of the kitchen in Dému. One is a picture taken of Lucien Segura in this last phase of his life, sitting on a garden bench with a dark branch fanning out above him. There is a sense of formality as well as disorder in the picture. And the disorder comes from the appearance of the writer—his unironed shirt, his moustache, which looks like something borrowed from an animal—though what is most informal is the openness of his face, as if it has just been blessed. His laugh, for instance—there is no attempt to hide the shaggy randomness, or even the unsightly gap of a missing tooth. This was a discreet man who used to laugh internally, in a hidden way.

On the righthand side of the picture is a dark blur, something unknown, like raw paint imposed on an otherwise immaculate canvas, or perhaps it is a bat in the daylight, caught flying between camera and writer. This is the only photographic capturing of Lucien's friend Liébard, or Astolphe, who turned on the photographer with a surprising belligerence when he heard the shutter begin to slip into place, turning so quickly that he was able to dissolve his appearance.

The other picture, taken on the same grounds, was snapped all these years later by the belligerent and blurred subject's son, Rafael. It is of the woman he met in the writer's house. He used her camera, and the image has been blown up to be the same size as the other, so it is, in a way, a partner to it.

We are much closer to the subject in this picture. Photography has moved in from the middle distance as the century progressed, eliminating vistas, the great forests, the ranging hills.

The woman's figure is naked from the waist up, moving forward, just about to break free of focus. The tanned body willful, laughing, because she has woven the roots of two small muddy plants into her blond hair, so it appears as if mullein and rosemary are growing out of the plastered earth on her head. There's a wet muck across her smiling mouth, and on her lean shoulders and arms. It is as if her energy and sensuality have been drawn from the air surrounding her. We look at this picture and imagine also the person with the camera, walking backwards at the same pace as the subject so that she remains in focus. We can guess the relationship between the unseen photographer and this laughing muddy woman, weeds around the fingers of her hand gesturing to him in intimate argumentative pleasure. This person who is barely Anna.

THREE

The House in Dému

The large clock above the mirrors at Le Daroles bar has remained at twenty minutes past eleven for the last two weeks.
The clockmaker has still not arrived, being somewhere in the
south, correcting time along the small villages of the Pyrenees.
He will come when he does with rags and oil and needle-fine
tools. He will lift the heavy machine into his arms, be guided
down the ladder by others, and place it on the marble counter of
the bar, intentionally taking up the prime space of trade in the
café. What will occur then is ceremonial. He will insist on his
taut espresso, and behave with a ponderous authority as if he
has been summoned into this town to correct the weakening eyes
of the mayor's daughter. He soaks petite flags of cloth in a sauce
of oil and with tweezers inserts them into the unseen depths of
the giant clock. . . .

They are a strange breed, clockmakers, some surly and insen-
sitive to all save the machine about to whir into life, some uncertain as poets about their gift. Because my stepfather—my
mother's second husband—was one, I have studied their natures.
He, my first clockmaker, never felt his talent as anything special.
There were just a few procedures to learn; now and then the Ital-
ians or Belgians would produce something that reversed the
cause and effect, but he did not feel himself to be in any way different from the market gardener in the way he spoke about his

work. And I learned the cautious and also incautious habit of my own work from him. You are given a trade, not a gift. There need not be intensity or darkness in the service of it. Still, I met no other clockmaker like him. By watching him, I learned enough to correct the pace on my own watch, but I would still take any failing timepiece to clockmakers in Toulouse so I could study the 'grandeur' they brought to their skill.

I love the performance of a craft, whether it is modest or mean-spirited, yet I walk away when discussions of it begin—as if one should ask a gravedigger what brand of shovel he uses or whether he prefers to work at noon or in moonlight. I am interested only in the care taken, and those secret rehearsals behind it. Even if I do not understand fully what is taking place. One of my pleasures, when I was a boy, was to ride alongside the Garonne to where four steam engines were set up on the riverbank, pumping water out for the city of Toulouse. In all that be-stilled countryside, where you could hear a single croak of a duck, the engines suddenly roared into life, like grand apes spitting and shoving against the edge of the water. I was hypnotized. It was as if they were adults in their noisy complex labours. It was as if they could bring on darkness.

The clock at Le Daroles in Auch was overtaken by fatigue at least once a year, and Chamayou, the proprietor, would send me a message to let me know when the clockmaker was expected, and I would travel to town for the procedure and stay at the Hôtel de France to witness the event. Up close, once the great object was on the marble counter of the bar, you could read the smaller letters on the clock face. A LaMarguere. The clockmaker wiped the appearance of mildew or foxing off the white portal of the dial and then lifted it off the mechanism. I, in order to remain close by, needed to appear humble—he insisted on a papal-like authority—and when told I was a writer, or at least was known to be a writer, he would speak to me rather than the other spectators, as if we were on another, professional level of existence. When it was clarified that I was a poet, my status slipped a rung or two and he muttered some line I didn't quite hear that got a laugh somewhere to his left, a laugh guided by his own.

The skill of writing offers little to a viewer. There is only this five-centimetre relationship between your eyes and the pen. Any skill in the divining or dreaming is invisible, whereas the clock-maker visiting Auch removed his dark cotton jacket and rolled up the sleeves of his white shirt, at which point I would part company from Claudile at the small round table by the window and come closer to the unrolled oilskin and its slim pockets that held tools and oil capsules, and his little flashlight for the machine's dungeons. Soon I was almost within the pleasure of his serious demeanour. I could imagine his even greater status in those villages in the Hautes-Pyrénées, towns like Laruns, Gavarnie, Ogeu, where he must have travelled as if on the raised authority of a palanquin. I enjoyed all of this. But I believe only in the humbleness my stepfather had, who would stop in mid-operation—on hearing a song thrush—and walk to a window to search it out. Or he would pass me one of his essential knives to sharpen my blunt pencils. He constructed objects for us out of those wheels and dials that were no longer being used, so they'd move like half-formal animals across the dining room table. He was not my father, but he raised me. I learned, I suppose, a manner from him. Also that any trade or talent could be shaped discreetly without the sparks of exaggerated drama. And yet, with all his modesty, he loved the grandeur of Victor Hugo— and those slow, obedient descriptions that walked towards revolution.

And he loved my mother. I saw him on the last days of his life lift that oil-scented right hand and enter its fingers into her ordered hair and rustle it free of its pins as if he had been offered velvet or the fur of a rare animal. Forever I hold that gesture. For me it was perhaps the last remembered pleasure belonging to him. It is the unspoiled core of whatever I know of love and family (and I have not been successful at the craft of it). Our shyness at embracing each other—it rarely happened—did not matter. I felt safe and comforted in his house. There was a calm, the two clocks in the house were silent but precise and we were safe in time. For just five years he gave us all that.

Marseillan

His mother, Odile Segura, had been born in Bagnères-de-Bigorre, where the Spanish influence whipped down from the Pyrenees fifty kilometres away. Miguel Invierno had crossed the Spanish border to work as a roofer in the town. She had been courted by him before he departed without warning a few months later with a trio of fellow Spaniards. In the village of Vic-Fézensac, to the north, there was a *corrida* every June, and each year she took her small child with her, hoping to find her lover among the crowd, but she never encountered Lucien's father again. Instead she married the clockmaker, and she and the boy came to live with him in his home outside the village of Marseillan.

The boy was four when he entered his stepfather's house for the first time. There, in its gardens, with the river's spark through the trees and a gardener's dog sleeping in sunlight, he learned to distinguish the voices of each field. Soon he had been taught which section of the sky to search for stars during different seasons and which tree it was that held a mockingbird. Each year, for their birthdays, his mother made *salade de gésiers*—a plate composed of a small egg upon salad leaves, with goose gizzard, potato, chives, and a grainy mustard that Lucien would find nowhere else. Each year, in the last week of May, she would give the house a spring cleaning, weed the garden, wash and iron her husband's shirts, and then gather the boy into a cart and travel to the *corrida* at Vic-Fézensac, searching the streets day and night, until she returned home empty-handed and with a mixture of disappointment and relief. The clockmaker never felt he reached the intimacy with his wife that existed between the boy and his mother. Perhaps he never was sure that, if his new wife did stumble across the Spaniard during the celebrations, she would return to their home.

With the stepfather's unexpected death, in spite of some inherited wealth, Odile Segura and the boy reduced their way of life. There had been little protecting the boy's world save for that careful man. Now Lucien became more cautious and secretive. In classrooms, the others heard his closeted speech patterns. He had spent too long conversing with just himself. As he grew older he had private words, as if collected twig by twig from an open field. He spoke a few sentences to himself about a rusted gate, or an animal's nervousness on entering a boat, and that spoken scene would become indelible to him. Already he protected himself with words, with the small and partial clarity they brought.

The Arrival

One evening at suppertime their silence was broken by the sound
of a cart. Their house was only a short distance from the journeying road, so it meant they had a visitor. But as the boy and his
mother rose from their meal, opened the door, and looked out,
an overburdened two-horse cart went past them and up the rise
of the hill. It struggled another hundred metres and stopped at
the one-room farmhouse that had been a vacant neighbour to
them for years. Lucien and his mother stood by the doorway,
halted in their expected greeting. They watched the couple in the
distance descend and stretch themselves, looking like mere outlines on the crest of the hill, a man and a woman. The farmhouse
had stood for years as the one inert obstacle on their horizon.
The idea that it was now to contain people was exciting to the
sixteen-year-old boy. It meant that he would have to be more
curious, and yet cautious with his own secrecies.

They gave the couple half an hour, and then, just before darkness, he and his mother walked over, carrying bread and milk
and candles, along with a few cuttings of meat. The man and the
woman were still unloading the cart. Beside the road were a
modest bed in two sections, two chairs, a painted table, an iron
stove and its L-shaped pipe. Amidst this minimal furniture and
one basket of clothing stood the man and what now looked like
a girl. As the couple turned towards the two who appeared, the
young woman reached for the man's hand briefly in some gesture or other—the boy could not tell what emotion was there,

within that movement. She looked slight and the man was heavy. Lucien had seen him pacing around the small building with grandeur, as if it were a walled city he had inherited and had somehow to revive, or teach a lesson to. The boy had been reading the Greek epics and in that moment these strangers felt to him like part of a foreign army or delegation.

If his mother had not been there, perhaps no one would have spoken, but she learned that their names were Roman and Marie-Neige. They had rented the farmhouse sight-unseen from the owner, who lived in Marseillan. Roman accepted their gift of food but refused any help in moving the furniture, even though it was becoming dark. He would do that alone. He'd already carried, while they attempted conversation, the sections of bed indoors. And the girl remained silent. Her mouth had made some movement when they were introduced, that was all. To the boy she seemed too thin, her dark hair cut short so that it barely reached her neck. He felt the man could have folded her into some part of his clothing and made her disappear. Lucien walked back downhill with his mother, turning for a last time before going in. The man had placed a lamp on the cart, and he was moving back and forth and blotting out the light every minute or so. Lucien went indoors and sat at the table and thought of what had happened. It felt as if his whole life had changed.

They discovered that the couple had been recently married. The wife did not seem to be much older than Lucien. For the first two weeks the boy and his mother rarely saw her, for she was as cautious as wildlife. His mother made every effort to befriend the couple, especially the wife. Perhaps she had glimpsed something in that young, stunned face. So Marie-Neige was eventually coaxed under Odile Segura's assured wing.

The girl would enter their home tentatively, as if she first had to learn the many rules that came with this scale of ownership.

The house must have seemed palatial. The boy was aware suddenly of the extra metre that rose to the ceiling, the extra
breadth and paces within each room. Roman seldom came, he
would be in the fields most of the day, but Lucien's mother
would bustle uphill to the farmhouse and invite the girl, who
appeared traumatized in her new role. He heard his mother say
to someone that Marie-Neige had nothing to do but clean their
little cabinet of a house and service her husband. Lucien would
ponder that line later, when he thought more about their relationship. She was as thin as a bride could be. In fact, she repre-
sented no sense of that word. Physically and in age she was
Lucien's equal—and he was only a youth. But she was married,
officially translated into an adult. She had the knowledge of such
a world, as if she'd earned some abstract honour in a foreign
place.

'Lean as a *haricot*,' he had described her to his mother's
friends when the girl was not there. And for a while, after that
burst of laughter, 'Le Haricot' was how they all referred to her.
He was showing off, and while it was the perfect naming, he felt
he had committed a betrayal. 'Well, she will soon grow some
bumps on her,' his mother said. And there was more laughter.

The Great World

The two families nestled gradually. His mother began teaching Marie-Neige to read. And on Saturdays, Lucien walked over to help Roman, digging turnips in the fields, or rebuilding a wall along the boundary line. To the sixteen-year-old boy, Marie-Neige's husband was an unknown force, the dangerous possibility of a figure of a father he no longer had. They rarely spoke, and didn't see each other during the week, for Roman worked in Marseillan or sometimes even further away. Meanwhile the youth was immersed in *The Black Tulip,* and one afternoon when Marie-Neige sat beside him in silence he decided to read the Dumas out loud to her. "On the way to his imprisonment in Buitenhof Prison, our Cornelius heard nothing but the barking of the dog and saw nothing but the face of a young woman. . . ." Le Haricot looked at him with her mouth open. He could not tell whether she believed he was inventing what he spoke or whether she was already hypnotized by the fragment. He continued. Marie-Neige was in fact a year or so older; yet as he read, she began to seem full of innocence to him.

From then on she wished to share everything he consumed from a book. During the late mornings, after helping with household duties, she learned the letters of the alphabet from his mother, and during the afternoons listened to this drug of stories as she and Lucien sat together on the porch or within the shade of the dwarf apple tree by the river. They had both grown up far from the intrigue of cities, and now they fell upon Dumas as a guide into those cities that were always in peril and where the sight of an emerald on a neck could betray a family dynasty. They accompanied horsemen who carried crucial documents across flooded plains and kept assignations with foes and lovers at midnight. The books were stuffed with unbearable love. "She gave a plaintive moan and fled, trying in vain to stifle the beating of her heart. Cornelius, left alone, could do no more than breathe in this sweet scent of Rose's hair, which lingered like a captive between the bars." Lying on the slim ribbon of porch, they felt at times that they could scarcely breathe, that there could be no normal life ever again.

He read as if speaking in tongues, with such adult knowledge he was like someone wise who had been wounded in a distant battle or by a passion. And it was as if she were learning of the great world through him—it was *he* (and he felt it himself) who was introducing Marie-Neige at court, or riding beside her from city to city under the moon. They discovered how it was possible to send a messenger pigeon as far as The Hague, which might change everything, though more often it was necessary to ride the great distance oneself. If Lucien hesitated, shocked sometimes by a woman's deceit or a violent beating in the fiction he was reading, Marie-Neige would interfere from within her silence, to examine what seemed to him a flaw in the carefully made fabric, and they would speak about it, discussing how, exactly, a man or a woman, a husband or a wife, might behave. For instance the line "What she wanted was beyond the power of this man, and she had to take him with his weakness." If there were aspects he did not fully understand, or was simply bored by, she would wonder out loud why that was. He realized she had a sly wit within her—just as she had her preferences for a specific musketeer's charm.

They came to know, in this way, about each other's interests and hesitations. She noticed how he raced over sections about childhood, for he found characters under the age of twenty too familiar. He already knew what youth contained. He wished only for the intricacies of adults and travel, war and battles, marriages. When he blurted this out to her he paused, embarrassed at the wall between them concerning that. She put her thin brown hand up to his cheek and kept it there not even a second. Someday you will marry. And then we will talk about that as well. No, he had said, We will not. I'm certain we will not. He stepped back into formality, so that they were like two flammable matches side by side in a tinderbox.

All this was during their first year together. By late afternoon Roman would have returned, and she would return to her real life. And he—he would race into the fields, cartwheel, aim at thin trees with a slingshot, and throw himself like a spear into the river. He'd burn through the water, eyes open in its darkness, certain he could find silver or a lost sword or a branch that would attempt to entangle him underwater. Something made him return to being just a boy in those moments after their separation.

She would go to her narrow back window and see him leap up to a branch. If she was helping Roman bathe at the rear of their house, soaping his shoulders, she might hear a splash that reached her from the distance of his world. If Roman desired her, if he returned tumescent and hungry, he would not even walk the few feet to their bed, she'd lie back on the kitchen table, her feet dangling, barely touching the floor, and he would crash himself into her, her hands gripping whatever edge of the table she could hold on to, half thrilled by him, their heads and shoulders under the swaying unlit lamp, the skin at her spine moving up and down against the wood, cushioned only by her open cotton dress. The boy would be hardly down to the river, and their coupling and mutual satisfaction would be over. Roman would put out his hand and she'd hold it with both of hers and he would pull her off the table into the air. He was an older, stronger man, nothing like the boy, and she saw his eyes lost in bitterness and frustration, in a fury about the state of their lives. He would fling a chair into the wall of curtain that divided their one room, and she knew it could just as easily have been her body that was thrown towards that dark corner. Once or twice she saw his personality in the musketeer, Porthos, and had even seen the possibility of Porthos in him, and that was her way of remaining faithful to all Roman believed in.

She was letting her hair grow longer. She felt tethered to their one-room farmhouse, and this was one small independence. She was rarely ever more than forty yards from the house, save when she went for her reading lessons or when Roman took her in the cart to the village.

The Dog

The boy was daydreaming by the window, enclosed by the deep sill, looking out. Gradually his eyes focussed into the distance, where there was a dog moving haphazardly. As it came closer he could see it was large and black. He mentioned to his mother, who was behind him, that the animal might be rabid, dangerous, and she came beside him and looked out for a moment and said, Perhaps. Don't go out. No, he agreed.

They were about to have lunch. He went to the north window to see whether Roman and Marie-Neige happened to be outside. He saw no sign of them, and returned to the first window and sat close to the glass and watched the creature. It was still ranging about, not barking, just moving as if it had a curse within. It charged towards the porch of the house, saw the outline of the boy's upper body in the window, and then retreated. It's going away, he told his mother. Good. The animal was rubbing its snout on the ground, then looked up and charged, bounded onto the porch, and threw itself at the window. Its paws smashed the thin glass and its forefeet touched the boy, and splinters speared his eye. He stood there for a moment, then fell to the ground. He believed the dog was in the house and the pain meant his face was being eaten. He couldn't scream. It was his mother who was screaming. She saw blood all over his face and shirt, and along the wall by the windowsill. The dog had pulled its paws back through the jagged glass and leapt back onto the dust in front of the porch.

She knelt by her son and touched his stiff body. The boy dared not move. She was screaming at him, assuming he had been bitten, but the boy made no noise, made no movement, and gradually she quieted down into frantic breathing. He couldn't see, and his brain read that sound as the panting of the dog circling him.

Then his mother left him, and he was alone on the kitchen floor.

In spite of the presence of the dog somewhere in the vicinity, she ran up the hill and returned with Roman and the young wife. Now his mother lifted her son's head and cradled it, and the girl stirred up a saline solution in a bowl and carefully washed away the loose blood, looking for the wound. There seemed to be no cut on his face at all. Finally she got to his left eye. There were two splinters of glass within it. He was staring up, unable to close that eyelid. Without pausing she plucked one of the jagged pieces out with her fingers, and his hand thrashed out. Can you see? But he could not. Even with the other eye? He didn't know, there was just pain. The socket of the other eye, the right eye, had become a pool of blood, and she could not tell whether that meant something, or whether it was safe, innocent. But for certain there was still another splinter in the left eye, which had gone deep. She did not think she could remove it, and wasn't sure if she should.

Roman carried him to the cart and placed him along the back bench so his head was resting once more on his mother's lap. She held a cheesecloth over his face to keep the dust away. The other two rode in front. Lucien's mother had brought the rifle, and it was there on the front seat between the couple.

After they had gone a few hundred metres, the dog appeared again, keeping its distance, following them. It was clear that the creature still intended to attack them. It ran beside the cart, snapping its jaws at the horse's hooves. They could see the blood, wet at its feet. Shoot him, the mother said, and Roman passed the reins to his wife, aimed and fired the rifle into the dust near the charging dog. The creature calmed suddenly and sat down as the cart raced on towards Marseillan, separating them from the animal. The young wife kept looking back, if not at Lucien, then at the dog in the growing distance. She had always wanted a dog in her life and had tried persuading her husband. Now she would never have one. She reached back and took Lucien's hand for a moment.

The doctor at the hospital, Monsieur Porcelain, was nervous and also certain of his authority. There was, he said, the possibility of infection spreading to the undamaged eye. He was determined to save some sight at least, and he convinced the youth's mother that the left eye be removed and that the socket, or 'cave,' that remained be cleansed thoroughly. This way no infection would reach the right eye, in its frail state. Lucien was not part of this decision, and for years he would remain bitter towards those who had defaced him.

By the time he came home, he could see faintly, just colours and shapes surrounding him. But that would improve. However, he was told he could not read for a year, and strangely, it was advised that during this period of time he must not cry. He was almost eighteen when this was demanded of him. It seemed that a cold anger was the only emotion allowed in response to the accident. He continued to blame the three who had taken him to the hospital in Marseillan. He blamed Roman for not killing the dog, so that it had disappeared before being tested for disease. He blamed Le Haricot for using a possibly impure saline solution on his eyes. Most of all, he blamed his mother for permitting the removal of his eye. He was behaving as if he were five years younger, and they found it difficult to make him respond in any way to them. He preferred to be alone in his room. In his anger he refused a false eye. As an adult he rarely spoke of the period when he could or should have been only weeping.

A month after the catastrophe some books he had ordered from Toulouse arrived in the mail. He had thrown them into a corner and walked back into his room. If there had been a fire nearby he would have burned them. His mother let them remain where they were until the girl came by for one of her lessons. Lucien was sitting on the porch when she approached him and announced the credits on the title page and began to read. 'Chapter One—The Three Presents of D'Artagnan the Elder. On the first morning of the month of April, 1625 . . .'

Everything froze within him. He refused to step out to meet her words. She was awkward with her accent, full of hesitations. He was aware this was equally or even more humiliating for her, this pretending to be worldly, this pretence that the Parisian prose style reflected her natural tongue. It was all that stopped the insult on his lips. But he could not give in to her. Tomorrow he would simply not come outside. The reversal of roles was embarrassing, galling. This neighbour's servant wife, who had been coaxed out of the quicksand of illiteracy by his mother . . . The book was on her lap and she was gripping the knife beside her that she was using to cut the pages. Black hair shielding her face. He could barely hear her voice mispronouncing the names of cities and lineages. All he was truly conscious of was her left arm quivering. He watched only that, would not be caught up in the story.

When she ended the chapter, she closed the book and without looking at him took it with her to her house. She didn't appear the next day. The day after that, she was helping his mother with some curtains when he asked her if she would clarify something he had missed, not understood within that first chapter. She looked up. 'I don't think I remember, I was too nervous.' There was a sort of response from him. 'Shall I go back and read it again?' 'No, just go on. Not knowing something essential makes you more involved.'

Roman undressed her, having drawn open the curtain to their bedroom so the kitchen light was on her. She was taller and stronger now, her long hair more womanly. When they wrestled on the bed he saw her confidence, her less passive enjoyment. Her arms pushed at him and she stared back as an equal, without shyness at what he was doing. When he came into her, her mouth reached up and bit into his beard and tugged him down to her. It was a duel more than the passion that had happened before, and in the half-light when they finished he could see the sweat on her, unaware it was on him as well until she leaned up again and licked the taste of it off his forehead, a gesture he thought performed by some stranger within her.

When he was asleep, she couldn't sleep. She lay there aware of the time rolling slowly and their bodies jammed against each other, her leaping mind awake. The light in the kitchen was still on, revealed by the open curtain. She looked for her shift and pulled it over her head and wiped herself between her legs. She bent over and watched Roman's face, so calm and content in sleep, which always surprised her. She believed this was when he was happiest, unaware of the world. Then she knelt by the bed and reached under it for her old towel and unwrapped the book within. She drew the curtain so he was in darkness, and sat down at the kitchen table and began rereading the first chapter. She was not one to be content with gaps in a story; she would discover its secrets and would tell her friend whenever he wanted or needed to know them.

Lucien began helping Roman build troughs for his pigs. At dawn and at dinnertime he poured gruel into the hog feeder and rubbed their backs as they ate in the twilight. All his life he would remember the texture of their taut skin, the tough bristles, their delicate leaps in moments of nervousness. A good number of years later, when he was called upon to give injections to soldiers in a Belgian village, he remembered the first needle he'd given—to a large pig whose mouth had become infected. He had needed to sidle the creature into a corner of the barn, then come up behind it and lift it onto its hind feet, so that it fell back helpless into his arms while he himself leaned back with all this weight into the stone corner. He held it that way with one arm for those few seconds, and with the other hand reached for the syringe and stabbed the needle into the pig's flank. Roman had told him what to do, and was watching all of this with a laughter that was rare but reassuring. And then Lucien had let the seemingly unconcerned creature loose.

The stories Lucien and Marie-Neige read together had become hers now. And he became accustomed to her voice, the way she read the fracas of a swordfight or described with unhidden amazement how the leaves in a book had been poisoned in order to kill a Protestant. The world out there was terrible with guile. The few times he corrected her pronunciation, it was done in no way to embarrass her but to protect her from embarrassment later in life among strangers. She read to him two or three times a week. They were equals again, sharing the alternative possibilities of a motive before it was revealed, arguing over the best musketeer, above all loving the fact that D'Artagnan, like him, was a Gascon and came from the Gers.

She saw him change as a result of his labour in the fields. She noticed his brown arms, his broken voice, its shrill husk falling away. He was no longer the boy she had first met. He had begun to move with confidence now, with the sureness she would never have. Again she hesitated within her world before stepping into the light and into the pleasure she got from him.

Charivari and Veillée

She had met Roman at a fair in the village of Saint-Didier-sur-Rochefort, and their marriage took place after an hour of bartering by an uncle who had raised her since the death of her parents. During the spring, all over the neighbouring valleys—in Perize, in Challons—there were marriage fairs. Marie-Neige was sixteen and Roman was in his thirties, and they sat at a small table while the scribe wrote out the marriage contract.

That evening whatever frail bond existed between them was met with derision by a gang of twenty or more who made up a charivari. It was a time when any union outside what was familiar was considered insulting to a community. A wedding too soon after the death of a spouse, a marriage between known adulterers, a marriage where there was a great age difference, would result in the humiliation of a bride and groom. If a woman was wealthy and a man poor, banners would proclaim the adage 'If the purse is big, a man will marry a bear.' When adulterers married, tumescent manikins were carried jostling beside them on the street. Some charivaris lasted two months; some, if the gangs were paid off, a few hours. Being poor and having no social power, Roman and Marie-Neige became easy victims. Although Roman was a powerful man, the manikin representing him depicted him as ancient and weak, and his young wife as a baby on his knee. There had been stories in the recent past of couples driven mad by a charivari; in one case a husband insulted beyond care stabbed to death the first jeering man he could reach with an awl. So that there was a wedding and then an execution.

All night her uncle's home was surrounded by torches and drumming and the bray of obscene songs. Roman stood for hours at the window, then slipped from the house before dawn and attacked two men who had been left to watch the house while the others slept, strangling one until he fainted and breaking the wrists of the other. He stood there alone with the bodies in the pasture. It was about five in the morning and there would be darkness only for a brief while more. His new bride came out carrying a lamp and he extinguished it. He put his hands on her shoulders and for a moment leaned his head against hers. Marie-Neige was dressed in the clothes of a boy and had cut her hair short. They did not go back into the house. They haltered her uncle's horse and walked with it silently through the village in the last of the darkness. When they were in the open fields he climbed on, reached his hand down, and pulled his wife up into the air and swung her behind him onto the animal. They rode south with the morning, the fields brightening around them.

They barely paused through the Ardèche, eating only what could be found on bushes, trees, and in vegetable gardens. Approaching Nîmes, they turned west and travelled through the departments of the Tarn and the Haute-Garonne, and by the time they reached the Gers, she had removed her boy's disguise and wore a yellow cotton dress. They found work at a fruit farm and slept with the other labourers in a crowded barn. The two had still not slept together as lovers, as husband and wife, and on the third night he woke her and they went into the warmth of an adjacent horse barn. The animals woke quickly, conscious of their presence, so there was a tense silence. He went up to each of the animals and calmed them, stroking their foreheads. Seven horses. Then he came back to the sixteen-year-old girl sitting on a bench, watching him. The light from the moon outside filled the rolled-open doorway. Crouching, he realized the floor was muddy straw. He went to the rain barrel by the entrance and washed his hands, then washed his arms and neck and stood in the night wind drying himself. She came out beside him and immersed her thin arms in the cold water, washed her face, carried scoops of it onto her legs.

All the landscape was blue around them. Years later, when Roman was in prison for assault, he would return to this moment, Marie-Neige bending to wash her legs and her feet with rainwater, her flesh a tint of blue, and the green fields blue, so the only thing another colour was the moon. He made her lean over the barrel and raised her yellow cotton dress but she turned around and looked at him and kissed the hands that had calmed horse after horse as if there would be all the time in the world, as if those seven animals were the only civilized creatures they had met since their wedding, in that place that now felt like another country altogether. He touched the soft and small delight of her face, then her neck and the dampness in her hair where she'd raked her fingers. She put her palms against his rough shirt and kissed the open triangle of his neck. After that she turned and put her arms out along the thick rim of the barrel where in the water was the moon and the ghost of her face. Roman moved against her, and in the next while, whatever surprise there was, whatever pain, there was also the frantic moon in front of her shifting and breaking into pieces in the water.

'*Who comes from afar, can lie more easily.*' But the next day someone they thought was a stranger recognized them and passed around the scandal of their marriage and Roman's brutality. Within half an hour they left the farm and that memory of the blue countryside at night. He proposed they travel as brother and sister, and they rode further west on her uncle's horse. For the next few weeks there was hardly any food to eat, and eventually she stopped having her period. The few times they did make love, when they could touch each other late in the night, there was little pleasure to be found anywhere within their weariness. They would be travelling most of the day, and the only thing alive in them was hunger. All they owned was a wineskin of water for thirst in the night. Neither could read, so if they wished to find work they needed to ask others. But they kept to themselves. The fairs they came upon were the only places they knew to look for work. At the village of Barran, west of Auch, they found themselves within the sounds of a great crowd. Around them were magicians, and craftsmen who could pull out your teeth, and soothsayers who would reveal your future as if it were a hidden serpent. She realized, seeing the stalls, she should have waited and sold her long hair so that it could have been made into a wig.

At the fair, the person who carried a live pig the greatest distance would win it, and Roman did so, collapsing beyond the others with the animal in his arms. He sold it to a farmer before he even got up off the grass, then changed his mind and promised it to the man for nothing in return for a job. The farmer agreed, and offered the pig-carrier and his gamine of a sister work in his fields and a place to sleep in his barn. A few days later Roman and Marie-Neige were invited by that man to the neighbourhood *veillée*. The communal gathering was held in a large chalk-walled structure. It felt like a night market or congregation, with the women sitting in rows, sewing and embroidering, peeling apples or blanching chestnuts close by the firelight. Further back the men repaired or sharpened tools, boasted and tossed pearls of rough wisdom. Roman sat with them, dressing hemp and burning the ends. A woman walked among them with a shovel of hot ash, from which they picked chestnuts and potatoes; another followed with a jug of mulled wine.

A *veillée* held the community together, it was where everyone volunteered work, even if exhausted. Outside was a defiant landscape where the crops hardly grew, where life was a constantly repeating wheel, so the truisms the men passed around had a clear-eyed meanness. *'Swineherd in this world, swineherd in the next.'* It was the only place where Roman and Marie-Neige ate properly. By the end of a day's work they were already in a state of exhaustion, but they donated hours to the *veillée* because of the available food. He could see her across the room, near the fire, involved with the night laundry, looking like a child among the other women. Courtships took place in the half-dark peripheries, even as lovers overheard the bitter wisdoms about desire. So that Marie-Neige was often approached by youths or men as old as Roman, while she twisted the wet sheets and hung them to dry against the firelight.

These were the most exciting days of her life. There was the adventure of disguise. And sleep was easy, without fear. In the barn, crowded with others, she felt a wall of security beside Roman, now forced to be platonic in his caring. When they wished or needed to make love, the lack of privacy and the seeming sin of brotherly love that surrounded the act made the tension and desire . . . magnificent. Every wish for sound between them was impossible and could be translated only into a half-lit glance. His hand on her back in the night, which had become gentle with this caution, was enough for her. So she would turn slowly from the blunt advances of others during the *veillée* and gaze towards the darkness of the workingmen, where she knew Roman would be watching her, and run her fingers through her hair and shrug.

And so wait for night. The hand on her shoulder. Touching the soft untouched back of her knee. They lay there, a brother and sister, silent and calm save for this brush of him against her. If someone lit a rush-light, its flood of ochre would reveal a nearness that might seem to have occurred accidentally during sleep. But hours of darkness cloaked them. She pushed back briefly against him and waited. He was already within her and held on to the stasis of this, did not wish it to end. A whisper. When he felt himself coming, his hand covered her mouth to silence it, though all noise came from the violence of his breath at her ear. And now, if a rush-light were held up in the middle of the great barn, the posture of the two would seem like a strangling, a brother in an old feud with a sister.

In the beginning this posing as siblings had made them anonymous to each other, but later, blindfolded this way, in a role, they knew each other's truthful desires. And what they discovered was not only conjugal love, but the quick danger of life around them. They were caught in the attempt at survival among strangers, these two who were strangers to each other. And they saw that anything, everything, could be taken away, there was nothing that could be held on to except each other in this iron-like world that appeared to stretch out for the rest of their lives.

Billet-doux

When Lucien Segura's mother died, a few weeks before his own wedding, Le Haricot entered the house, for the first time uninvited, drew a chair beside the coffin, and rested her head against the black pine. She would not move away. She had been befriended and had grown magically in the shadow cast by this woman. And then with the recent imprisonment of Roman, the result of his assaulting a carpenter in Barran, Marie-Neige had been close to losing their farmhouse, until Lucien's mother had paid the rent. Thus, when Marie-Neige keened and wailed beside the coffin, Lucien believed she might in part be fearing the loss of her home, and he had taken her aside and told her it was still hers and he would cover the rent; she stared at him with a look of scorn and turned away. She sat down in the chair again and put her head against the black pine. Lucien realized he had insulted her, misinterpreted her sorrow. After that he did not see her for a long time, and when he did she would not speak to him. Nothing he could say would remove the damage.

In the years between their first meeting and his wedding, there were two indelible versions of Marie-Neige that Lucien had been unable to adjust and combine into one, as if gazing into a flawed stereoscope. There was the seventeen-year-old woman in a yellow cotton dress. She wore it constantly during those early years in the fields, while carrying water from the river to the barn animals, or when visiting their house. And then the person now ten years older, who had become this woman, with Lucien almost unaware of it. If he was conscious of any growing in those years, it was more to do with himself, his tentative beard, the removal of his beard, his mother's pallor. Not her.

Now, with the insult, he felt he had lost her. Marie-Neige would scarcely acknowledge him. But there was a moment at his wedding when she surprised him by touching his shoulder and, as he turned, slipped into his arms wordlessly to dance. He was more startled than was courteous. But she did not seem to care. He said something to break the tension, nothing really, a bit of small talk, but she did not answer him, just looked up and watched his face, watched this essential friend who was now finally married, like her, who had once said they would not talk about it. Her expression then was the quizzical and knowing look an animal can give, as if she already knew what excuse or evasion he would provide. So he forgot words for the rest of the dance and held her not too close, in order that he could look at her properly. He could feel the 'bumps' his mother had joked about years before. She wore, of course, a simple cotton dress, but one he had never seen. And her thick black hair was combed precisely, clean as the night. He leaned forward and smelled it. The smell of the river. Marie-Neige had taken care, even with this simplicity, in preparing herself for his wedding. It could be she had spent as much time as the bride. And now they were dancing, both of them unconcerned with any rules to do with steps, and remembering it had been his mother who had taught both of them how to waltz.

He thought her beauty came because of her familiarity to him, though this was not the person he had grown up with. When he put the two mental photographs of her onto a stereoscope, side by side, he could see echoes of a look. But there was also a tug in him, a recognition that within this woman was a private nature he always felt close to. It was not just her face and body. He assumed he was marrying the face and body he wanted and desired. But here was something much larger, more confusing, here was a whole field, yet more intimate, a heart that was beyond him, who had chosen Porthos among the musketeers, and he had never understood why.

And as the music ended he saw her, like a woman in a romance, pull from her cotton sleeve a note that she pushed into his breast pocket. It would burn there unread for another hour as he danced and talked with in-laws who did not matter to him, who got in the way, whose bloodline connection to him or his wife he could not care less about. Everything that was important to him existed suddenly in the potency of Marie-Neige. He could tell what the shallow frieze of the wedding party that surrounded them would continue to be, and yet the one he knew best—he could not conceive how she would behave or respond to him in a week, or even in an hour. She had stepped into more than his arms for a dance, had waited for the precise seconds so it was possible and socially forgivable—the sunlit wedding procession, the eternal meal—and she had passed him a billet-doux as if they were within a Dumas. The note she had written said *Good-bye.* Then it said *Hello.* And then it reminded him that *A message sent by pigeon to The Hague can sometimes change everything.* She had, like one of those partially villainous and always evolving heroines, turned his heart over on the wrong day.

Night Work

Time passed before he saw her again. Lucien and his bride left Marseillan and journeyed north, to the forests of southern Brittany, then Paris, and when they returned three months later the formality of his relationship with Marie-Neige had hardened again. He had entered the central and compromising realm of a marriage; he had also realized that, if he was going to be more than just a married man, he had to take his own work seriously.

He wrote during the late mornings and afternoons in what had once been his stepfather's workroom. The view from that window still held most of the natural world of his childhood, though the river was hidden now by overgrown trees. Then, after dinner, when his wife or any visitors had retired, he returned to its quiet and darkness, and before turning on the lamp, allowed himself to become conscious of the smell of the clockmaker's oils that had once filled this space. He sat there weighing what was already written, half-dreamt during the day, until he fell on a scrap of sentence, something uncommitted, that would open a door for him. He worked for much of the night, aware of the darkness beyond his lamp. Only the pen and notebooks were alive, the rest of the world somewhere in the cliff-fall of dreams. Now and then he heard words spoken into a pillow in a far bedroom, a clue of another reality, like a juniper root shifting within the earth. He read out loud to himself, the way she had read to him, when his mother was alive, when Marie-

Neige was seventeen, and Balzac was still too difficult for them. They'd entered the great world this way. Was he in such a place now?

He pushed the glass doors open and walked into the night so the coldness filled his shirt. He noticed the square of a lit window on the slope of the hill. There was a tightrope between the two farms, and below it an abyss.

In-laws

He was never fully certain as to what made him write. He had seen his mother dance at her wedding with the clockmaker, just a few embraced steps. And once with a cat—his mother dancing with a cat in a meadow, he remembered that. It had become for him this delicious, witnessed example. It was a way he could enter the world as himself.

The few women who knew him well (a mother, the neighbouring woman) saw how his early success altered him. He turned from uncertainty into a more determined and more private youth. He camouflaged his life. He seemed to them like a creature who had slipped into a mistaken garden of celebrity. He was now in a well-lit place, such as those zoos in distant countries where one is able in the hours of night to witness the behaviour of animals that assume they are cloaked in darkness.

When he had been about to marry, his fiancée's family recommended a fortune-teller for them, someone who was known to predict accurate fates to those living in the village. The man read their stars and then whispered some safe sentences about the future. They were about to return to the sunlight of Blaziet when the seer grabbed Lucien Segura's sleeve and asked, 'You are a good gardener?' No, he said, refusing to reveal his profession. The man looked at him with disbelief, then let go of his arm. Lucien and his future wife left the curtained parlour and walked arm in arm for an hour or two along a road banked with poppies, and into a marriage that created two daughters. There would be years of compatibility, and then bitterness, and who knew when that line was traversed, on what night, at what hour. Over what betrayal. They slipped over this as over a faint rise in the road, like a small vessel crossing the equator unaware, so that in fact their whole universe was now upside down.

Essays were being published in cities about his career, his craft, his psychosis, his landscape, the lack of close friends, his secretive and diverse nature, his soul. They reproduced maps of the town of Bagnères-de-Bigorre, and the Fan of Gascony, and Marseillan. Every local cleric, neighbouring butcher, and mailman came out from the quiet corners of Lucien Segura's world with a story or an insight that would expose his silence. It turned out that his wife had kept a journal of fury towards him. He had assumed their relationship was affectionate. He read a few pages and realized how each of them was truly invisible to the other. He saw the disfigured man who was portrayed. He was the nocturnal animal in that night zoo, revealed in the darkness, who growled or bit his fellow creatures and ate his children.

Sometimes he lost that crucial part of himself that allowed him to feel secure. *Segura.* The irony of his name was not lost on him. The safe world disappeared. One of his daughters, it was probably Lucette, would enter the darkened parlour and witness him with a thin plaid blanket over his shoulders. She had been sent in to make him talk and bring him away from himself. Papa! Her mother had insisted she carry in a plate of food, but the girl did not place it on his lap. She was sixteen. She wished to be an accompanist, not a messenger, desired only to spell him through the darkness. He knew darkness well, all the footfalls within it. She sat on the floor, her back against his legs like a spaniel, as if she were owned by his silent body. Lucette remembers the heat in the room, the boredom of the hours there, until she recognized each minimal gesture of his as a kind of talking.

She began to speak about what she feared, what drove her to jealousy, what she imagined of the future, and eventually Lucien muttered how he himself had behaved when he'd been caught as a boy in a similar place or with a similar fear. He would never recall for certain which daughter had been with him that long day in the dimly lit room with its small window, when he had felt the thin blanket was his only skin, when only a careful breathing could release the rubble of what he contained.

He recalled a metal pencil box he had owned as a child, he remembered the young *grisette* he once shared a train carriage with, whom he would name Claudile in three of his books. Her companion was dangerous, she told him. The man had kept her captive, jealous of her friendships, and had overthrown her sense of perspective. There was no one to give an alternative opinion that countered his. Lucien sat across from her in that train carriage, and they spoke as if the oldest of friends in a night brasserie. She seemed wise in all things but her acceptance of this man. How easy it was to be caught within another's personality.

He wondered whether he was like that to his own wife, knowing how dark their union was. When he returned home he considered his role within the family, recognizing the controlling element in himself. It was true he had found himself more compassionate and empathetic to the woman he had spoken with on the train for those three hours. He already missed her, even in his busy life. He began to invent the days and nights of this woman without having taken a single step into her life. For more than a year he wrote of Claudile and her belligerent companion, the rooms they lived in, her visits to meet a writer in Auch for desire, and for a few thin luxuries. He watched and described her exhausted face during sleep, the pace of her breath during sexual excitement, the obsessive reading of the books the avuncular writer smuggled to her. He lived almost fully in her world for a year. When he completed the trilogy of tales about Claudile, he opened his study door and it felt to him that an era had passed. He found a chaos of in-laws around him on the estate at Marseillan. He was responsible for a many-headed family, and this left him unable to act for himself anymore.

❧

It is difficult to recognize your own vices in a son-in-law. He ought to have watched over the youth from a more neutral zone. If Lucien was objective about what he was witnessing in the young man, he could have blown whistles and surrounded the monster. His daughter would have hated him for a season, but all would have ultimately been perceived and resolved. Yet he felt mocked and finessed by the man, an up-and-coming poet, whom Lucien once caught winking at his patriarchal role, which the young suitor did not believe for a second, any more than Lucien believed in the man's flattery and attempts at family courtesy.

Whereas the truth of what was occurring was more anarchic. His daughter Lucette, now twenty-two, was engaged to Henri Courtade. His nineteen-year-old daughter, Thérèse, was being courted by the young poet Pierre Le Cras. Regarding these romances from a parental height, Lucien could recognize an essential truth. Pierre Le Cras was drawn more to the graciously mannered Lucette, and she was clearly unable to let go of any glance that he threw towards her. Lucien watched their smothered gestures. He witnessed a hand's pressure in the passing of a napkin, the too-long stare as Lucette entered the rowboat, the sharing of songs at the piano. And there was the photograph that recorded everything. During a gathering when everyone was formally watching the camera and no one was looking at *them*,

Lucette and Pierre gazed openly at each other, forgetting the witness of the camera itself. Lucien kept the evidence of this now permanent gaze in his workroom.

Perhaps he should have remained silent with this knowledge. There is no need for a father to oversee his daughters' territories for them. Adult children are no longer children; they know more than they appear to, they can put up with more than a parent thinks. But Lucien took these betrayals upon himself, coaxing each clue from the shifting group around him. The lovers would hold their breath as he walked the corridors of the large house at night. The youth had gall and the charm of an *arriviste,* and disarmingly, he was a good poet. Lucien Segura did not know what to do.

When Lucette confided to her father that she was pregnant and that her wedding needed to be moved forward, Lucien insisted they take a walk across the fields and discuss it. But once alone with him, Lucette refused to admit to Pierre's existence within her emotions. She stared at her father's seeming madness when he brought up the young poet's name, and took shelter in mentioning the very goodness of her own fiancé. Then she referred casually to the possibility of her sister's marriage in the near future. Lucien began to doubt his suspicions; perhaps his cast of mind had become jaded over the years. It was to be a brief walk, and Lucette was married three weeks later, and at the wedding he performed like a contented father. For all he knew, she had ended her affair with the talented, deceitful poet.

Shortly afterwards, Pierre Le Cras published a remarkable sequence of poems dedicated to his future wife, Thérèse. They were vague enough to prevent any physical identifications, so the poems had a 'universal' quality. But at the same time the emotion within the verses was heartbreaking and generous, and soon Paris was celebrating the young writer. All this led to plans for a second wedding. Thérèse was ecstatic, her mother delighted. There was, Lucien felt, a fever in the household. It was all a false portrayal. He watched them and listened to them and saw no awareness of an alternative truth. The true portrait was the photograph in his study, where the two lovers simply watched each other openly. This man had swept into their home as if under a protected spell, which Lucien could not control. Lucette had grown up with a natural grace and politeness, rising from her chair for any new guest or messenger. She was determined to be a writer like her father, constantly improving herself, perfecting herself, just as she would carefully erase her faults on a page and pencil in a better rhyme or metaphor. In recent years, she had even helped him clear away a sentiment or two in his own work. He'd watched her small bony hand brush away the curled fragments that contained the erased phrase from a page of his, so that she could write in a more modest word, asking him tentatively with her eyes if *this* might be better. Sometimes with a work, such as an astronomical treatise by Flammarion, he would purchase two copies so he and Lucette could read simultaneously, so they could share the landscape of the same book as each of them roamed through it. She had come to think like him, he believed.

But during the capsizing months on either side of the two weddings, he felt everything change. He knew that while Lucette did not wish to harm her sister, she would enter the bedroom of Thérèse's intended and favour him in the dark. They would make love disguised within the shell of a travelling *diligence*. She would be in the garden shower—under which she had bathed as a child—at a certain hour and would tie the gate closed with a string or ribbon, knowing he would be there, already undressed. They synchronized their journeys to Paris, and drank absinthe and slept together drunk within their hotel room. They consumed dark coffee and stayed up all night writing. They were cautious, and yet nothing kept them apart.

Besides, she was already married to the sweet and lackadaisical Henri Courtade, was she not? And yet here was her sister's suitor, languid and brilliant, quick-hearted, for he was humorous with all of her family, not just her (which Lucette loved in him), deceiving them all so that he could be close to her.

'If you will not break off your engagement,' Pierre Le Cras had warned her, 'and marry me, then I will slip into the stockade of your family in any way I can.' 'I dare you,' she had responded. 'I shall propose to Thérèse,' he had said, 'and if she will not have me, I will become an architect and build a house for your father, or become the gardener for this estate.' 'Tante, our neighbour, keeps an eye on the garden.' 'Then I will become your father's biographer.' 'He wishes for no biography, he's famous enough.' 'Then I'll make you pregnant and hell will break loose.'

There were scarcely any rules for the two of them. Or there was only one—whatever allowed them to be together. 'If I have a child, then it must be yours,' she said. That became the second rule.

She accepted everything about him, ached for him.

I want to . . . Let me. This.

Here?

Yes.

She knelt on the turned earth, they were in someone's field, he came into her mouth, and she stood up again. Around them suddenly was the rest of the world.

Lucien was halfway up the steps to the garden tower when he glanced down and saw his very pregnant daughter bathing under the shower, shielded partially by a birch. Few used the shower anymore, not since the children had grown up. When they were young the whole family bathed there during summer months. Lucien paused and watched the quick movement of Lucette's hands as she soaped herself, and all at once, in that moment he became happy and was at ease. He accepted whatever the love was, and wherever it came from. He had at one time surely been as foolish as they were. What did it damage? There was in the end an order, even to this.

He was certain his daughter was pregnant by Pierre but things would be all right. A torch of desire sometimes sprang up in the strangest half-lit rooms, but a family could somehow envelop and contain that. He knew this from his own life. He continued up the steep iron stairs, looked down once more, and saw Lucette run her wet hands through her light brown hair, darkening it. Then she seemed to hear something and she turned her back and bent over, and the slim naked body of Pierre Le Cras stepped between Lucien and her.

What had been innocent—a celebration!—abruptly made him a voyeur. His daughter's forearms and open palms were flat against the mildewed wall as Pierre tugged her white hips and shoulders towards him, his body digging into her again and again, and again as if she were the very centre of the universe. Lucien thought of her small hand brushing away the erasure rubbings from his pages.

He turned quickly to go down the flight of stairs to the level of the earth, to the normal perspective of a human. Ten metres up, you saw over walls, witnessed an unexpectedly revealed house. You were a writer in mid-air. It was what Japanese artists called the 'lost-roof technique.' Cursed with omnipotence, he had seen the blunt truth of their romance. The girl he had carried in his arms during a childhood nightmare now had the needs of an adult. It was something a father should not have shared, although as a young man he had bathed with this same person under that very same water spout.

She had been as tall as his knee.

There were nights when Lucien startled himself awake at his daughter's wildness. How had she, the one daughter he had known as obedient and well mannered, evolved into such a person? Was it simply that Pierre was the man she demanded above every other principle? There was this live coal of desire on her tongue that had altered her, so that she could no longer be sheltered by the husk of a family. And he realized he loved even more this proud indelible daughter, his Flammarion companion, who had leapt beyond him into the life of this dangerous stranger, a man he was unable to like except through the knowledge that Lucette had placed herself in the cup of his hand, just as she had bent over and moved back into his body, defenceless with pleasure in the garden shower.

Sometimes truth is too buried for adults, it can be found only in hours of rewritings during the night, the way metal is beaten into fineness. Whereas children are a generation with immediate clarity. He could not comprehend how the sequence of poems by Pierre had been so powerful and believable. He did not understand how his two daughters seemed so close and yet uncareful with each other. Once he had pockets full of wisdom to give his children. Had he not been the one who taught them where exactly to climb a fence, or how much to feed a dog?

◊

Perhaps he'd 'done enough' in his life, as a novelist said to him in a salon before the war. She meant he had written enough to be significant, or at least he had as much chance of being significant as one could expect in a literary career. Even then it was not what he wanted to be comforted by. Fame was not what he wanted, fame was as foreign to him now as it had been when he was twenty. He'd protected himself from it by becoming a splintered creature. (When he made journeys, he would go with one friend, never two, then bid farewell and meet the second acquaintance in Lapalisse perhaps and walk with him into Burgundy.) Anyway, he had been dancing with that bird-slim novelist at a salon on the avenue Hoche, one of her hands on his shoulder, the other a light goose-wing at his neck. These were gestures towards possibility, and he had often imagined her as a lover. She was a graceful writer who had her own honours in her career. But for Lucien, writing was a place of emergency. He wanted what he had done those first few times, without awareness, when the page was a *pigeonnier* flown into from all the realms one had travelled through. There had been the gathering then, the thrill of diversity. There was no judgement. He had not sought judgement when he began to write, but it had somehow become crucial to his life. When all he had wanted was to dance with no purpose, with a cat.

Le Bois de Mazères

Years earlier, before the death of Lucien Segura's mother, the belfry of the church in Barran was renovated. Roman, agile for such a thickset man, was one of those hired to work on the fifty-metre height of it, where he would receive better money than could be earned anywhere else. Hanging within a rope harness, Roman hammered loose and ripped away the rotten sheeting, revealing gradually the skeleton of the twisted tower. Then he and others, their bodies roped to pulleys, entered the old belfry and in the darkness strengthened the structural braces, and laid new octagonal floors at each level.

They worked inside the tower for two months, while the high gales and snow raced over the plain and swirled among them. Then they came into sunlight and hauled up fresh sheets of wood and rebuilt the outer structure. Roman at this time was as hazardous as the work he was doing. He had rarely worked alongside others. When he returned to the ground he'd swagger, as if drunk, free at last of the tension of balance. All day he had hung in a bat harness or stood on a single spike on the edge of the air, while around him was all the universe of the Gers. He could see the many brown paths that wove towards the forest, and Auch twenty kilometres away, and the route he took each night on his horse in the darkness back to the farmhouse. Arriving around eight at night, he would eat a meal with Marie-Neige, and be awake by five the next morning to return to Barran. If not for those solitary night rides, if not for Marie-Neige and their quiet talk as he slipped into sleep, he felt he would have gone mad. By seven the next morning he was attached once again to the structure, riding it, clinging to wood that had been cut down in the thirteenth century. All that winter he worked against the sloped roof. Still, the most difficult hours were when he came down before darkness and there was the need to test himself on the ground in a different way, as if to hold on to the earth.

During the night, snow came in the darkness, and Roman and Marie-Neige woke to a brief white land. In the Gers it snowed and then melted with the first sunlight, so the green landscape of fields and forests soon returned. But when Roman rode towards Barran, it was still early, and his horse left a path in the whiteness that arced up to the forest. He always took the route through the Bois de Mazères. Travelling this way, through the great acreage of trees, he could reach Barran in less than an hour. He rode, the low branches with their new weight grazing his shoulders, so snow fell onto his lap, his thighs, the rump of the horse. Eventually he let go of the reins so the horse selected its own route, and would remember it when they returned in the darkness.

Then Roman would lie back and look up into the green crosshatched tapestry. For those minutes, lost under the shifting world, he was a boy, doing what he had done as a boy. The reins were loose at his knees and he thought of nothing. Because he was a man who could not read and who rarely spoke except when there was a necessity, every gesture that occurred around him magnified in meaning, and was full of angles of introspection. A silent hesitation by Marie-Neige, or the tone of a sentence from an authority at the church in Barran, said almost more than was necessary. Thus the low, easy swoop of a magpie, with some bright object in its mouth, turned slowly within him like something grinding in a mill.

Bird life had hardly been awake when he'd entered the trees. A first chirp from above had fallen like a splash down towards him. But now the oaks and beech trees repeated melodies and verbose plans, so it felt as if he were moving through a market-place. For Roman, a cow or a pig or a scared hound revealed itself with sound and posture—they were no different from humans. He could read the expression that told of a broken claw or a thirst. But birdsong was the great mystery he had come to love. He aligned himself within it, its vast architecture, which contained all forest life and the life of a sky. Wherever Roman worked, he had found time in his day to enter a copse or forest.

The light of the open field hit him as he left the trees, and he sat up on the horse and saw in the distance the twisted belfry of Barran. He was a man who appeared to ignore everything around him. Whenever Lucien spoke with him, asking him what he thought were essential questions, Roman seldom gave an answer if he felt it could be discovered or pointed to instead. It was only when Lucien had retreated from all of them, his face cut by those splinters of glass, that Roman felt close to him. Since his marriage he had never trusted strangers. In a narrow street, coming upon others, he would stiffen so they could pass around him. He owned almost nothing, but would have fought a legion to protect the one or two or three possessions he had— some furniture, including a bed and a table, the two horses, the pigs he boarded—as well as the things he felt he had a right to, the arms of his wife, the path he took in the forest. Everything else was a stranger to him, possibly against him.

At night, when he returned to the farmhouse, the two lamps Marie-Neige had lit and hung above their door frame allowed him to leave the roadway and ride across the fields, and as he came over the rise, up out of the valley, and saw them, he gave a long howl like that of a wolf, and she would know he was near—so that sometimes Lucien and his mother or sometimes Lucien's fiancée would believe there was a creature skirting the two farms. No, there are no wolves, Marie-Neige would say if asked, never revealing the source, and they never believed her certainty. It was in a way the tenderest communication between her and her husband.

At Barran, Roman tied on the leather apron, with its pouch for nails and hoop for a hammer, and ignoring everyone climbed the ladder up the side of the belfry until he was back in solitude once more, with nothing but a jarring wind and the echo of his hammering and voices that shouted below him like the barking of foxes. It reminded him of the charivari, those hoots in the darkness. Such wordless events and small gestures converged on Roman in this way. Up there, high on the belfry, he recalled the image of that swooping magpie with something stolen glittering in its mouth, as if it had been a sign.

There was a suckling child carved out of wood in a nearby church at Monteyzal that he took. The embroidery on kneeling stools hidden among pews, that he cut and pulled free. Portraits of saints from walls. A marble bowl. A rug. An ebony cross. A felt-covered ledger. In Fontanilles and Douelle and Brouelle and Malemort and Senilla—everywhere he rode, he fell upon ancient churches empty at midnight, alone in their small grandeur, unheated and in darkness. So there were nights when he did not travel the simple twenty kilometres to the farmhouse, but rode into those villages on the periphery of the great forest and entered churches, slept in their darkness, and took what he needed or what he felt the churches did not need, the lace, the rims of silver from a portrait, a graven image; he brought them to a clearing in the Bois de Mazères, and waited until there was faint light. Frost covered everything. The passereaux and the rapaces were awake already with tentative songs in the dark. He dug up his previously buried tarpaulin and added to the cache the new things he had taken. He would trade such objects for plants and grain and clothing.

The final stage of work on the belfry was the slate covering. Slates had been brought from the Angers region and were to be installed without overlap. The men hammered them on with rifled copper nails. Ten metres below the cross and the rooster, Roman balanced himself on a single spike. He could see the forest of Mazères in the northwest, shaped like a green cloverleaf in all the whiteness, for snow fell deep and unseen into those trees. Whatever he had taken from the churches was buried there, save for a painted wooden flower he had pulled off a carved saint's blouse for Marie-Neige, a stolen thing like a live alouette in his pocket.

He paused in his hammering, and looking into the distance saw Marie-Neige on horseback. Even with all that space between them he could recognize her shape as she and the animal nudged forward on the last half-hour of their journey to Barran. She would never get to tell him, after the fight that occurred shortly afterwards, why she had come to Barran that day, what news she wished to bring him. He saw her foreshortened figure tie up the horse and begin walking towards a group of carpenters. He imagined the men gazing openly at her; she was the only woman there, it must have been brazen. Then they had looked up, pointed to the tower, and he heard laughter. For a long time he did not move, high on this strange tower that people insisted had been created originally by a sudden and perverse wind or by the madness of a roofer in love.

Fields

Whenever Marie-Neige returned from visiting her husband in prison, she walked the periphery of their two fields—one that surrounded the barn like a horseshoe, and a larger one that sloped uphill. Roman had boarded horses and pigs for neighbouring farmers, and this had brought in minimal subsistence. Now, with him in jail, she could hardly keep up. But walking the property at dusk made its possibilities clearer. She could live on what she grew within the horseshoe and turn the larger field into a market garden. But she had to learn how to replenish the fields. The animals they boarded had ripped open the earth. So she began to fork manure and vegetable remains and fire ash into the earth, and took the wagon to the slaughterhouse in Marseillan to bring back offal and the remnants of carcasses, which were like gold. Needing a darker, loamier soil, she sprinkled chimney soot over the rows where she had planted cabbage, dragged lime and ammonia through the claylike soil, and used cow dung where it was sandy and horse manure where it was chalk. Some of this she already knew. The rest she discovered in a monograph she borrowed from Lucien's library that showed how earth was renewed in an old battle zone. All this reminded her of the book where Cornelius tried to grow a perfect black tulip.

She bundled weeds at the edge of the larger field and let them dry, and a week later heaped them all into a fire. The acrid smell drifted downhill to Lucien's house and slipped into his workroom, so that he came to the window and watched her in the distance, outlined by smoke and flame. She trod seeds into the earth instead of broadcasting them with her hands. They called this *plombage* in Lucien's military monograph. She cut down brush and left just a few fruit trees along the fences. In the new vegetable gardens, she discouraged sparrows by laying out white cotton along the seedbeds, and dissected earthworms and dipped them in nux vomica, then slipped them into mole holes. She was as gentle with seedlings as she was brutal with pests. She loosened the moist earth and carried the bundle of shoots in her cupped hands as if it were a fallen bird to be returned to its nest. She saw her work now as a path through the seasons, seeding onions and celery between February and April, leeks and winter cabbage from May to July.

She was older now. She had wept when she married, and then had seen her new husband try to murder someone during the darkness of her marriage night. He was a man who had grown up with the harsh etiquette of self-protection he had witnessed on a farm. But the world they were in was harsher. And Roman was now in a prison, having attacked a man near the square base of the belfry, almost killing him in a rage of jealousy. It had taken seven men to hold him down. As if he were a stag. When he had looked down at her among the carpenters from that great height, he did not know she was pregnant.

Marie-Neige visited him every week in his cell in Marseillan. A month after he was imprisoned, while walking home, she had a miscarriage. She lay down in a stranger's ditch and lost all of what she and Roman had created. She got up after an hour. One rich thistle had been growing next to Marie-Neige, and it became burned within her memory. She tied two sticks together into a cross and planted it by the roadside, gathered whatever was there into a fold of her yellow cotton dress, and brought it home and buried it in the horseshoe-shaped field near the house.

She saw her life then for what it was. There would always be this pointless and impotent dreaming on farms, and there would always be a rich man on horseback who galloped across the world, riding into a forest just to inhale its wet birch leaves after a storm.

'Where is your yellow dress?' Lucien asked when giving her a lift into Marseillan, and her answer stuttered into silence. One evening shortly afterwards, she and Lucien talked for long hours into the night. Roman was still in prison, and she believed she herself did not have much more than the fate of a mule. She spoke to Lucien about everything, confessing her poverty, and he admitted his unawareness. Even though he was her closest neighbour, he had been preoccupied by his own life.

He went to Marseillan and bought the property she lived on outright from the Simone family, partly with money and partly with an exchange of fields. A day or so later, everything was notarized and he walked up the hill to her farmhouse with the papers. He saw her by the well and called out her name, but she did not move. She kept staring down into the well. He came up to her, and her focus of intent hesitated at the sound of his voice and she turned to him. She had heard the news that someone was buying the farmhouse. He took her hand and she jerked it back. But he would not let go. He pulled her that way towards the house. It was the way Roman persuaded her into sexuality, and her heart beat fast from embarrassment for both of them. For him, her friend, as well as herself.

He made her sit at the blue table. It was the table he would take away from that small farmhouse some years later, and it became the dearest possession in his life. She sat on his right, and he spread out the bill of sale in front of them. He went over all the clauses, reading them, explaining them. It was something other than shock when she noticed her name. She'd been given nothing in her life, on even the slightest scale.

Then, a few minutes later, only halfway through the document, she relaxed, and he sensed it immediately.

What is it? he asked. She shook her head and kept reading the paper before her. There'd been no gasp of breath or gesture, but he was so familiar with her nature he'd recognized the sudden lightness. What is it? he said again.

She watched him, smiling. Nothing, she said.

It was not connected with this grand gesture and the gift of property, but some realization by her that made the acceptance of it possible. They were old allies. And only she knew why, when they sat down side by side at the table, she had known automatically which of the two chairs to sit in. It was so his good eye would be next to her and could share the page they read together, while the other eye—his blindness, at all their differences in this life—was far from this intimacy.

She made a sparrow's dinner for them, and needing something to praise, he praised the freshness of her well water until she was laughing at him. He was always too shy and tentative to speak about his own work. Instead they discussed her plans for the fields, and that night, when he returned home, he took down the military pamphlet from his library shelf. He could sense her excitement about the farm's possibilities, now that she owned the land. At one point during their meal he even said what had crossed her mind already—that she was now entering the world of the grower of the black tulip. She nodded. They were as close as that.

And though she spoke that night far more than he did, she knew in essence all about him, the range of his successes, his two daughters, his wife. Then, just before he left, as he stood up she asked him to sit down again, and she told him about the miscarriage, and how she could not stand it. She could not stand it. She could not stand it.

One solitary light in the room over the blue table. And him putting his hands out to reach for her thin fingers that had nothing in them.

Thinking

As close as she was to Lucien, the idea of physical passion between them had not existed in her mind. Her frolic of a dance with him at his wedding had been just that, a bookend to signal the end of their youth. They had been taught the steps of a waltz by his mother in the barnyard, who had stated that, if they were reading about life in Paris and Fontainebleau, they needed to practice their social skills, and that the three essential areas of training for a musketeer were horsemanship, swordsmanship, and dancing. Lucien's interpretation of a dance, confirmed by his studying of engravings, had been that it was an act where you pushed the shoulders of your partner until you both reached the far end of a room, while the girl suspected dancing meant simply intermingling for a period of time under the spell of musicians. His mother had needed to educate them both.

Still, the two of them were cautious around each other. In spite of their proximity, they had their own lives and separate beliefs. When Marie-Neige reconsidered his accident with the dog, she felt as if that partial blindness must have already been there in him. For someone so intuitive and empathetic, he was, for instance, unknowing of the true nature of his wife, believing that if there were errors in the marriage the cause was in him. And he was a dreamer in terms of his compassion, unaware of how the world was knit together unequally, so that the radius of his generosity was short. He had never veered much into the real world.

She knew little of the great world herself, less perhaps than he did. There was for her no life outside her home. Every evening she sat in her kitchen, then slept in the bed behind the curtain. She could not write to Roman in prison about what she felt for him, about her hunger for him, because he was unable to read. She wished she had taught him, the way she had been taught, so he could escape his solitude, but he had always returned from work exhausted. When darkness came, she washed herself at the barrel of rainwater by the barn, then walked with the lamp towards the house. She'd pick up a book, but as soon as she sat down with it she fell asleep in her chair. She never got used to reading in indoor light, although every evening she attempted this. It was already a pleasure to rest in a soft chair and hold a book in her hands. Sometime later, after the lamp burned down, she opened her eyes. Perhaps the smoke from the burned-out wick woke her. She stood up, gathering her senses into almost clarity, and went through the darkness to her bed.

War

Because of his partial vision Lucien Segura did not fight in the war. He volunteered instead to be part of a commission that studied disease and trauma along the battle zones near the Belgian border. He arrived at the front with treatises and reports he'd translated from German texts of new rehabilitation techniques, but he was ignored by the young overworked doctors. Around him was the chaos of troops being destroyed by mortar and starvation and, above all, fear. They needed something else, not someone to study them. While he continued to file reports, he began working in the hospital tents. Within a month he had become another person, one of the anonymous wave of soldiers and attendants, his face gaunt, the goatee spread into a rough beard, while the impatience and anger in the missives he continued sending to Paris meant that they were seldom read, just buried in files.

He caught the diphtheria in his second year. At first he had a mild fever, then difficulty swallowing. Two days later Lucien could barely talk, unable to make even the sound of a murmur, his palate paralyzed. The tissues of his neck were swelling and he was fighting for every breath. In the medical tent he could see others bleeding from their mouths and noses and guessed this was also a portrait of him. Lucien had been a passive and fateful man; now everything in him fought to overcome the exhausting pain, so that he could think clearly. He knew the disease's first twelve days were the most unforgiving and dangerous. He knew too that there were other diseases prevalent in the camp and insisted on sleeping in the open, crawling outside to avoid the circling air of the wards. There was no solitude there, among those on the path to death, and he needed privacy to hold on to what strength he had. He swallowed only liquids that were certain to have been boiled, and refused offers of unknown water.

The military reported his likely fate in a letter to his wife and she arrived, barely recognizing him among others in the sanatorium at Épernay. She discovered, when he was able to speak, that she could not understand his thought processes, or his bitterness like a poison towards the political world. He demanded she leave him alone with his 'companions,' though in reality he was fully solitary, studying only himself to be aware of the shifts in his illness, in the desire to survive.

After twelve days, he and the others who were still alive were made to live alone in tents, made to wash themselves and prepare their own meals. They were still toxic. They still carried the 'plague in the throat,' the white membrane that might suffocate them. The Spanish called it *garrotilla*—1613 was 'the year of the *garrotilla*.' He felt he knew more about diphtheria than anyone else there, and he was vain and proud of this knowledge even as he was prostrate on the mud floor of his tent. Leeuwenhoek in the 1670s had discovered the microbes through a microscope, 'shooting through spittle like a pike through water.' A brother poet. American colonists saw the disease as 'the fruit of strange sins,' an act of God that would ravage and thus cleanse the new world. All responses to diphtheria were medieval until Napoleon's army was being devastated by it, and he was forced to offer 12,000 francs for the best study for prevention of the disease. The essay that eventually resulted, by Bretonneau, which located the false membrane in the throat, would remain a classic of clinical medicine. Then Agostino Bassi, who studied diseases in silkworms, theorized the doctrine of parasitic microbes. But along the Belgian border, in 1917, and in the sanatoriums, there was still no cure, little more than prayer.

Lucien Segura was still alive. There were days of delirium, then stillness, when he would lie on his narrow cot exhausted, just looking at the back of his hand. Or at the cover of a romance, one of several appallingly written books regularly left by soldiers outside his tent, until one afternoon someone left him Balzac's *Les Chouans,* a story of 'love and adventure.' In his feverish daze, Lucien could swallow a volume a day.

The solitude at Épernay gradually released him from the everyday world. He witnessed only what he saw through the open flaps of his tent. Once he overheard a strange rustling that confused him as to what was occurring outside until an officer was revealed attempting to fold up a large topographical chart. Sound, and thereby imagined plots of sound unwitnessed by the eye, became important. . . . He was lying on a daybed at Marseillan listening to the gradual approach of crows, and then their bickering in the poplars. He remembered the familiar hoofbeats of Marie-Neige's cart horse, the rustle of the outdoor shower as it sprayed onto the earth, muted now and then by a body that stepped into it. He could make out the sound of scalpels in the medical tent being placed back onto rubber sheeting. There was a dying man's cough three tents over, and in it the hidden fear that Lucien could recognize. He had these maps of sound, and they taught him to locate distances, to distinguish a footstep on mud as opposed to dust, or whether a voice was moving towards him or away.

He continued writing his reports, hunched over in the tent. And with what remaining energy he had, Lucien wandered back into his youth, his half-formed adulthood, reconsidering incidents that might have altered him as this person here, now, under such dark skies. It was as if he had been handed a mirror for the first time and could see what he held only faintly in his memory. Those nightly seductions of Madame de Rênal in *Le Rouge et le Noir,* had they taught him something? Or deceived him? His dance with a light-boned writer. The Dog. The past was gate-less. An overlooked life came rushing into his dun-coloured canvas tent, till then so full of the certainty of death. It was November now, and at night many were dying in the constant rains. He had saved a partially used flashlight but would not waste it on the darkness except in an emergency. He knew that, like him, it was a mortal thing.

He thought, strangely, not of his family but about Marie-Neige, with whom he had rarely spoken since his marriage. For a series of nights his mind leapt with excited freedom all around her. He would recall something and force himself to journey across the episode again, slowly. He had seen her rise from sewing and arch her back, slip her left hand up within the sleeve of the other arm and tug at the muscle there. If he had been more relaxed as a man, he would have crossed the room and kneaded the muscle free of its stiffness. There'd been some sibling-like desire in him towards her. He began sorting the evidence of that. Where he had turned right, he now turned left and entered a room with her, or helped her carry bundles of laundry when it started to rain—they rushed into the house, their arms full, his shirt and her blouse speckled, no, *sodden,* with rain. She picked up a towel from the basket and dried his hair. His palms rested on her thin shoulders while his head was bowed towards her, aware her taut body was made up only of essentials.

In Épernay that November, all that kept him warm were her shoulders. His mind reached forward and lit them like a gas fire. He'd been a secretive man for most of his life, and now was disconcerted by the secrets he had kept from himself.

Furlough

The furlough allowed him ten days. He returned home and it was midsummer and the August storms, or the threat of them, came every night. Sometimes there was lightning but no rain. His thoughts and emotions were loose in him, random, similar to the abrupt cuts of light in the sky. He would walk in the fields by the river long past midnight, unable to lose his wakefulness. In the house, his wife and daughters were asleep. He had been home three or four days and was still not used to the quiet, was not used to the chance of a suddenly lit room while he waited for the nightmare or the dream. The lack of the war was like a frozen river around him. There was security only in the past, with Marie-Neige always somewhere, in the symmetrical rows of her garden, or steering a wheelbarrow full of wet clothes back from the river.

What had touched him most on the day of his return was her greeting, the odour of the mud on her hands as she reached up to touch his new beard. He wanted to thank her, somehow, for saving him during the days and nights in Épernay. But he was cautious, fearing his strange obsession about her during the month of diphtheria was nakedly evident.

He sat at his desk organizing his reports, hiding everything he felt. Twice he walked to Marseillan and back. The town had been devastated, losing almost all of its men in the German war. It was a village of widows. Marie-Neige told him Roman had been released, but only into the war as a soldier. Lucien wondered what his old neighbour had been told he was fighting for.

At one or two a.m. he'd still be awake. He would dress and go outside and walk to the river. He'd leave the footpath as if splashing into long, coarse grass, and a wave of insects would lift around him so that anyone could be conscious of where he was by their sound.

Another night. In his bed he could hear thunder, the formal distance of it. He listened for rain but it did not come, and the frustration hovered alongside him till he fell asleep. Then thunder again, like a cynical, dry hand-clapping, and he was awake, with hope once more.

Another night.

He had his shirt off and stood among the noise of cicadas and grasshoppers. The ochre colour of a lamp came through the trees like a lit vessel being carried over the sea. When she reached him they both were still and quiet, as if intent on listening for some pronouncement or signal in that hesitation, and then the silence was lost, as the chirp and clatter of insects rose like dirt once again into the air around them. There would be no privacy even here, even now, after all this time in their adjacent lives. A wakeful nature surrounded them. A mockingbird at a height beyond their reach in the new branches (he would never see the bird) was consistent and woeful.

The lamp hung from her fingers beside her dress. But they said nothing. As if they knew that darkness was also a liquid, and just one uttered word thrown out would ripple back to the house. He held her hand and walked with her to the edge of the river. She dimmed the light, just enough so they could find this place again from the water, then moved away from the burn of the lamp and undressed and walked into the river. He could hear her wading movement. A few minutes later they faced each other. When his weaving hands touched her underwater, he pulled back in a courtesy or a shyness, she couldn't tell which. Lucien could see no edge to the sky, not a star. He moved into the deeper darkness. He had not swum in a night river since he was a boy. He was with his sixteen-year-old self, and it was a while before he became aware of her absence.

Marie-Neige was on the shore, near the light, a tin outline. She lifted the lamp above her head and called out his name and he said *Yes* and she turned. She could see the ribs on his thin body as he came into more and more light. She placed the lamp on the grass and picked up her cotton dress and began drying her hair, so it was no longer plastered around her face, then came nearer to him and rubbed his hair dry with the dress. So now they looked as they did in a room, or across a table, no longer appearing as strangers to each other. On his knees, behind her, he pulled her thighs back to him in a slow rocking, as if he wanted her now to search for him, the heat of her cave onto his coldness, missing each other, and she said his name again and he moved into her, her softness and the unknown warmth.

How many stories were read between them in which they had discovered the codes of eventual love and said nothing in their shyness. She'd barely been touched by him—his cupped hands once on her shoulders, his hard grip when she pulled the splinter out of his eye, his holding her small hands across a table. It was as if they had both known what all this would be like, these doorways and reflections of each other, this cautious modesty and the secrets of herself she had hidden from others. All that witnessed them was a lamp in the grass. She moved back onto his lap so she could control their movement, slow him into more intimacy, so his hands could hold the quiver in her stomach and there could be an equal pleasure. They heard nothing, not the sterile thunder or the mock of the bird or the million insects carelessly yelling. Just their breath, as if they were dying beside each other.

Return

There is little record of Lucien during the final year of the war. He disappeared back within the anonymous fabric of troop movement and field hospitals. In those final months, while he was stationed near Compiègne, one letter of hers got through to him. Who knew how many she might have written? But he assumed this was the first since he had seen her during his furlough. The note was about Roman, how she had recently met him, and how she had been relieved that they had been close, able to talk easily. Roman was still a bear of a man, and she hated the idea of him imprisoned once more within a regiment.

For some reason Lucien did not write back to her. Perhaps he had already imagined and written every kind of letter in the voice of those other soldiers when he had helped compose their messages to wives and lovers, using so many verbal emotions that honest literary empathy did not exist in him anymore. He no longer trusted words. He wrote a few notes to his wife instead, about the moral state at the front and the dangers that might come with the winding down of the war.

His own family was living temporarily with his wife's relatives near Paris. The countryside around Marseillan was rumoured to be unsafe with illnesses, and there were mercenaries now, and deserters breaking into homes and farms. The only order seemed to be within the last official gestures of war. In the towns and villages there were continual incidents of violence caused by poverty and need. Lucien had no idea what his family's life near Paris consisted of. But in Compiègne he was recording what he saw taking place around him daily, witnessing the deaths and even suicides. Priests forgot the names of those they were giving last rites to. He himself had prayed dutifully over dying strangers, and they had looked up at him with disgust. He had scarcely enough time to think about Marie-Neige. He had lived and relived so much of their life together before that last journey home. Now he had to somehow keep himself alert, keep himself safe, be aware of exactly what was taking place. One night someone tried to kill him; he woke up being strangled, and this man was not even the enemy.

A few days before the war was over, the soldiers were allotted train passes, but with a warning that all transport was slow. The journey home could take weeks. He looked at a map and realized that with a horse he could return to Marseillan and see whether the house was safe; later he could take the train and meet his family in Paris. He looked for an animal he could buy, anything that would allow him to leave the war zone sooner, eventually bartering for a horse that might take him a day's journey. Further away from the front, he could probably buy another. He strapped up all his documents and left everything else behind, medical texts, clothes, the utensils he had needed till now. There would be clothing at the house, and he could shave and bathe there before eventually going on to Paris.

At Montargis, he traded the horse as he had planned. With luck it would be only three more days, and he would reach Marseillan late on the third or fourth evening.

There was bright sunlight everywhere but it was cold, and

what he was wearing did little to keep him warm. At an abandoned farm he found rolls of burlap that he cut and fashioned into a cloak. The animal was not healthy, they had to move at a slower pace than expected. He found himself losing his judgement. By the late afternoon on the second day, Lucien was fading into half-sleep, then waking unsure of where he was. He was lost for two hours in a river valley. He discovered himself suddenly riding through a field of onions and dug some up with his hands, ate one, and saved the rest in a pannier.

In Figeac, a farmer sold him a bowl of milk, which he gulped down. He saw virtually no one on the roads. A man on a horse passed him, going the other way, cradling a dog in his arms. The rider said nothing, did not even look at him. He too must have been fearful of gangs. Lucien realized he should have waited for a troop train.

The next night was colder, and Lucien shook, as he had with the diphtheria. He kept looking at the whiteness of his breath to convince himself he was alive. He believed it would be the last thing he saw in his life. He woke in the unending darkness and lit a match to see the time and whether his breath was still there. The horse, near him, had not moved. It started to rain and he gave up. He slept or passed out, he was not sure which.

When he woke in the morning, his body was stiff from the coldness of the ground. He could hardly rise. He turned and saw the horse calmly eating grass, its head coming up slowly to gaze at him. He walked beside the animal for more than an hour before he was able to mount it. This must have been the fourth or fifth day of Lucien's travels, and he was skirting the forests whenever he could because he feared encountering strangers. Though what did he have that they would want? Then he thought of the documents he was carrying, and the awareness of them made him step back from his torpor. What he had was more than himself.

It had been dark for many hours when Lucien reached Marseillan. Everything was closed. He went on the last ten kilometres. It was unlikely there would be food at the house, maybe some cans, or dry food, but at least he could bathe and sleep. Or perhaps Marie-Neige would still be next door. He had no knowledge about where Roman was, or whether he was alive, or home by now. The animal was slowing down, and he got off and walked beside it, needing to generate more energy and heat in his stiffening body. The dampness in the air filled his cloak. He knew his mind wasn't right. For some time he had been thinking his mother would greet him. Then, when he remembered, he began to believe she would welcome him as a quiet ghost. She would welcome him and feed him, have his bed made. There would be a fire.

He walked up the road to the farmhouse in total darkness. The world around him was moonless, not a star. Not one candle flame. He let go of the animal and just stood there. Then stepped up onto the porch, found his way in, and soon had his house awake with light. He moved from room to room, speaking loudly to himself, every now and then saying a name. He removed the damp burlap coat and saw himself in a hall mirror. It was so long since he had seen himself. The clothes he put on now seemed too big. He looked from a window and there was no neighbouring light. So they had gone too. The rise of hill was black. A paraffin light or a candle would have shown.

He went out into the dark and led the horse to the barn to feed it. Returning, he smelled something, the remnant of a fire. Smoke could have come from more than a dozen fields away, caught in a pocket of the wind. If there had been rain, smoke would have been pounded down and a thread of it might have remained in the grass. But he wanted to make certain no one was next door. This was his homecoming, and he had not seen a soul in the village or for most of the days of his ride. And not even his mother's ghost had met him. He walked up the hill into that black landscape, leaving the lights on behind him.

There was no wagon or horse in their barn. He knocked at the farmhouse and waited. He lifted the latch and walked forward slowly until his thighs touched the table. He knew the table. He knew its old blue colour when it existed there in daylight. So often he had sat there playing cards, or talking, when he was younger.

Lucien had no idea where they could have gone. He called out both their names. First Roman's, then hers, although he rarely used her name when they spoke. It had always felt too formal for what there was between them. Even her simple, lovely name. He thought he heard a cat. He walked to the cupboard where they stored candles, and swept his hands back and forth on the shelf. He lit one and it warped light onto the walls. He heard the cat sound again and, carrying the candle, drew back the curtain that separated their bedroom. She was lying on her back like a corpse, covered in a black blanket, her head moving from side to side. He saw a spasm overtake her, and the cat noise came out of her. She was alone in the farmhouse, and there had been no light or heat. But when he touched her forehead his hand slid off the slickness, she was perspiring so much. This was chills and fever. Marie-Neige? He whispered her name as if he did not wish to disturb her, as if at the same time he needed to wake her discreetly, without scaring or confusing her, so she could be aware of his presence.

Where is Roman?

All her lips seemed able to do was blow out air. And when he bent over and looked at her closely, her eyes kept edging over—as if signalling—to something behind him in the other part of the room.

He had thought during his journey to the farmhouse how much he wished to talk with her about what he had witnessed in the war these last few months, when he had felt the presence of her within him. He needed to realign himself alongside her. If they found themselves alone, then perhaps they would lie in a bed and sleep together. But that path had now changed beneath his feet. He needed to care for her in her fever. He began telling her about the time he was alone, when he had been ill and delirious in his tent and all that had saved him was his history with her. Marie-Neige's eyes stilled for a moment, then she convulsed, so much her head rose off the pillow; then she lay back breathing hard, twice as exhausted. In Compiègne, he had seen horses with the 'thumps,' whose bodies convulsed because of the lack of calcium.

I saved you? she said, barely audible, as if to herself, as if he did not exist there except as somebody she was imagining.

Yes. It was as if you were the only one who would visit me in that cold tent.

He lowered the candle he was holding to the floor and placed his palm on her forehead. It was still damp, her hair wet. He raked his stiff fingers through her hair slowly, again and again. It was a gesture he used in love, and now, sensing this was a comfort to her, he did not stop.

Most of the light the candle gave off collected on the low ceiling of the room, so they were dark outlines to each other. Now and then a glint on her cheekbones. She was about to convulse again and he held her shoulders. Her body jerked up violently, then fell back, a stone figure in a vestry. She must have felt capable of death. She drifted somewhere, and he sensed he had lost her. He left the candle where it was, on the floor beside her bed, and returned to the kitchen and lit another. 'She's with us,' his mother said, beside him.

He ripped up some old cardboard to use as kindling and opened the iron door of the stove. There was a slope of wood, cobwebbed, against the wall, and he lit the fire. Where was her husband? It felt to him that the house had been deserted for some time; the stones on the wall and the floor held an old cold. The cracking and banging of the burning wood woke her, and he heard her say, *Roman?* He came back and wiped her face dry with the blanket. 'Lucien. It's me. Let me change your bedding, it feels as wet as you.' 'It doesn't matter,' she said. In the cupboard he found a flannel sheet. It looked familiar. His mother must have at one time handed it down to her. He spread it over a chair in front of the fire.

He opened a can of soup, put it on the stove, then brought the warm sheet to her. When he pulled the coarse blanket down, her chest heaved as if freed of the weight, and her head came up coughing with each spasm. She was bent almost in two, a naked hairpin. When she lay back, the shadow of her ribs broke his heart, her thin whiteness reflecting the candlelight from the ceiling. He wrapped her in the warmed sheet and covered her with the blanket. Then he brought soup to the bed and began spooning it into her. She was drinking it eagerly.

Roman.

No. It's Lucien.

It's Lucien, she repeated slowly, as if confusedly shifting dance partners.

Yes, he confirmed. Where is Roman? But as he said that, he saw he'd lost her again, her mind elsewhere, in the shadows.

He must have fallen asleep in the chair. When he opened his eyes he couldn't see her. He thought he'd just felt a hand on his shoulder. But the candle wavered then, and he saw her face on the pillow, looking at him. Her eyes signalling something. *You, my friend. You have to take me out. Do you understand?* She closed her eyes again, giving up, as if she'd been shouting at him through thick glass. He didn't understand. But she kept turning to him for help, there was something else. *Do you . . .* Suddenly he understood. He was a fool. The blanket wrapped tight around her, he gathered her into his arms, crossed the room, pushed the door open, and carried her into the cold night. He didn't have a light with him, but he knew where it was—the small shack that was the outhouse. 'Thank you,' she was saying. 'Thank you, Roman.'

In the cubicle he lifted the blanket so she could sit down, and then sat next to her so he could hold her upright. After a minute she nudged his arm. All right? She nodded, with almost a smile. Again he gathered her like a frail branch and carried her to the farmhouse, and put her back into the bed. She was already asleep, and calm; he drew the curtain across so she would not be wakened by daylight.

He woke in the morning, his head on the kitchen table, his eye against the blue of it—the scratched and cut-into blue, a history of them all. So he knew where he was, coming out of the deepest sleep, in the instant of waking.

He sat up in the chair. Light from the east window revealed dust across the floor. He noticed the stove and went forward and touched it tentatively, but it was cold. There was a pan on it with the remnants of solidified food. He stood there not moving. The room, the air, was so still that he felt he could not be existing within it. He could hear nothing. He looked down at his feet, then at his hands held out in front of him, to make certain he was fully alive.

All he wanted to hear was a cough, or the movement of a bed-spring. He walked forward and looked at the bare faded land-scape of trees and a river depicted on the curtain that cut the room in half. As though it was another spectrum of life he could now almost enter. He had not breathed for so long. He drew the curtain back and there was nothing there.

Say Your Good-byes

He walked into Marseillan and at the police station discovered that what he had warmed and carried in his neighbours' house was a splinter of memory or light within himself. Marie-Neige had died during the last months of the war. And there was no longer evidence of Roman in the records of the prison. He had enlisted, but they were not sure he would ever return, even if he was alive. Lucien walked back to the farmhouse alone. For the first time in his life he had no one around him. He did not have a neighbour. His neighbours' home was empty. He slept that night in the one room that had belonged to her and Roman. He sat at their table. He rode his horse into Marseillan and gave it away, then went by train to Paris, collected his family, and brought them home.

Lucien Segura completed the report on his time in the military camps and field hospitals, exposing what he had witnessed there. The first chapter was read, then the report was shelved. Almost no one read the work. His experience was questioned. How had this writer moved from a complex, finely tuned poetry to a blunt, coldly prepared vendetta? It irritated the literary populace of Paris, and they hoped once again for the slim volumes of verse. But he knew poetry would demand everything from him.

Roman did not return. And Lucien moved his workplace from his stepfather's room into Roman's farmhouse. He began to write again, and as he wrote he waited for her arrival, usually halfway through a book, long after a location and a plot had been established. She entered the story sometimes as a lover, sometimes as a sister. And in this way he spent most of his days with Marie-Neige as an ally in the court, or as a village girl who saves the hero without his being aware of it. Marie-Neige as a lost twin, Marie-Neige as a jongleuse the central character falls in love with, who, disguised within her craft as singer-acrobat, robs the great châteaux of the Bordelais, Marie-Neige who in one book guides a blind father out of a foreign city.

Often there was in these fictions a finite love or an unrecognized affection. But for the most part Lucien gave his readers the happiness of a resolution. As the stories were completed, he mailed them to a small press in Toulouse, where the success of the books brought stability to the publisher. With the printing of these tales, the central characters became popular public figures, especially as no one knew who the author, 'La Garonne,' was. Lucien had composed them in secrecy, in much the same way he had walked and dreamt as a boy surrounded by copses and thickets and rivers that had been his true intimates. The books hardly seemed the work of a well-regarded poet, or the author of the bitter jeremiad on the recent and already forgotten war.

The adventures had a hero who was at times awkward and at times gregarious, at times cautious, at times foolhardy. Before he plunged his rapier into a villain's heart he would fling out the line 'Say your good-byes.' Whenever readers saw the line 'Say your good-byes,' they would know the very necessary death would occur in the next paragraph. It was a signal for final music as 'Roman,' after slaying the Count de Guispelle at the Académie Française and nailing a proclamation of motive to the imperious oak doors, leapt from the second floor into the waiting hay wagon driven by a Mathilde or a Melicante or a Marie-Neige.

Roman was an inconstant hero, witty with his lover and sullen with his enemies, but sometimes quick-witted with his enemy and sullen with his lover. He never seemed to be fully understood by his author, and so no one could ever be sure of him, not even his accomplices. In a later century, he might have been considered manic-depressive or bipolar, but in his time in France he got away with it. Often he went into depressions or was violent. He rarely proclaimed his anger out loud, instead hiding it (rather unfairly, some thought) from his victim, who was therefore unaware of the stalking and hunt. During the last third of a book a villain's financial empire would crumble, his allies would turn against him, and le Conte de Porcelain would remain in the dark about which of his vices someone had taken exception to—a badly timed application of the *droit du seigneur,* perhaps, or the eviction of a sick family, or some financial razzle-dazzle with a publishing house in Lyons that had bankrupted all but Porcelain. This policy of silent anger was the reason Roman was forced in his last act of retribution to nail proclamations onto some nearby surface, before he and Marie-Neige and the sidekick Jacques (more about him later), who were the central trio of each book, galloped away at the end of every adventure.

The Dog in the Gartempe River and *The Yellow Dress* swept through France. Meanwhile no one, even within his family, was aware of the link between Lucien Segura and the author of the Roman stories, that whore of popular success who somehow seemed to understand the intrigues of the publishing world too well for the comfort of many within it. And the swordsman Roman was not beyond quoting the poetry of Verlaine or Pierre Le Cras out loud in the middle of a fracas, sometimes mockingly, but usually with a sense of recognition of their worth. In one novel, he strolled through a famous art gallery in Munich, humming Don Ottavio's 'Dalla sua pace,' his fingers stroking the textured paint. So while people read him for swordplay and romance and moral vengeance, they absorbed everything else. Roman's obsession with art and poetry was strange, and may have had to do with the fact that he was illiterate. The verses he sang or recited were taught him by his seemingly unworthy companion 'One-Eyed Jacques,' a libertine and socialist, who bandaged Roman's wound when his arm was slashed open—if Marie-Neige was nowhere to be found—and who was also a master of disguises: he would infiltrate enemy courts sometimes as a foolish dauphin, sometimes as a wealthy countess. There were many sequences in the novels when Jacques and Roman wrestled around campfires over the subjects of poverty, foreign wars, the Black Goyas, incest, the selling of children, Balzac's Vautrin, and the banking system in Paris. Their adventures always took place alongside the events of the day.

All this, until the very last book, when Marie-Neige succumbs, dying in an epidemic while Roman is off adventuring in Brittany, so only Jacques is with her in the final hours. He has discovered her alone in her farmhouse, overtaken by a fever. Slowed into confusion, barely able to breathe, she keeps asking for Roman in her last hours. She whispers to the old ally Jacques to assist her in getting a message to Roman, and there is nothing Jacques can do but lie. He nurses her, changes the sheets wet from the fever, and feeds her. In the last hours, as she drifts off, he undresses and takes from a chest the clothes of Roman and puts them on, and cuts his long hair and darkens it. He enters her room noisily as her lover, wakes her and speaks in his voice so that in the haze of her vision she sees *him*. She beckons him to lie beside her, and the old degenerate sidekick, who knows and loves these two people more than any others, enters the bed beside this village queen he has travelled and worked with and conspired alongside all these years. At all those campsites in the Ardèche or the Loire, during their adventures in earlier works such as *The Girl on a Horse* and *Baptiste's Breath*, he has slept on one side of the campfire while Roman and Marie-Neige slept together on the other.

She whispers to him now, touching his hair, looking deep into his tired, caring face. It looks to her almost like the Madonna's in this semi-darkness. He whispers back, reminding her of their times in the past, of the sunlit afternoon when the two of them travelled with Jacques through a grove of oaks, and the clicking branches sounded like rain, of a river swim, of his love for her. . . . So he accompanies her into her final sleep. He kisses her mouth and lies in the bed beside her all that dark night, until the first grains of light, when he is able to see her again. She has hardened into the position of an effigy, and the heat of fever that consumed her has departed with her soul. But there is also a dry whiteness on her lips he did not see before. And so he waits for more sunlight to fill the room and pries open her mouth and sees the flecks of white sores on her tongue. Diphtheria has been sweeping into villages and killing children as well as those who nursed them. When Roman returns from his adventures in Brittany to the farmhouse, he is surrounded by this truth. The disease has destroyed the two who are dearest to him in his life. It is not war or finance or greed or power, all those easily corrupting things, but this small membrane of death in the throat.

It was to be a horrifying conclusion for those readers of the Roman adventures, and what actually became of Roman remained a mystery. As readers left the final pages of *Whiteness*, he disappeared, and Lucien stopped writing, near the village of Marseillan, at his neighbours' table. The seven adventures of Roman came to a close. Lucien had said all he knew and remembered about Marie-Neige in these stories, the sound of her wheelbarrow, how she lit a fire, the moment of a yawn, the way she had talked about a thistle in a ditch. She was within him now.

He diverted a modest sum of francs into a new account. He collected some notebooks, climbed into a horse-drawn cart, much like the one his mother had used to search for the lost father in the *corridas* of Vic-Fézensac, and disappeared, barely a mustard seed in his pocket. He would not write again.

A half-year later he used one of his notebooks to keep score during a card game in Dému with the boy named Rafael. There are three notebooks (one of them blank) in the archives in the Bancroft Library at Berkeley. There are some childish maps indicating where he had planted certain vegetables in his new garden. '*You are a gardener?*' the fortune-teller had asked him. There is a scale drawing of his house and property with its small lake and avenue of trees. There is an illustration, in another hand, of how to make a nest for insects by partially stripping a cob of corn.

One afternoon, in Lucien's last garden in Dému, the boy mentioned that he was reading the series of adventures about Roman, but Lucien Segura said nothing. He simply took the book from him to see what Astolphe's son was using as a bookmark, then responded that he had heard of this writer of escapes and revenge, of love and adventure, but he had not read him.

'We have art,' Nietzsche says, 'so that we shall not be destroyed by the truth.' For the raw truth of an episode never ends, just as the terrain of my sister's life and the story of my time with Coop are endless to me. They are the possibilities every time I pick up the telephone when it rings suddenly, some late hour after midnight, and I hear the beeps and whirs that suggest a transatlantic call, and I wait for that deep breath before Claire will announce herself. I will be for her an almost unrecognizable girl save for an image in a picture.

Every evening our father used to walk the property of our Petaluma farm before dinner, until finally, on the far hill, he would step from the dark shadows of the trees and come down in the last sunlight. We always saw him do this, although he never knew he was being watched by the three children. One evening a fox appeared behind him, running up and down along the edge of the copse, but my father, looking the other way, ambled down into the valley. Claire saw it first and nudged us. The creature moved lightly, as if on springs, barely glancing at the human near him. My father, sensing something was wrong, paused. He turned then and saw it, and began to walk backwards, cautiously, keeping it in view, the fox moving with its light step as if mocking him, back and forth, back and forth, on a different tangent.

With memory, with the reflection of an echo, a gate opens both ways. We can circle time. A paragraph or an episode from another era will haunt us in the night, as the words of a stranger can. The awareness of a flag fluttering noisily within its colour brings me into a sudden blizzard in Petaluma. Just as a folded map places you beside another geography. So I find the lives of Coop and my sister and my father everywhere (I draw portraits of them *everywhere*), as they perhaps still concern themselves with my absence, wherever they are. I don't know. It is the hunger, what we do not have, that holds us together.

∾

I see Lucien Segura for the last time with the boy Rafael, who recalls the old man sitting out of doors in the glare of the day. Rafael appears with bread. They tear up the loaf and eat it with an onion or some herbs. If Lucien is thirsty he walks over to a pond, immerses his hand, and lifts it cupped to his mouth and drinks. This is how I remember him, Rafael tells me.

Lucien must have walked into that depression of the earth that was once a *mare* and sat at his blue table, the only furniture he had brought with him in that journey by cart. A few years earlier at Marseillan, in the middle of describing a tense scuffle of a swordfight, he had suddenly become curious about how long and how wide the table he wrote on was. He began measuring it with his hands. From elbow to fingertip twice, and then twice from wrist to fingertip. So the length was slightly over a metre. About one metre in width. It was made out of two pine boards, with a narrow runnel down the middle, where they joined. The table always a fraction below his notebooks, always out of focus as he wrote. The six nails that held it together, the colour of the paint, that exact height for him to bend over, as if over a mirror, to see what could be found. His constant companion.

Astolphe's boy would turn up and sit on the stool across from him, with his grin, his desire for, it seemed, every possibility in this world. Perhaps Lucien himself looked like that when young. Like a slim combed hound, mouth open, breathing fast with eagerness, hoping for everything. Even rain would not keep the boy away. Lucien would look down from his bedroom window and see Rafael arrive, and see him shelter himself for a while under the oak tree before leaving. He was curious about what Rafael would remember of their afternoons. Would it be the card games or his own fragmentary thoughts like half-told secrets? Or his avuncular air, the holding of his hand above his good eye when the sun fell onto him like a weight? Would he be even a fragment in the boy's future?

He would see Rafael coming towards him, pause, and turn back to the herb garden. *No. Come here,* he'd say out loud. And the boy would return and sit across from him. And what Lucien had been remembering disappeared into his clenched fist.

Then even these friends left him.

Rafael's father strolled down the driveway of plane trees with two horses he had received in exchange for something. (The object of trade was in fact one of Lucien Segura's peacocks, which a distant farmer coveted. The disappearance of the bird was not noticed yet; it was whimsical in its wanderings and may simply have followed a layer of warmth that came after a storm. And as far as the old thief was concerned, to separate an owner from fish or fowl or undomesticated hound was not quite robbery; there was always the opportunity for it to return, even from seven or eight farms away.) So Rafael's father walked guiltlessly beside the house where sumac bordered the walls, whistling, in contrast to his earlier departure at four a.m. in silence, when he carried the struggling bird—it was almost a mammal, he thought—within his long coat.

Lucien witnessed his return, his head alongside two nodding horses, and not wishing to inquire too directly, waited until the next afternoon, when the family crossed the small lake in the boat, to ask what they were doing with the new animals. They were going to live further north for a while, he was told. They gave no reason and he did not ask for one. Perhaps there was easier commerce there, or the father needed to evade a rumour of his existence in the area. And 'for a while' was as precise as they wished to be about the period of time they would be away. A few days later, shockingly soon to the old writer, the entourage rumbled along the narrow path beside the house and then departed along the straight lane between the trees. It was almost dawn, and Lucien in his narrow bed listened to the muffled clang of pans at the end of each sway of the caravan, and Aria's clear voice talking with the boy. When he came outside and stood there ten minutes later, he detected a faint remnant of cigarette smoke that had caught against the rough brick of his house.

After they left he must have remained, alone, through the dark fortnights of the moon, the arrival and departure of winter. The vegetable garden slept under snow, revealing only a frail fence, and a tent, a pyramid of stick and cloth where the travellers used to store their tools during other seasons. He walked one day across the hard and brittle vegetable beds and entered the tent's light-filled emptiness and simply stood within it. It had been Aria's garden. He would often see her early in the morning. The mist would slowly lift and she would be there on her knees plucking away snails or dead leaves from the soft, damp earth after night rains. It was as if she had been there all night in that posture of almost obsessive prayer, waiting for the darkness to lift, and then for the white mist to disperse, until Lucien saw her in her green shawl.

He was still Lucien Segura, after all his years, after all these changes and escapes. He was, he realized, still more responsible to the boy he had been, than to the father he had become. In spite of everything he had not been a paternal man. But here, where the late-winter storm fell on him, protected by this thin pyramid of a tent, with its hidden bulbs and grains frozen under the snow that would be alive again in the future, he saw he had used up his life. He stood in the shelter that had belonged to Aria, and then walked back to the house, and the only footprints were his; there were not even those of the peacock, whose warm three-toed feet would have revealed the green under the snow.

The lake throws up a sparkle between the trees. Lucien takes a moment to struggle into his cardigan and walks into the shadows of the oaks. He does not feel this present life is real without the boy. The essential necessity of Rafael. They have shared things cautiously. He has reached for some fragments of his life to give to this almost adopted boy, and in return Rafael has described the eclipse he and his mother witnessed near Plaisance, its terrible wind that was more terrible than the darkness. And what Lucien wants now is a storm.

Among all the great works of art he stood before, as a younger man, was *Ivan the Terrible and His Son Ivan,* by the painter Ilya Repin. He has remembered it all these years. The old despot cradling the son he has killed accidentally with a blow to the head—and the patriarch's eyes on fire, and all around him the future darkness. A week later, in another city, there was another painting, another nightmare, Peter the Great interrogating his son for conspiracy, and in the father's eyes a sure knowledge of the young man's guilt.

He will never know what becomes of his children. He will not know whether he has nurtured them or damaged them. A girl travels down the long California valley in a commercial refrigeration truck, hardly able to speak, as a result of her fear or her bravery, listening to every word of the good stranger. Lucette in Paris sips absinthe with her lover. The boy Rafael will meet me, a woman from the New World. . . . And Coop? And Claire? Will these children, in their eventual cities, turn out to be the heroes of their own lives?

I have recently been reading, in a monograph, a haunting thing about a missing father. 'And so I hoped that someone would come, a man, why not my father, at nightfall. He would stand in front of the door, or on the path leading from the forest, with his old white shirt, the everyday one, in shreds, dirtied by mud and his blood. He would not speak in order to preserve what can be, but he would know what I do not.'

Oh, this older need for a lullaby, not a storm.

He comes out from the shadows of the trees and walks the length of the meadow until he reaches the edge of the water, until he stands beside that oldest of boats. He remembers finding it in the grass that first morning in Dému, believing at first that the struts were the ribs of an animal. It lies in the mud, and a loose knot ties it to a tree. Rafael often sculled across the lake in the evenings, for no reason but glorying in his energy.

Lucien pushes the boat free of the mud shelf and strides beside it through the cloudy water and climbs in. He turns his back to the far shore and rows towards it. He can in this way travel away from, yet still see, his house. Water laps up between the boards, and he feels he is riding a floating skeleton. He is able to distinguish the shape of his small home in the quickening dusk. He wants to stand, to see everything clearly, and at the very moment of his thinking this, a board cracks below him, like the one crucial bone in the body that holds sanity, that protects the road out to the future. His gaze holds on to this last, porous light. Some birds in the almost-dark are flying as close to their reflections as possible.

ACKNOWLEDGEMENTS

My thanks most of all to Susie Schlesinger, and to Jean-Hubert Gailliot and France David, for the help they gave me during the writing of this book. Thank you also to Bill and Sakurako Fisher of San Francisco and San Anselmo; to Theresa Salazar, Anthony Bliss, and David Duer at the Bancroft Library at Berkeley, California; to Alfredo Vea of Oakland; to David Ben, with his magical talents, in Toronto; to Glen Garrod and Ruth Winningham, Dave Walden, and Janis Arch in Nevada City, Lake Tahoe, and San Francisco. To Sandra Compain of Quincy; Rick Simon at Coach House Press, Toronto; Madeleine Duffort and Paulette Latarget of Barran; Guy Bodéan in Dému; and Oliver Maack in Petaluma. To Caroline Richardson and Susie Schlesinger for horse lore. To Robert Creeley and Roy Kiyooka. To E. F. C. Ludowyck, many years ago. To Karen Newman, Lucy Jacobs, Agnes Montenay, David Warrell, Alexandra Rockingham, Mary Lawlor, and Julie Mancini; the architect Jon Fernandez, video-installation artist Douglas Gordon, David Young and Anthony Minghella, and Baltic Avenue. As well as Graham Swift—for his care of a river. Also Le Daroles bar in Auch and Jet Fuel in Toronto.

Thank you to Katherine Hourigan, Diana Coglianese, Lydia Buechler, and Anthea Lingeman at Knopf. To Anna Jardine. To Ellen Levine and Steven Barclay. To Donya Peroff and Tulin Valeri. Thanks to Quintin for her research, and Griffin and Esta and Linda for their comments during the last stages of the book. To Sonny Mehta and Liz Calder, Louise Dennys and Olivier Cohen. And, once again, a special thank you to Ellen Seligman, my editor, at McClelland & Stewart in Toronto.

*

The lyrics Cooper sings to himself at the card table are from the song 'Johnny Too Bad,' originally recorded by The Slickers in 1970 and written by Derrick Crooks, Roy Beckford, Winston Bailey, and either Delroy Wilson or his brother Trevor Wilson, depending on the source. The line of song quoted on page 118 is by Tom Waits, another line by The Lovin' Spoonful appears on page 46. The song 'In Delaware, When I Was Younger' is by Loudon Wainright. The song 'Um Favor' (partially described on page 73) by Lupicinio Rodrigues in essence began this book.

The passage on page 273 about 'the father at twilight' appears in *Le paradis perdu/Paradise Lost* by Marc Trivier (Yves Gervaert Editeur, Bruxelles, 2001, © 2001 Marc Trivier), used by permission. Nietzsche's original line is '*Wir haben die Kunst, damit wir nicht an der Wahrheit zugrunde gehen.*' J. M. Coetzee's slightly different translation of it in his speech when accepting the Jerusalem Prize led me to it. Two lines of a poem by Lisa Robertson from her book *Rousseau's Boat* (Nomados, Vancouver, 2004), used by permission, appear on page 143. The comment about 'archives being an utopia' is also by her. The phrase 'sweeping the translator's house' appears in Brenda Hillman's book of poems *Cascadia* (Wesleyan University Press, 2001). The sentences from Alexandre Dumas's *The Black Tulip* appear in the translation by Robin Buss (Penguin). The remark about Colette's 'amorously selected words' on page 142 is by Francoise Gilot in her book *Matisse and Picasso* (Bantam, Doubleday, Dell Publishing Group, 1990). The conversation about the author of *Sophie's Choice* possibly uses remarks by William Styron.

*

Thank you also to the following works: *A Military Garden*—a pamphlet written by Georges Truffaut, with the collaboration of Helen Colt, in 1919; Eugen Weber's *Peasants into Frenchmen: The Modernization of Rural France 1870–1914* (Stanford University Press, 1976)—from which I drew some historical data on chariveries and veillées, as well as 'sayings'; *Miasmas to Molecules* by Barry Wood (Columbia University Press, 1961); *The Great Central Valley: California's Heartland* by Stephen Johnson, Gerald Haslan, and Robert Dawson (University of California Press, 1993); *Rush for Riches: Gold Fever and the Making of California* by J. S. Holliday (University of California Press, 1999); *Belles Saisons,* the writing of Colette assembled by Robert Phelps (Farrar, Straus & Giroux, 1978); *Blessings of the Wind* by Tad Wise (Chronicle Books, 2002); *The Tevis Cup* by Marnye Langer (The Lyons Press, 2003); *Road Hustler* by Robert Prus and C. R. D. Sharper (Kaufman and Greenberg, 1979). Some descriptions of the First Gulf War that Dorn mentions during the game of Texas Hold 'Em are drawn from *Martyrs' Day: Chronicle of a Small War* by Michael Kelly (Random House, 2001); Kelly was killed during the Second Gulf War. Annie Dillard's lines on page 141 appeared in *The American Scholar,* Spring 2004. The information about *gotraskhalana* comes from Wendy Doniger's book *The Bedtrick: Tales of Sex and Masquerade* (University of Chicago Press, 2000).

A Note on the Type

The text of this book was set in Sabon, a typeface designed by Jan Tschichold (1902–1974), the well-known German typographer. Based loosely on the original designs by Claude Garamond (c. 1480–1561), Sabon is unique in that it was explicitly designed for hotmetal composition on both the Monotype and Linotype machines as well as for filmsetting. Designed in 1966 in Frankfurt, Sabon was named for the famous Lyons punch cutter Jacques Sabon, who is thought to have brought some of Garamond's matrices to Frankfurt.

Composed by North Market Street Graphics,
Lancaster, Pennsylvania
Printed and bound by Friesens,
Altona, Manitoba
Designed by Anthea Lingeman